S. M. Zas-Rey

About the Author

JOHN BARLOW was born in West Yorkshire, England, in 1967. He studied English Literature at Cambridge University and has a Ph.D. in Applied Linguistics. He has since taught at universities in both England and Spain. He lives in Hull, England, where he is at work on his first novel.

Eating Mammals

Eating Mammals

Three Novellas

JOHN BARLOW

Perennial

An Imprint of HarperCollins Publishers

For Susana

¿Recuerdas donde comenzo todo esto?

This book was originally published in Great Britain in 2001 by Fourth Estate, an imprint of HarperCollins Publishers.

HarperCollins books may be purchased for educational, business, or sales promotional use. For information please write: Special Markets Department, HarperCollins Publishers Inc., 10 East 53rd Street, New York, NY 10022.

First U.S. edition published 2004.

Library of Congress Cataloging-in-Publication Data

Barlow, John.
    [Novellas. Selections]
    Eating mammals : three novellas / John Barlow.— 1st ed.
        p. cm.
    Contents: Eating mammals—The possession of Thomas-Bessie—The donkey wedding at Gomersal.
    ISBN 0-06-059175-7
    I. Title

PR6102.A764E24 2004
813'.6—dc22

2004040898

04 05 06 07 08 RRD 10 9 8 7 6 5 4 3 2

Eating Mammals

My career began with two strokes of good luck – fate you might say, because as instances of good fortune none could have bettered them. After the war, towards the end of which I served as a cook in His Majesty's land forces, I returned to England and, armed with the ability to knock up a wholesome bully beef stew for three hundred, presumed to pass myself off as a chef. In my new, ill-fitting suit (we all got a new, ill-fitting suit) I talked my way into the kitchens of a modest hotel in Scarborough, and several years afterwards found myself working in one of the superior hotels on the Yorkshire coast. I won't tell you where, because about a decade later, at a moment when I gained some brief, local notoriety for swallowing slugs, my former employer there wrote to beg me never to divulge the name of the place to another living soul. Quite right, of course, although by that time I had completely forgotten the name of the establishment, and his letter served only to remind me of it.

Anyway, whilst I was working at this hotel as third chef, in which role I took charge of breakfasts, I found myself one morning called to the table of a guest in order to receive his compliments. His name was Mulligan, a regular customer, and familiar to us all, not by the frequency of his stays so much as by the dimensions of his body. He was, quite simply, enormous. In his tweed suit he resembled a well-tailored tree trunk, a huge lump of man. One would not have called him fat, although there was certainly more to him than meat and bone. No, not fat. Even as he sat, motionless but for the steady working of his jaws, one could tell that he wasn't a *wobbler*, that when he stood up his belly would not flib-flab around in front of him like a sackful of jellyfish. From head to toe he had achieved a condition only dreamed of by the obese, and scorned (somewhat jealously) by bodybuilders everywhere: *firm fat*. And underneath that magnificent outer layer there resided also an ample musculature, sufficient muscle indeed so that, had he been alive today, Mulligan would have been at least an American wrestler, and at best a great film star.

But as luck (for me) would have it, he was neither of these; he was the fêted Michael 'Cast Iron' Mulligan. And that morning, as I picked bits of uneaten bacon from returned breakfast plates, examining them for teeth marks before setting them aside for a quiche, he wanted to speak to me.

At that time I knew no more about him than what I saw, and that included what I saw him *eat*. On this particular occasion he had consumed enough porridge to fill a bowler hat, ham and eggs sufficient to keep a team of navvies on the move all morning, and half a loaf of toast. But, then again, he had done so the previous morning, and as far as I was aware my cooking had not improved miraculously overnight. So why he wanted to speak to the breakfast chef I could not guess.

I approached his table, where he was sipping tea from a china cup, as delicate as you like. As if to mark my arrival he dropped a lump of sugar into the cup with a pair of silver tongs. Then he looked up at me.

'So you're the breakfast chef,' he said, in an Irish accent which teetered between seriousness and levity, as if everything had two possible interpretations. 'Well, many thanks indeed for another fine meal. Yes, many, many thanks.'

I accepted his gratitude somewhat awkwardly, not quite deciding on an interpretation.

'And,' he continued, pushing a vacant chair towards me and lowering his voice, 'I am in need of a little assistance, and you look as if you might be the right man for the job.'

I sat down at the table, and noticed that there was a pound note slotted under a side plate. He let me consider its possible significance for a moment, then went on.

'Today,' he said, then stopping to drain the last of the tea from his cup, 'I have a little business, a professional dinner if you will . . .'

I nodded, still looking at the money.

'. . . a rather special affair, for which I am to provide the liquid refreshment.'

I was about to tell him that access to the wine cellar was strictly by arrangement with the manager, having (incorrectly) deduced that he, like many others before him, baulked at the prices on our wine list and fancied some vino on the cheap. But I was a rather timid young man, and before I could summon up a suitably tactful form of words to explain that every thief has his price, and that mine was three pounds a case, he took a small piece of paper from his waistcoat pocket and placed it in front of me. On it was a recipe, handwritten and with no title:

fresh orange juice	3 pints
fresh tomato juice	3 pints
pure olive oil	1½ pints
honey	½ pint

Whisk until all ingredients combine. Leave to stand. Whisk again and decant into eight pint bottles.

Whatever else he might have been, then, there seemed little doubt that Mr Mulligan was severely constipated. *And do you wonder!* one might add, although just how constipated a man can be, even a man the size of a tree trunk with the appetite of an elephant, was perplexing indeed. And why the home-made remedy?

'I see that you find this something of a strange request, but I assure you that it is quite harmless, quite innocent . . .'

He nudged the plate with the banknote under it towards me.

'And if you can supply me with the eight bottles by five this evening, in my room, there will be another small gift awaiting you.'

My eyes must have accepted the offer on my behalf, since he sat back in his chair as if the deal was now done. Carefully, I extracted the note from under the plate and stood up.

'Oh,' he added, 'and, please, *olive* oil; of that I really must insist.'

In those days, not so very many years after the war, and with rationing only just out of the way, oranges enough for three pints of juice was a tall order. Even before I reached the kitchen it occurred to me that procuring wine was a far easier sideline than juicing six dozen oranges clandestinely, not to mention the tomatoes. As for the oil and the honey . . .

My career as a cook had been touched by the cold, pinching hand of rationing, so without hesitation I set to the question of spinning-out: I pulped the tomatoes and added sugared water and ketchup (for some reason more plentiful than the real thing); I ran to the sink, which mercifully was still piled high with unwashed breakfast plates, and rescued a good half-jug of fruit segments in syrup, not all orange, but at least citrus for the main part; I collected the dregs from two or three dozen glasses, and got more than a cupful of fruit juice, albeit of mixed origin; then, from the fruit store, I grabbed a couple of dozen oranges.

In a corner I got to work, grinding down the fruit-flesh with an ancient mincer (aha! If only I'd known!), sneaking cupfuls of concentrate and the odd can of tomato juice from the stores, pulping and grinding in an anxious frenzy. The oil was a dilemma, but also the making of me. In it went, pure olive oil. There was secrecy in it, and no great abundance in the supply room. And all the time that pound note looked less and less like good value. Curiously, though, I felt a certain pride, almost a reverence for the task, with Mulligan's words echoing in my ears: *Oh, and, please,* olive *oil; of that I really must insist.*

And so it was that, as casually as possible, I stood over a pan of pure olive oil on a slow flame, and carefully stirred in a half-pint of honey, mimicking as far as I could manage the slow arm movements of someone heating milk and eggs for a custard. Oil and honey are at best distant relations and, although once heated through the emulsion had a not

7

unpleasant taste, the oil did tend to rise. However, the job of introducing the sweetened oil to my juice mixture posed more acute logistical problems, and in the end I carried the lot off to my bedroom in a steel bucket. I whisked and whisked until my arm went into cramp. To my surprise, the stuff combined tolerably well, and although one couldn't have said that it was a tasty concoction, neither was it all that bad.

Then I returned to my quiches and the luncheon preparations, leaving the bucket hidden inside my wardrobe. Six hours later I whisked the mixture again and put it into eight milk bottles.

At five minutes to five I began my furtive scurry through the hotel, the heavy crate of bottles in my arms, avoiding the main staircase entirely, sprinting along old servants' corridors and up dark, winding stairwells only used in emergencies. When I arrived at Mulligan's room, sweat had begun to trickle down my forehead and into my eyes, and as he opened the door I was blinking maniacally. Before I had chance even to look at him I had been yanked inside, and the door closed behind me. The room was full of the charming, intermingled smells of cigars and cologne, and in one corner hung a purple velvet smoking jacket, which, since Mr Mulligan was wearing a waistcoat and trousers of the same fabric, I guessed was part of his evening dress.

He fussed around with his cigar, unable to locate an ashtray, and finally popped the burning stub back into his mouth. From the wine crate he extracted a bottle, examined the colour of the liquid against the light from the window, and sipped. He murmured his approval, before replacing the bottle.

'Not all fresh, especially the tomatoes, but a fine olive oil at least,' he said, nodding towards a table where another pound note awaited me. 'And that comes with my sincere gratitude, young man, to be sure it does.'

But I didn't take the note. I wasn't going anywhere until I'd had an explanation. Although in retrospect it was pure naivety which led me to such presumptuousness. Michael Mulligan, as I was to learn, was not a man whom one obliged to do or to say anything. If the King himself (the Queen by that time, actually) had desired something from him, it would have been requested formally, as a polite favour. In my ignorance, then, I stood my ground until an amused curiosity crept across his face.

'I can see,' he began, sitting down in an armchair and gesturing towards another, 'that you want explanations, not cash.'

He laughed, not the big belly laugh one might have expected, but a high-pitched, impish giggle. I sat down and waited for him to continue.

'That in itself is commendable. Here,' he said, offering me a cigar.

I accepted it, lit it as one would a cigarette and, for want of knowing better, sucked heavily. All at once my lungs were full of burning rubber and dark, sizzling caramel, and my stomach lurched and tore itself in all directions, my throat near to rupture as I forced repeated vomit-spasms back down. Not only did I avoid vomiting but, to my amazement, neither did I cough.

Mulligan looked on with interest, and as I recovered from my first taste of a Havana, he said: 'Now that sort of thing I find really *quite* impressive. You neither coughed nor were you sick, although even your evident pride has not been sufficient to keep your face from turning green. One doesn't, by the way, inhale the fumes of a cigar. But I digress. Keeping it down! That's what this is all about, my friend. The mixture which you prepared will help me to do likewise this evening.'

My head swam uncontrollably, and I was too debilitated by my lungful of smoke to make any response.

'I have a rather unusual dinner ahead of me,' he continued. 'And your fine mixture will ensure that not only can I get it down, but that I can *keep* it down. Tonight, I will be eating furniture.'

I looked at him, but quickly diverted my stare; I realised that I was in the company of a madman. However, the newly-lit cigar in my hand smouldered, and from what I had often seen in the hotel dining room, a cigar of this length and thickness was going to go on smouldering for quite some time. From its tip a fine strand of blue smoke curled off into the air, but too little and too slowly, and I willed the thin ring of ash to speed up, to eat its way down the filthy stick with more visible speed, as a cigarette consumes itself in a gusting wind.

I desired only one thing more than to escape his smoke-filled room, and that was to confirm that he really had said such a thing. With this information I would quite happily have fled, cigar in hand, back to the hot, frenetic security of the kitchens.

'I am an eating specialist,' he said, and again I hardly knew how earnest or capricious I was to take him, 'although, if I say so myself, of a rather exclusive kind. Not an *attraction*, in the normal sense. I do not actually attract people. My performances are entirely private affairs. But perhaps you have seen something of my profession, or heard of it at least?'

I assured him that I had not, shaking my head vigorously.

'And in the pub, or at the fair, have you never seen men competing to be the fastest with a yard of ale, to the delight of all around? And have you never heard of the great pie-eating competitions, of tripe-swallowing and the like?'

I had to admit that I had.

'Well,' he said, turning his palms upwards humbly, 'every profession has its amateurs, its quaint traditions and its side-street hobbyists. And every profession has also its experts, its virtuosi, its aristocrats. I, if I may be so bold as to say so, am of the latter category: a gentleman eater.'

And thus he began a narrative which took us not only to fine, seaside hotels in the north of England, but across the great oceans, to places and societies which, even in the depths of despair during the war, I had hardly dreamed existed.

*

Michael 'Cast Iron' Mulligan left Dublin in 1919 and followed many of his compatriots to the New World. A combination of charm and immense size and strength led him quickly into the public relations departments of New York's finest bars and restaurants; that is, he became a liveried bouncer. However, he began to make a name for himself not through the grace with which he could remove drunks from the premises, nor the unerring discretion with which he could explain to a troublemaker just why he ought to make his trouble elsewhere, but after the evening's work was done, whilst eating with his colleagues. Here he showed a talent for food and drink which amazed and frightened all around him. At first they thought he was just a hungry boy from the countryside feasting for the first time on good American food. But it continued, day by day, week by week, the quantities growing steadily. In the early hours, when the last of the customers were slamming taxi doors behind them, the band packing away their instruments, the kitchen would fill up with staff – waitresses, doormen, musicians – all waiting for that boy Mulligan to eat.

Such feats soon got him talked about, and not just below stairs. Before long the fine clientele of the restaurants and hotels where he worked got to hear about him, and wanted to see the greedy Irishman in action. However, the genteel nature of these establishments meant that demonstrations of this kind could take place only behind closed doors. Vaudeville, and more especially the freak-show business, was full of swallowers of all descriptions, and no association with such lower forms of entertainment was desired. So, before he knew exactly what he was getting into, Mulligan was performing nightly for enthusiastic private parties of rich New Yorkers, eager for any novel and diverting spectacle.

In those days he was strictly a quantity man. And his act came immediately after an audience had finished dining. That is to say, it came at the precise moment when, to a tableful of gorged, drunken socialites, the very sight of someone eating was in itself revolting. That such a sight involved almost unbelievable amounts of food merely exacerbated the monstrousness of the performance. To Mulligan it was no more than an extension of dinner, and each evening, after the show was over, he would pat his groaning stomach and shake his head with incomprehension, quite at a loss to explain his

12

growing celebrity. Night after night it went on: a basket of fried chicken, a bottle of champagne, a plateful of sausage, a quart of beer, two dozen lamb chops, a trifle ('a mere trifle!' as the script went) followed, as if to confound the disbelievers, by another, identical trifle ... The act came to its climax when, plucking a single rose from a vase, Mulligan made as if to present it to the most glamorous woman in the party and then, feigning to prick himself, would say: 'Why, this is a dangerous weapon! I better take care of it!' With which he would promptly gobble down the flower together with stalk (which he had de-thorned earlier), to the amazement of the city's finest.

One evening, after a particularly successful show in which he had performed a routine entitled *Americana* (forty-eight hot dogs, one for each star; thirteen slices of apple pie, one for each stripe; twenty-eight cups of punch, one for each president; and a brandy for Lincoln), he was approached by a thin, fragile man who spoke in a strange accent, and who had the eyes of someone who expects *yes* for an answer. Laden with a stomach full of borrowed patriotism, yet happy with his performance, Michael listened with great interest to the proposal: Paris, twenty dollars a week, more varied work ...

He was soon on a steamer to France, earning enough money through drinking competitions in the lower-deck bars that when he disembarked in Europe, he had more than two hundred dollars in his pocket, which he spent immediately on fine suits of tweed and velvet.

On arrival at his new place of employment – another unmentionable hotel, I'm afraid, since it is still there, almost unchanged they say, although of course I have never set foot in the place – he found a rather different kind of job awaited him. Amid the grand opulence of banqueting halls, their walls covered in immense oil canvases and gilt-framed mirrors, and occasionally in the private suites of the hotel's more extravagant guests, he no longer ate his way through a fixed menu, but rather devoured whatsoever was requested of him. This, then, was the meaning of more varied work.

'I was the greatest!' cried Mulligan from his armchair, pounding his chest with a cannonball fist and laughing out loud. 'The act was pure theatre, pure spectacle. After dessert was well under way, I would arrive and sit at a place laid for me at the table, this place having remained ominously and threateningly vacated throughout the dinner itself. There I would assume a pose of impervious indifference to those around me, who, I should say, often included not only crown princes, sheikhs and ambassadors, but also the shrieking, guffawing minor nobility of any number of European states, not to mention the greatest actresses of the Parisian stage, to whom clung more often than not one or another chuckling millionaire. Yet, before my steely, unforgiving expression (in addition to my size), these diners usually appeared a touch intimidated, with those nearest to me the most humbled.

'And here we worked an excellent trick. The story went that I had been rescued from deepest rural Ireland (my red hair, which in those days I wore long, added zest to this detail), where I had been brought up almost in the wild by my grandmother. Moreover, I was profoundly deaf, and could communicate only through a strange language involving tapping one's fingers into another's palm, a language known only to my (now deceased) grandmother and the idealistic

Frenchman who had brought me to France on the death of my grandma. This man had become my trusty assistant – the young lad was really an out-of-work actor from the provinces, so out-of-work, indeed, that this was his first job in Paris – and each night he acted as interpreter for Le Grand Michael Mulligan.

'"Ladies and gentlemen," he would announce after my silent presence had generated its usual disquiet, "Monsieur Mulligan hopes that you have dined well, and will be pleased to consider your suggestions for his own dinner this evening."

'Now, a curious thing is that the powerful and highly placed citizens on this earth are frequently the most child-like. Thus, whereas these guests were prone to exaggerated, uncontrolled enthusiasm once they had become excited, it was not unusual at the initial stages of my act to encounter a nervous silence. Eventually, someone, an inebriated eldest son over from England for the chorus girls, or a fat German banker too pompous and drunk to know timidity, would shout out, "A sardine!" to great and relieved hilarity all round. My assistant would tap the message into my palm. In return, Le Grand Michael Mulligan would consider the request solemnly until the laughter had subsided, and would either give a controlled, deliberate nod, in which case the specified item was called for, or would decline with a slow shake of the head, glowering in the direction of whoever had made so contemptible a suggestion.

'And thus the evenings were enacted. The audience soon lost its coyness, and God alone knew what would come next. "Five locusts!" someone might shout, to the derision of the rest (in fact, we did have a small selection of dried insects, awaiting the order of any guest well known for his generosity), but through the derision an alternative would usually surface. "Well, if not locusts, how about worms?!" At which point my assistant and I would go into a protracted communication, resulting in the announcement, "Mr Mulligan will eat only one worm, since he says that he already has one, and another will keep it company!"

'That one always got an enormous laugh, but the laughter would turn to screams of horror as a long, wriggling earthworm was placed before me, and I sucked it up like a string of spaghetti.

'My twenty dollars a week turned out to be good business for the hotel too, since all petitions to Le Grand Michael Mulligan were billed to the requester. A very good business indeed. And in this way, sadly, I managed to bankrupt more than one person with my stomach.

'I had, very early on, developed a penchant for beluga caviare, which could, as you can imagine, have perilous financial implications. Yes, in this way I turned several of our best guests insolvent, although for the most part I think they probably didn't realise until the following morning. Yet it is a poor, sad-faced English gentleman for whom I harbour most regret. It happened on a particularly slow night, with no one of consequence (or imagination) in the house. My evening's work had run to a mere bucketful of cherries, a fox's tail (from a stuffed animal in the hotel lobby), and a side of pork belly, which I had rather enjoyed. Throughout the evening I had noticed, at the far end of the table, a man in a crumpled dinner suit, whose expression of empty fatigue had deteriorated by stages to one of inconsolable despair. With the mood rapidly leaving us, I was keen to secure one final request. Apart from anything else, I was still hungry, and my paltry *menu sélectionné* had thus far provided me with but a snack. Finally, the despairing English gentleman drew himself up from the nearly horizontal slouch into which he had fallen, and getting (somehow) to his feet, raised his glass.

'"My dear Mulligan . . ." he began, as those around urged him to retake his seat, ". . . fine, fine, noble son of the Emerald Isle . . ." at which point he belched, but I took no offence, ". . . I tonight stand here, a poor man . . ." ("You'll make another million, Quentin! Sit down, old boy!" came a shout from someone further down the table.) ". . . I have made and lost a great fortune. Yes . . ." he gulped down some port, ". . . but you, you of the fine orange hair, dumb to the heartless world which you neither understand nor whose vices, my dear sir, could you comprehend . . ." At which point he rather lost himself . . . "Err . . . ehm, but think not of this world, good man!" he rallied. "It is not worthy of your attention. Michael Mulligan, I toast you, and with my final sovereign I invite you to share with me my final dozen oysters."

'With this he raised his empty glass and held still, save for some involuntary listing, awaiting my reply. I communicated with my assistant, and indeed this time I really did use a form of secret language, for the message was unusual, and in truth it was rather a rash one.

'"Mr Mulligan will toast your future success, sir, not with a dozen oysters but with a dozen *dozen* oysters!"'

Here Mulligan took a long, pensive draw on his cigar, watching the rich smoke spiral upwards from his nose and mouth, spilling out into thin, flat clouds which hung in the air, forming a plateau across the hotel room.

'That,' he said wistfully, 'turned out to be a touch imprudent. A dozen oysters, two dozen, even six dozen, I had swallowed on one occasion. After all, seventy-two oysters are no heavier nor occupy more space inside than seven or eight braised pig's trotters, or a couple of ostrich eggs. But a gross of the things . . . Ha! It was the undoing of me, two nights running! And as for the poor Mr Quentin, we never saw his face again. Who knows, perhaps he is paying off the debt to this day.

'Ah, yes! Paris in the 'Twenties! How much I learned there, how much I learned. How much I ate!'

From his armchair he recounted more incredible tales, of churns of milk in Belgian monasteries, a grilled lion's paw in Baghdad, sinkfuls of pasta ('Tubes, my boy, the biggest possible! Pound for pound they look more!'); of a forty-five chitterling marathon in Brittany, ten kilos of roast cod in Bilbao, seven pickled mice for a bet in Marrakech. And he told me also of the people, those fine clients of the hotel, who sought a little extra zest to their dinner parties in Rome, Kabul, Delhi, London, Frankfurt, inviting him to their holiday entertainments in Goa, Rimini, Monte Carlo and Thessaloniki. On a visit to Tokyo he had consumed so much sushi that, in listening to him, one felt as if one were floating on a sea of raw fish; in Constantinople his ability to finish off an entire roast goat in little over half a day had so enthused one of the dignitaries privileged enough to witness the spectacle that Mulligan was presented not only with a belly dancer for the night, but was invited to extract and keep the bulging ruby which adorned her navel. Along the Magreb he had sucked the eyes out of more dead animals than he cared to remember, and the glittering rewards for such fripperies were staggering indeed. To crumbling European castles he had travelled, there to gorge on whatever his noble amphitryon decreed: seventeen pairs of bull's testicles at the table of the Duke of Alba in Salamanca; inconceivable quantities of sausage for any number of gibbering, neurotic Central European counts; regular sojourns to the seats of the Dukes of Argyll, Dumfriesshire and sundry other Scottish lairds, each one desperate that Mulligan improve upon some or other haggis-eating record, or simply curious to know how quickly their national dish could disappear down the throat of one man. For a time he was in huge demand in the USA, where he set a string of records for chicken and ribs throughout the Southern states; he amazed the Romanian Jews in New York with his evident partiality for ridding any restaurant of all its chopped liver and the relish with which he glugged down whole pitchers of schmaltz as if it were . . . well, metaphors are hardly appropriate; the Ashkenazim wouldn't have him, but he didn't mind, there were plenty of other sects, plenty of other religions, to astound; he even did a promotion for the pro-Prohibition Methodists, drinking the body weight of a six-year-old child in lemonade, presumably to illustrate that purity and excess can coexist. He repeated *Americana* for countless gatherings of businessmen, and in one particularly prolific afternoon's work notched up a record of sixty-two hot dogs (even before Babe Ruth's achievement) at a public demonstration sponsored by Wurtz's Wieners, a Chicago sausage company owned by one of those immigrants who really *wants* you to mispronounce his name.

'Then the Depression hit,' he continued, 'and the profession of gluttony suffered something of a downturn. The rich

19

became preoccupied, and the poor became hungry. Overnight, or so it seemed, no one wanted to see how much *more* than a normal man I could eat. Now it was a matter of just *what* I would eat beyond the normal. On its own this was nothing new for me. After all, for the better part of a decade a great many of the things I had sent down to my stomach could have been called food only through a very liberal understanding of the word, or by a desperately hungry person: in Oxford I had feasted on a sturdy hiking boot, prepared in advance, not *à la Chaplin*, but in vinegar and wine, and then slow-roasted in butter and olive oil; somewhere else (I forget) a mackintosh, curried; a canary in its little wooden cage (I mean, *and* its cage); a large aspidistra (leaves *au naturel*, stem and roots flambéed) . . .'

On he went, and as the list became more and more preposterous, my astonishment and incredulity grew in equal measure. This man, I told myself, was not only mad but also a great fabulist. However, I must tell you, before we go any further, that The Great Michael Mulligan was, in recounting these stories, very far from invention, for the truth was that he had eaten things far more extraordinary, more extraordinary indeed than he dared mention.

But how, you ask, can a man chew his way through a boot, or a raincoat? How, come to that, could he possibly sit down to a chair? Well, you yourself probably possess all that is necessary to achieve such a feat. A mincer, and a good dose of oil is all that you need. Mulligan had begun with a small kitchen mincer, to which he had fitted the finest, most durable blades available, and which was quite adequate for turning all manner of small items into an ingestible mince.

With the addition of larger and more powerful machinery, the toughest boot could easily be turned to a leathery crumb. And is that so hard to stomach? Have you never heard of Peter Schultz, or Jean-Paul Kopp? The former ate a Mercedes-Benz, the latter a biplane. Both employed the simple expedient of filing and grinding away slowly at the object in question, swallowing the resulting dust little by little along with a suitable internal lubricant. The aeroplane sounds impressive, no doubt, but it was really only a matter of time, and in the two years it took from propeller to tail fin, Mr Mulligan would have eaten his way through enough household items to furnish a decent sized parlour.

Over the years the great man designed a number of hand-operated grinders, with higher and higher gearing ratios, so that, along with the toughest and best grinding blades available, he was capable of turning wood into sawdust and small amounts of worked metal into perfectly edible filings. He never touched glass (although some did), but he was occasionally tempted by a china cup and saucer, or a particularly fine dinner plate.

'All of which explains my need for the mixture which you so expertly prepared,' he said, drawing his story to a close. He examined his pocket watch and stood up. 'You see, my friend, I really am going to eat a chair this evening. For Freemasons, I'm afraid, dullards to the last, but times are hard. And now I must prepare.'

He smoothed the velvet of his waistcoat down the vast, arcing curve of his stomach and went over to his jacket. I bade him goodnight and, with my head full of the most extraordinary tales of gluttony, as well as the effects of my first cigar, I wandered out of his room. I forgot my pound note and made my way back down to the kitchens quite without knowing which route I took, so immersed was I in a thousand new turns of the imagination.

That was my first stroke of good fortune: a chance meeting with a true king of his craft, a maestro fêted the world over, The Great Michael 'Cast Iron' Mulligan.

*

When I arrived back in the kitchens, I found the place unusually quiet. Dinner preparations were being conducted in a strangely subdued manner: hard beating had become feather-light whisking, brusque chopping replaced by slow, painstaking slicing, all eyes turned downwards. Either some-one had died, I thought, or someone had got the sack.

At that moment I heard a crash nearby. I looked down; a metal bucket lay at my feet. I realised, rather too late, that I had abandoned it in my room. Immediately I deduced the source of the abnormal quiet. Chef, from whose hand the bucket had fallen, knelt down and ran his finger around the inside of it. He closed his eyes in mock appreciation as he sampled the sweet, oily mixture. Then he stood up and faced me. He was a big man, but I was bigger. In a kitchen, though, physical size is of little consequence, as well I knew.

'Three questions,' he said as a sharp, aching silence fell around us. 'One: have you by any chance read tonight's menu?'

Instead of pronouncing the sentence with its appropriate interrogative intonation, though, he punctuated his delivery with a cuff to the side of my head, delivered with the full power of his considerable upper body. My ear crackled and buzzed, and immediately half my head began to numb over. Of course, I had not read the menu, yet I had little doubt that it included recipes proclaiming their citrus content, or their basis in finest Italian olive oil.

'Two: did you use *the whole bottle of oil*?'

The singular form sang out ominously for me. I began a forlorn nod, but even as my head dipped for the first time I felt my jaw rocket back upwards, as his forearm swung into my face, my teeth slamming together with a sliver of tongue still between then. I felt no pain, but, incredibly, a slight sense of relief that I had already survived two out of three.

'And finally,' he shouted, breaking into an exaggerated goose-step and circling me several times, 'DO YOU KNOW WHERE THE FUCKING LABOUR EXCHANGE IS?'

He bawled it into my ear from behind me and then, grabbing me by the collar, pulled me off balance and punched me three times in the back of the head as I went down.

Then nothing. And even from the floor I could detect quite clearly the horrified stillness in the kitchen, spatulas sinking unattended into batter, whisks suspended in mid-air, dripping half-beaten egg on to the floor. The blood ran cold from the side of my mouth, almost as cold as the icy floor onto which it trickled, and then the various sites of localised injury began to get their screaming messages through to my brain.

'We need that veal stock in five minutes, eh!' Chef called out suddenly, breaking the silence. Back came a clipped reply. And things returned to normal. Some of my colleagues threw me sympathetic glances as they stepped over my crumpled, aching body. But no one offered assistance.

By slow, agonising degrees, I made my way to the door, and got myself to a low crouch. Then, as I stumbled out of the kitchen, a young trainee who I had come to know

23

hopped out after me, making sure nobody had seen him, and asked: 'What did you do with it? Everybody wants to know, especially Chef. It's been driving him mad, but he's too proud to ask. What the hell were you cooking?'

It was a second or two before I recalled.

'Mulligan!' I said, more to myself than to my friend.

'What?'

'Le Grand Michael Mulligan! I cooked him a chair!'

I reached his room just as he was about to leave. He ushered me back inside and helped to clean my blood-smeared face. I attempted to explain what had happened, despite my damaged tongue, and then, suddenly, as he dabbed my chin with a damp towel, he furrowed his brow as if something striking had occurred to him.

'My word!' he said, patting first the top of my head and then his own, 'you're almost my height! Not as broad, naturally, but, *by Jiminy*, you're no stripling either!'

With that he dashed over to the wardrobe, pulled out a black dinner suit and threw it at me.

'Put that on, my boy, and forget your woes. You're coming with me!'

With not a moment's hesitation I changed into the suit. It hung about me like an untethered tent, but the length was not too far off the mark, and all in all it lent me an almost eccentric aspect.

'The car's ready,' he said, lighting another cigar and consulting his watch. 'Tonight, you will be, let's see . . . Captain Gusto! Yes, that's it! Captain Gusto, assistant to The Great Michael Mulligan!'

And that was the second stroke of good fortune to befall

me that day: to be beaten senseless by a furious chef and, as a consequence, to be invited by Mulligan, the great man himself, to share the stage for his most enduring act.

The car was a shining Rolls-Royce. I climbed inside, and Mulligan backed his ample frame in through the opposite door and on to the driver's seat, which had the appearance of being rather flatter and less bouncy than the others in the car, somewhat like an over-egged sponge that has risen enthusiastically and then turned sad in the oven.

He reached behind him and took one of the pint bottles from the crate on the back seat.

'Care for some?' he said, before polishing off half its orange contents. 'I have a long evening ahead,' he added as way of explanation.

On the way to the event I tried to get him to elaborate upon the stories he had told me earlier that afternoon. At last, perhaps somewhat exasperated by my incessant questioning, he said: 'My art is something which really must be observed. No manner of description will suffice. Have patience, and you will see . . .'

'Seeing is believing,' I chuntered, as an errant strand of incredulity wrapped itself around my thoughts and introduced doubts not only as to the true nature of his act, but also about where this monster fruitcake was taking me.

Mulligan brought the car to an abrupt halt, right there in the middle of a twisting, coastal road. I lunged forward, sliding to the edge of the shiny leather and getting halfway to an involuntary squat in the footwell. His wry, twinkling eyes had turned dark, all fire, and stared menacingly into mine.

'Seeing, my friend, is comprehending. Seeing is understanding.'

And with that, his eyes still fixed on mine, he reached behind him for the half-finished bottle, and proceeded to empty its contents down his throat.

We resumed our journey, and my apprenticeship began. From that day on I began my education in the lore and history of our trade. Mulligan would talk about the distant past, of old, famous, forgotten names: The Great Eusebio Galante, Franz 'Fledermaus' Pipek and Rocco 'La Rocca' Fontane; of Sammy Ling ('He'll eat anything!') and his predilection for neckties; of who'd eaten most; of scandalous, illegal records set in the back streets of hardly remembered Bavarian towns; of the rotten and the rancid, eaten and (allegedly) digested for a bagful of the local currency; of the unfortunate demise of Henry 'Tubby' Turns; of the great American masters like Nelson Pickle, who at the height of his powers had eaten a grand piano (baby, no frame) in little over nine weeks as a promotion for a new Detroit music store – those were the Prohibition days, great times for professional gluttony! – poor Nelson, who came to Europe to give eating demonstrations at the great German beer festivals and died of alcohol poisoning after assuming that beer was beer the world over and drinking a keg of Belgian Trappist in a single weekend for a bet.

That night was also to be my first appearance on stage with Mulligan. The evening began inauspiciously. After a long drive we finally turned into the forecourt of a large, somewhat podgy Edwardian building. He smiled and said, 'Well, Paris it's not, and it's no palace. And, I *assure* you, there will be no crown princes in the audience! But this, for tonight, is work.'

We unloaded some heavy wooden crates from the car and wheeled them around to the back of the building. A cheery but nervous man in a tight-fitting dinner suit greeted us, a glass of gin in his hand, and led us into a large, modestly elegant dining hall. The place smelt of Sunday school, but with the added aromas of overcooked meat and aftershave. Forty or fifty place settings announced, by means of the sorry array of cutlery at each, a rather strained attempt at luxury. The man with the gin pointed to a small semicircular stage at one end of the room.

'Everything is as you requested,' he said to Mulligan, looking around the hall a little anxiously. Mulligan himself surveyed the tables, and then turned his gaze to the stage.

'Yes, yes indeed. All appears to be in order. Quite acceptable. So, there remains only that small transaction which my accountant constantly reminds me must never be overlooked . . .'

The gin man stared down into the glass.

'We do . . . you know, it was rather felt that, that . . . that *that* would normally come after . . .'

His voice tailed off. Mulligan said nothing. The three of us stood there, a very distant murmur of cocktail chitchat in the background, Mulligan's amenable, matter-of-fact smile fixed on his face. After a handful of long, cringing seconds, the poor chap reached into his breast pocket and drew out a brown envelope.

'You'll find it all there,' he said in a soft, defeated voice.

'Ah, splendid!' said Mulligan, bursting into activity. 'I'll make you out a receipt—'

'No, no, that won't be necessary,' the other replied, hitching down his jacket and turning away. 'If you could begin after coffee and be finished by twelve,' he said over his shoulder as he started out towards some elaborate double doors at the other end of the hall.

Mulligan opened the envelope, smirking.

'The people one meets in this job! I don't know! Get me another bottle of the mixture, would you?' he said, quickly thumbing through what appeared to be a considerable wad of banknotes.

Our preparations that evening were meticulous. On the little stage we erected the apparatus, each of its separate cast-iron pieces removed one by one from the crates and taken from their wrapping of soft, oily cotton cloth. I assisted where I could in the assembly of the main frame itself, a four-legged structure which bolted down on to the bottom of the largest crate, which itself unhinged on all sides to become a sort of stabilising floor for the machine. From then on I was useful only in passing the maestro one greasy rag bundle after another. He pushed, slotted and clamped such a number of cogs, grinding cylinders and levers on to the growing contraption that I began to wonder if he was going to attach wheels and a petrol tank and drive off into the distance.

Mulligan's concentrated industry began to yield results. The nascent iron structure slowly grew into *The Machine* – the very largest hand-cranked mincing machine you could possibly imagine. If, I told myself, just if he really does plan to eat furniture this evening, just if, then at least he has something which is of potential use. I peered down the funnel and saw huge, menacing teeth poised like bunches of iron knuckles, ready to pound raw granite to a crumble, or so it seemed; I peeped around the back at the intricate system of gears mounted around a series of progressively smaller grinding chambers; I studied the tiny opening from which the mince would emerge, hardly bigger than a bottle neck. The Great Michael Mulligan, then, was going to eat a ground-up chair.

Still in shock, and for the first time truly believing that such a thing could be done, I looked around the hall, wondering where the chosen item had been positioned. Surely, but surely, it would be a special chair, its legs partially hollowed out, or made of balsa wood. Meanwhile, Mulligan put the final touches to The Machine and gave the plaque bolted to the funnel a brisk polish. *Mulligan & Sons* it read, gleaming brass against racing green. Later I learned that his father, the owner of a Dublin foundry, had disowned his son Michael on learning of his new career as a 'bloody glutton'. The plaque had been sent secretly from Ireland by a brother.

Mulligan stopped and admired the plaque for a moment, and then came up to me and stood by my side.

'Now, Chef, why don't you select a nice, plump chair for me?'

For the duration of the dinner itself we sat in a back room, glad not to be partaking of the paltry feast which four dozen Freemasons were busy praising through grinning, shiny faces, each one of them eager no doubt to disguise their disappointment. Mulligan decanted six pints of the orange liquid into a tall, vaguely Egyptian-looking jug, and took occasional sips from the one remaining bottle. He explained the part I would play: I would be dumb, although only for effect, not as a stated disability. To this I had no objection, since I am by nature a retiring person, and of course my tongue was still throbbing. I was also beginning to feel unwell, although I would later recognise this as stage fright.

The rumbling, masculine conversation out in the dining hall turned by degrees to a controlled, middle-class raucousness. They sang a song, or perhaps it was a hymn, it was hard to tell, and there were a few short speeches which were greeted with hearty approbation. Then The Great Michael 'Cast Iron' Mulligan was introduced, to a combination of polite applause and a good deal of muttering.

Suddenly, perhaps for the first time in years, the sundry magistrates and bank managers, the police officers and provincial lawyers assembled to celebrate their collective worth, were confronted with a man whose most evident baggage was a bunch of superlatives, enough to pour scorn on the very loudest boasts of English Freemasonry: the biggest man they had ever seen, almost certainly, and without doubt the handsomest giant; the most outrageous suit, and the most booming yet also the sweetest voice; the most confident, the most endearing, perhaps even the wittiest man they had ever encountered. And, of course, the most intimidating, whose great strength and power manifested itself at each moment, evident in the very slightest detail of his movement, in the way he would stand behind someone's chair and rest an enormous hand delicately on that poor soul's shoulder, and in the way he had of running his eyes casually up and down a whole row of men, as if to register in passing how, even en masse, they might consider it prudent to grant him their most careful respect. He was also, as far as any of them knew, the richest man in the room; not one of them would have failed to notice the Rolls-Royce outside, as they climbed out of their Morrises and Austins in twos and threes, or strode up from the bus stop, dicky bows peeping out above the collars of well-worn overcoats.

He began by praising his hosts for the splendour of their banquet, in that same lyrical tone which edged back and forth between seriousness and whimsy, and which, little by little, drew each diner up in his chair, stiff with expectancy, enthralled and rather embarrassed, yet unable to take his eyes off the great man. Mulligan himself wandered amongst them, stopping here and there to pluck a sugar lump from a table and pop it into his mouth. He recounted some of his more modest feats of ingestion, keeping it simple, letting each man present believe that he too could, just possibly, have eaten his way through a whole suckling pig, or four brace of pheasants; keeping it also within the bounds of human consumption, the six dozen oranges some-where or other, the ninety-nine sardines, the gross of oysters (although he omitted the aftermath). I think for the main part he made these stories up; the Great Mulligan was no more likely to go to Seville to eat a paltry seventy-odd oranges as he was to go to the barber's for a shoe shine. But he knew how to start, how to create atmosphere, taking and manipulating the assembled Masonic consciousness, running and developing it around the tempting notion of all-encompassing gluttony, as a great maestro takes a single theme and weaves from it a mesmerising sonata.

His discourse ran on and (it must be said) *on*. By subtle increments, though, he began to challenge even the most credulous before him, with tales of monstrous extravaganzas of consumption, of quantities measured not in numbers, but in *numbers of crates* and *sackfuls*.

The first snort of disbelief was heard quite suddenly, from the back of the room, and was followed immediately by the shuffling sound of an audience losing all faith in the act, the sound of embarrassment as a magician's illusions are *seen through*, of a comedian's jokes becoming hopelessly predictable. Mulligan played on this, indeed he appeared to relish it, and the louder the (still somewhat muted) cries of derision, the louder he talked above the noise, and the prouder and more outlandish his stories became. He laced his performance with a finely judged pathos. Waiting. Waiting for it.

'Nonsense! *Codswallop!*' came the full-voiced cry of contempt from some way off. Mulligan, caught mid-sentence, stopped and looked around to identify the source of the outburst. The room fell dead quiet, as forty-nine pairs of eyes watched one enormous, silent face move from shock to a hurt, childlike indigence, as if the Irishman had been found out, and his pathetic lies derided as the vulgar stuff of a fairground sideshow.

The chap who had voiced his doubts looked down into his coffee cup and shook his head, aware that, slowly, and without another word, the great man was approaching him. As luck would have it, the author of those first outspoken criticisms was a short, tubby fellow, rather red in the cheeks, and a true wobble-pot of inflated self-importance. When Mulligan got up to him, he bent down and whispered something in the man's ear. Tubby got to his feet, cowering under Mulligan's huge bulk.

'This man,' he boomed, standing behind his victim and draping both his arms ominously over the shoulders of the smaller man, 'this man, gentlemen, believes me to be a liar.'

Stifled gasps as the dread word rang out around the hall, and Mulligan's reverse bear hug tightened, so that the little chap's ruddy cheeks turned purple.

'A liar,' Mulligan repeated, emphasising each syllable with a good, solid slap of his hand on the chest of the wilting individual caught up in his embrace. From the shadows at the back of the stage, where I was sitting, horrified and amazed in equal measure, I noted that those most proximate to Mulligan wore concerned expressions, trying with no success at all to treat the whole thing as a joke, whereas those further off appeared to find the scene wildly amusing, nudging each other and sniggering like schoolboys, although their animated delight was for the most part silent.

Then Mulligan's face lit up. He broke out into the broadest smile and released the short, fat man. Spinning right around on his heels twice in uncontrollable joy, he announced: 'I have a plan!'

More murmurs now from the tables, some of which seemed to indicate a resurgence of boredom and embarrassment with the act.

'Sir,' Mulligan continued, talking to the little man, 'I cannot eat you' (amusement all around). 'No, we all have our standards' (hoots of laughter), 'but I can perhaps regain my honour. You will at least permit me that small favour?'

The man in question was too abashed to do anything other than nod. Mulligan cleared away a few plates and glasses from the place setting in front of him and, picking Tubby up like a child, sat him on the edge of the table, his little legs dangling down like a puppet's. A concerned kind of laughter stirred around the hall, whilst Mulligan fussed about, apparently looking for something. He turned all of a sudden and, tripping over the vacant chair behind him, fell to the floor.

A few wisps of cruel laughter could be heard, and other diners looked on with pity. Further off conversations grew afresh, as if the act were already a rather tiresome irrelevance.

'This is it!' came a deafening cry from the ground. Everyone stared, but instead of Mulligan getting to his feet, they saw the chair rising slowly into the air. Then Mulligan stood up, the chair held high above his head. 'This, my friend,' he said, and brought the chair down, holding it right in front of the little man's nose, 'this is what I will eat tonight! I will eat your chair!'

With that he marched over to the stage, on to which there now fell some light, illuminating not only myself, but also the imposing form of The Machine, which lay shrouded in red velvet.

Inside my baggy dinner suit I prickled with sweat, desperate to get my part right, and at the same time feeling a certain complicity with Mulligan, who even now was tweaking and poking at the audience's disbelief and mercilessly burlesquing the pity directed towards him only moments before.

'Gentlemen,' he shouted, twirling the chair effortlessly in one hand like a toy, 'although I am twice the man of anyone here today, my teeth are my weakness. Once, in Torquay, I no more than nibbled on a hatstand, and got a cracked molar for my troubles.

'But,' and here he swept away the red velvet, revealing what on first sight perhaps most resembled a pygmy combine harvester, 'I will swallow this chair tonight . . .' (chuntering and some giggles from the floor), '. . . wood . . .' at which he snapped a leg off with his hands and tossed it to me, '. . . seat . . .' ripping a little of its fine gold braid from the edge of the chair's cushion, '. . . and screws!' flicking with his fingernails the tacks which held the seat's ancient cloth in place (only brass, quite thin). Gasps from the floor at the word *screws*. Many hands dropped down to feel the girth of chair legs; half a dozen men scrambled to put on their glasses and, having done so, stared all the more urgently at Mulligan, and then at the chair they were sitting on. The short, fat man, utterly mesmerised by Mulligan, slipped down from the table, never taking his eyes off the stage, and procured himself a vacant chair from the side of the hall. He retook his place at the table, lit himself a cigar, and settled back for the entertainment, apparently believing that his own ordeal was over – in this he was correct, for Mulligan was no bully – and in addition feeling perhaps just a touch proud of himself.

'You will, I trust, allow me a little light refreshment?' Mulligan asked, pouring himself a pint of orange liquid from the Egyptian jug and taking a sip. With that he gave me a nod. I dropped the chair leg into the funnel and cranked the long iron handle. At first nothing happened. The series of gears transposed my efforts into a slow, menacing rotation at the bottom of the funnel, but as fast as I might wind the handle, nothing happened. Then, little by little, the leg in the funnel began to move, turning and twisting, slowly at first but then with more animation, bobbing and dancing in the teeth of the grinder. The handle stiffened as the sound of cracking, splintering wood filled the hall, and the chair leg began its long, painfully slow journey through the mechanism. I worked frantically at the cranking handle, and even from the stage I could sense that there was not a single movement anywhere else in the place, all eyes on the top of the chair leg, which poked up above the rim of the funnel, but was gradually disappearing from view.

Wood moved steadily through the various crushers and grinders, but with more wood always entering from the top the job became harder, and soon I was lunging at the crank handle twice, once to wrench it up towards me, and again to push it back over for another revolution, throwing my body halfway back round with it.

Mulligan laughed out loud.

'Some day,' he said, turning to the dumbfounded men before him, 'this young man here will be as strong as an ox. But it will require work, oh yes, and a very special diet.'

Then he was off again, regaling his audience with more stories: of the time he had eaten a beehive, comb, honey, bees (fried), the lot; and the occasion on which, purely as a party trick in Hollywood, he drank the bathwater of a certain film star's six-month-old baby.

Was all this true? Was any of this in the least *possible*? You may well wonder, and from time to time, as I recall the great man's orations, those most expansive, most outrageous, most boastful claims, I too sometimes wonder. But there, in front of forty-odd men of sound mind, with Mulligan's sweet, hypnotic voice, and the low grinding of The Machine as it crunched, splintered and powdered solid wood, ready to assuage the gargantuan appetite which this extraordinary man proclaimed of himself, in those circumstances, in that hall, no one doubted a single word he said.

And I ground and I ground.

At last it arrived, the slightest trickle of powder, although really it was more a dry, gritty pâté, which dropped from the pert sphincter of the big, iron digestive tract like pale, crumbly mouse droppings. Only then did I notice *where* it dropped: on to a large platter, a gleaming oval of fiery, crimson-hued gold, which was positioned directly beneath the grinder's nozzle. (A present from an ecstatic maharaja after he had witnessed one of Mulligan's regular appearances in Paris.) The platter was a part of the stage set which he kept concealed until the appropriate moment. On the large shining oval the pile grew fractionally. Feeling somewhat ashamed at my own performance, I redoubled my efforts, and before I knew it Mulligan had thrown another leg into the funnel, to resounding cheers from the floor. However, the cheers soon fell away to nothing as, pulling a golden spoon from his pocket, he stooped down and collected a sample of the chair dust, inspected it for colour and aroma and popped the loaded spoon into his mouth. There he remained, crouched and absolutely still; without thinking I stopped cranking, my incredulous eyes, like those of everyone else besides, on the great man. (Later, he commended me on this little detail, which, I have to admit, did add somewhat to the drama of the moment.) He moved his jaws in a slow, ruminating fashion, and then, after an appreciative mumble, smacked his lips and sprang to his feet. Taking a quick drink, he announced: 'The chair, gentlemen, is exquisite!'

Shrieks and hoots greeted the announcement. Mulligan held up his hand for silence.

'Compliments to the chef,' he said, turning and giving a solemn bow in my direction.

More howls, and great applause. I returned to the crank handle, and Mulligan set to breaking up the rest of the chair. By the time he had got down to the seat, I had ground a tolerable amount, perhaps something more than a whole legful, and the pile of sawdust had grown to a dusty pyramid which covered half the platter.

He indicated that I stop grinding. With plate in one hand and spoon in the other, he shovelled the stuff into his mouth. He made as if to masticate for a moment, then put down the spoon and took a long draught from his glass of liquid. And swallowed. The audience chuckled, as if to say, *Yes, yes, that was funny, you really did swallow a mouthful of the stuff*. But he followed it with another mouthful, and then another, eating greedily, swilling it down with the sickly orange liquid, until nothing remained on the golden surface but a powdery film, turning the warm glow of the metal dull.

I recommenced grinding, and he, after refilling his glass, strolled amongst the tables in the hall, exaggerating, boasting, joking, until the next course was ready.

By the time he came to his fourth plateful, both his eating speed and the enthusiasm of his audience were on the point of waning. A true master eater, though, is not simply one who can swallow, but one who can make that swallowing an entertainment. So, he descended with his golden platter into the audience and offered some of the fare to a tall, elegant-looking gentleman near to hand. The man declined, but the one next to him dipped his tongue in, and through his expression alone confirmed that it was indeed no more nor less than sawdust. Another gallant offered to eat a whole spoonful and, attempting to follow the example of Mulligan, poured a full glass of port into his mouth to accompany the dust. He chewed and chomped, and with great industry tried to swallow the mixture, but to no avail; the whole lot came back out and was deposited into a large, white handkerchief which, curiously, he stuffed straight into his jacket pocket. Another, less sober individual thought he might upstage Mulligan's comic performance, and took a pinch as if it were snuff, but succeeded only in half choking himself.

Then we had the evening's tough. Permit me here to indulge in a little amateur psychology. I have, over the years, observed many gatherings of men (women, for some reason, are seldom to be found in great numbers at these events), and it is unquestionably the case that whenever groups of men congregate there is a tendency for one man to emerge as the tough, the hard type. Unlike the playground tough-boy, the adult version is seldom the leader of the group, and never at the centre of things. He may in fact say and do very little. Often he is neither the richest nor the most powerful; neither the most respected nor the most heroic; he is in fact more often than not the dullest, and his presence is only ever really valued if trouble erupts and reliable fists are needed. Anyway, in the company of Mulligan, even in sight of him, the local tough would often disappear from view completely, receding further than normal into the anonymity of the group. However, over the course of an evening, these types invariably sought some means of proving themselves in face of a seemingly harder, bigger, greater man. Let us say that in this respect Mulligan, quite without wishing it, constituted an unfortunate stimulus-to-act for these men.

On this occasion the fellow in question was a tall, grim-looking thug in his mid-fifties, not unlike Mulligan in build, but a degree or two smaller in all departments. A scowl had adorned his face all evening and now, just as Mulligan made to return to the stage, this man stood up, to a variety of rumblings, mutterings, and not a few *sit down!*s. But he stood firm, a pudding spoon at the ready, held down at his thigh, inadvertently, I believe, although it looked for all the world like a deholstered pistol. He stared straight at the platter.

Mulligan was not one for humiliating people, no matter how disagreeable they were, but this chap had certainly set himself up for a rather large slice of humble pie, although in this case of a rather unusual recipe. Mulligan had no desire to crush the poor man's infamy, yet what could be done? He marched over with the golden plate and, rather obviously *half* filling his spoon, offered it to the new challenger. Not to be put off with insults, the man brushed Mulligan's spoon aside and grabbed the platter, spilling a good deal of dust down his suit in the process. He dug his own spoon into the pile and brought it up to his mouth, spilling about half its load. Having tipped what remained into his mouth, he repeated the operation two more times, both times resulting in significant spillage, although at least proving beyond doubt that his mouth was indeed full. After returning the gold plate to Mulligan, he strode over to the stage, slowly and with his chest out in front, and took a long draught from the Egyptian jug. The liquid ran down his chin, staining his collar a salmon pink. When he could absorb no more liquid, he returned to his table, stood face to face with Mulligan and swallowed. Three times. After a period in which his hard face

turned red, and then white, he took up his glass of port and
drank that too.

Mulligan led the tumultuous applause. With the platter
held out in front of him, he shook the man's hand vigorously,
managing to spill a good cupful more dust down the front of
the chap's jacket without anyone noticing. Then, more as
a joke than anything, he offered the plate again. Somewhat gingerly, Tough then helped himself to a more modest
spoonful. To cheers all around, he slugged down someone
else's wine greedily and, after another long and protracted
swallowing, sat down, bringing his diverting cameo to a
close. However, his contribution to the evening's entertainment really only ended some twenty minutes later as he was
dragged out of the hall, groaning the word *mother*.

Then we were down to the seat. Somehow I didn't expect
him to eat it, horsehair, brass tacks and all. But in it went,
Mulligan tearing bits of cloth and stuffing from the main
structure and dropping them into the funnel. The grinding
became easier, and even the brass tacks, which were the
very final items to go in, seemed to cause no problems.

As soon as the last remains of the seat had disappeared
down the funnel, Mulligan made a furtive adjustment to The
Machine and whispered: 'Carry on turning!'

He had cut off the supply, with a good deal of the chair
still inside the grinder. Within seconds no more of the
fine, wispy grounds of horsehair and velvet accumulated
on the gold plate. Nevertheless, I continued cranking, and
he made an elaborate pretence of ensuring that everything
had been minced up, and that the last crumbs of chair were
ready to eat.

Whilst munching them down he delivered some amusing

41

observations on the nature of horsehair, it being but inches away from real meat etc., and once or twice, in great pain, removed a mangled brass tack from his mouth, holding his jaw in agony, and then offering it to a nearby member of the audience. Of course, the tacks from the chair were all by now ground down to a fine powder, or, indeed, were still inside The Machine. The mangled ones were from a supply of such items secreted in his jacket.

As the last spoonfuls of chair went in and, with much apparent effort, went down, I became alarmed at the great man's obvious discomfort; he walked ponderously, and held very still whilst, with a slow, tense concentration, he attempted to swallow. One felt that he was bunged up solid with sodden dust, and that each new mouthful found its way no further down than the back of the throat, where it lodged itself, tickling the uvula and impeding the flow of his breath. By this point his stomach was so distended that he appeared to be in constant danger of toppling forward; I am convinced that, for one horrific moment, every person watching believed that Mulligan was about to perish there on the stage, as his huge bulk ground to a final halt. The sawdust, it seemed, had set firm inside him.

And there he remained, utterly still, his eyelids drooping heavily like those of a man passing quietly from drunkenness to unconsciousness. Finally, his head turning painfully slowly towards the silent ranks of dinner suits, he said, in a quite unconcerned manner: 'I think I need a drink.'

After innumerable pats on the back, and calls of *Bravo!* and *Good show!* he finally opted for a place next to the small, tubby man, who grinned like a delighted child. He accepted a glass of brandy, and nibbled at the few petits fours which were left, in evident high spirits and answering the questions thrown at him with the best humour he could: *Have you ever eaten a horse?* ('Yes, but I made sure it was a filly!') *What about an umbrella?* ('The spokes get in one's teeth!') *Snakes?* ('By the sackful, my man! Nothing better!') *A window?* ('Let's draw the curtains on that question . . .') *The complete works of Dickens?* ('Not to my literary taste, but I did sample the pulped score of *The Pirates of Penzance*, and found it rather toothsome!'). Et cetera, et cetera.

Thus, my introduction to the art of eating had been, by preposterous good fortune, the very best possible. Mulligan stayed at the table with the Freemasons just as long as it took for everyone to realise, with incredulity still framing their thoughts, that this man really had ingested, had *dined* on a chair. Just long enough also to confound the widespread suspicion that he would dash straight off and expel the contents of his stomach down the lavatory. Indeed, he was eating again, and accepted at least three glasses of port from the excited company around him.

At last, with beaming, happy faces bidding him goodnight, and several dozen earnest handshakes and garbled declarations of his damned brilliance duly acknowledged, we began to dismantle The Machine. The process was over almost as soon as it was begun, since (as I subsequently discovered, to my eternal gratitude) the contraption was designed not so much for its compactness in transit as for the speed with which it could be returned to its crates. We were packed up and ready to go even before the last, drunken stragglers in their crumpled jackets and cock-eyed bow ties had staggered from the premises. The low-growling Rolls-Royce carried us away from the Masonic hall and into the darkened streets and lanes of northern England.

And it never occurred to me to wonder where we had been, east, west, city, town, village. The single point of reference I can offer is that, a good many miles from the place in question, behind a hedge on a secluded country lane, someone deposited a curious mound of damp, orange-coloured sawdust.

'Did you think I was going to sleep with that lot inside me?' he said, rather superciliously as he climbed back into the car and we headed off into the night.

*

For the next seven years I accompanied Mulligan around the world, although by this time his world had reduced in splendour and opportunity considerably. He never replaced the car, or the suit for that matter. But he kept going. And with the maestro's approval I undertook some freelance appearances of my own, during the increasingly long breaks between his own performances. Having neither the reputation nor the contacts which Mulligan could rely on, my own career began not in the homes of crown princes and cinema actresses, of shy millionaires with glamorous Riviera villas, but in obscure towns, unheard of village fairs, mostly in dark, faceless corners of Europe, and at the odd German festival where a hushed-up sideshow of bizarre and illegal acts would be organised for those of perverser mind than the sausage munchers and beer swillers.

Captain Gusto (for, after my impromptu baptism by Mulligan, I felt no urge to change the name) specialised in a modest eat-all programme. He would invite those assembled to offer up items for consumption, at a price. With each object offered he would state the cost of its ingestion, inflating the amount beyond the perceived pocket of an individual when disinclined to consume, and keeping it reasonable when the thing was more manageable. In return I paid a site rent to the fair, circus or freak show in question. I was, if you like, an itinerant beggar to Mulligan's aristocrat. But we both ate.

For the main part, though, we travelled together with The Machine. There was an endless supply of stories, mile after mile in that old, majestic car. Names and feats which amused, surprised or saddened, like poor Henry 'Tubby' Turns, who died in a sideshow tent in Pittsburgh whilst trying to keep two rats down, out of pure professional pride, and even against the wishes of those half a dozen appalled Pittsburghers who'd paid to witness it. Our conversation would also touch on more recent times, to the decline of our trade and the rise of public opinion against us, to arrests and the lack of offers of work from travelling shows, the short-lived interest shown by television and the tragic cases of those who made it big on TV only to find that they were subsequently pursued all the more assiduously by local public health officials eager to stamp out the whole business. He warned me that things would only get worse.

He was right. Since then I have probably spent more time in local jails and courthouses than in hospitals. And hospital is by far the *better* place to be from time to time. In hospital, you say? Yes! As the mountaineer can expect the odd broken leg, and the tennis player his eponymous elbow, so the eater is no stranger to the stomach pump and the enema bag. Nor does he fear the liquid shakes of gastroenteritis, other than through the loss of income which it implies. No, from experience I can affirm that I would prefer to be bound over by a surfeit of sawdust than by the local magistrate any day of the week.

But, alas, it was the latter which haunted my working days and meant that every trip, every performance, each appearance of Captain Gusto and his Marvellous Mouth required the planning and precision of a bank raid. And this, I need hardly tell you, made the job itself all but impossible. In the end one ingested not at one's leisure, as the great men did, slowly, drawing the audience in with a series of grimaces and exaggerated, faked gripes, staggering and holding your stomach as if it were about to burst and spill its contents over the incredulous onlookers before you. It was more a matter of gulping the stuff down with one eye scouring the audience, seeking out the blank face of a health department official, and with the other watching out for the approach of the fairground manager, come to tell you that he's been forced to close you down (although never to return your site fee). Captain Gusto and his Marvellous Mouth have, if I were to tell the truth, scarpered from more places than he (or I) would care to remember, sometimes with the marvellous mouth still chewing.

But back then, in the Rolls with the great man himself, who could have resisted? Could you, sitting right next to Mulligan himself, the tingling anticipation for that evening's performance already in your stomach, have thrown it all in for a steady job?

Working the fairs did have its benefits. For the main part, what was offered up consisted of the same things which the crowds themselves were eating. Someone would toss me a half-eaten apple, and I, pretending to examine it minutely, would quote a farthing, or the equivalent. The coin would be passed to me, and I would begin munching. If there came giggles from the audience, then perhaps I might discover a worm in it, or that it was rotten pulp on the inside. That didn't matter, for the humble apple would attract attention, and more pricey morsels would then come my way. Someone would pick up a sausage from the ground, covered in mud, and I would swallow it down for a penny, my mind fixed with hard determination on the thought of Turkish delight or smoked salmon. Once, in eastern France, a whole bunch of hysterical schoolboys passed me their sandwiches and, for a trifling price, I ate the lot, to the great disapprobation of the adults present, who scolded both me and the boys for such a foolish waste of good food. Another time, at a small and somewhat uncivilised country fair in the old East Germany (for the Iron Curtain was invariably lifted in those out-of-the-way border towns, where, to be honest, I have always been most in demand), a group of drunken young men threw me their half-eaten salamis and other, less appetising, varieties of cold meats. I ground the lot up and got it down in no time. That didn't satisfy them, and they went off in search of more entertaining provender, returning with a couple of ragged, inedible (or so they thought) cabbages, and an armful of dirty, mould-ridden potatoes. They had no more money to offer, but on the understanding that I envisaged absolutely no problem in chomping my way through the vegetables, the lads persuaded a great many of the prurient, grinning bystanders to cough up their loose change until, weighing the money in my hand, I gave a solemn nod and began to grind.

On that occasion, as on many others, I had to ask myself, 'Well, did you think I was going to sleep with that lot inside me?' The problem here, though, lay in making a sufficiently swift exit after consuming that item which one most desired to see coming out the same way as it went in. It was a matter of orchestration, of balancing the need to tread the ground of the astonishing, to excite and amaze, to encourage the proffering of extravagant objects; of balancing this with the requirement that, in general, a thing really worth the distasteful task of consuming was, by definition, the *last* thing which one would want to eat that evening. Afterwards, it was simply a matter of vacating the place as quickly as possible.

Meanwhile, the number of Mulligan's own appearances dwindled. One began to perceive in his comportment the slightest flutter of arrested fatigue. His appetite remained strong, but he strained under the effort of summoning up that visible relish which was always the most striking feature of his act. Without a doubt he wanted a rest, although the word 'retire' I mentioned to him only once.

'Retire!' he bellowed straight back at me, gasping under the sheer preposterousness of the suggestion. 'Retire? And what, might I ask, would The Great Michael Mulligan do in retirement? And where? One of those little retirement homes on the coast? Eh? Those prisons for the wrinkled and the incontinent? Eh? Eh? Perhaps with the occasional biscuit-nibbling demonstration, or championship Grape Nut chewing in the afternoons? Is that what you mean?'

I did not mention it again. But as his performances became more laboured there came a point when not just I but also some of his more enduring clients began to see in his feats of consumption not the old majestic confounding of one's senses of the possible, but an ageing man in a faded velvet suit eating furniture.

Then one night the inevitable happened. For the first time in his long career, the cruel, ignominious shadow of normality fell upon Michael Mulligan. It occurred during a performance for a bawdy and foul-mannered bachelor party, an evening which the great man had agreed to only as a personal favour to the groom's father, and which was to include the famous chair-eating routine. Part-way through the act, with two legs and a good section of the chair-back already ingested, he turned to me. His face had gone pale, and threads of sweat wound their way down his forehead. Above the raucous noise of a roomful of young men too drunk to appreciate either his repartee or the feat of ingestion being undertaken for their entertainment, he said to me: 'I'm full.'

Quite calmly he took a piece of wood which he had been on the verge of throwing into the mincer's funnel, and held it out in front of him. Then he dropped it. The wood made a muffled thud as it hit the stage, and the sound attracted the attention of a few revellers. There Mulligan remained, staring out at the audience, frozen to the spot, his mouth shut firm. His eyes tripped slowly from one young man to the next, each in his dazzling new dinner suit and claret-spattered shirt. One by one, table by table, their garrulousness fizzed away into silence.

He held their attention for a second or two, nothing melo-dramatic, but enough to register a kind of paternal authority. Then he spoke.

'It appears, gentlemen, that you find the act of eating a chair quite ordinary, quite . . . beneath your contempt indeed.'

Someone chuckled, as if to confirm the fact.

'*What!*' shouted Mulligan, as loud as I had ever heard him, looking straight at the source of the noise. The man in question shuffled; as if in jest, he made to hide behind the shoulder of his nearest companion. But nobody seemed to share his joke, and the truth is that he really did cower. I watched the poor boy's head drop and his whole body shrink behind the protection of the human shield.

Mulligan turned to The Machine and fished all the loose bits of chair from the funnel, tossing them over his shoulder theatrically, and making sure that one or two smaller pieces found their way into the crowd.

'Grind her through,' he said.

I began to crank again so as to empty the contraption; meanwhile, Mulligan fumbled in his pocket.

'Don't move a muscle, *boys!*' he sneered over his shoulder.

He pulled out a screwdriver. Returning to his audience, he continued.

'Right, you bunch of drunken morons . . .' (some murmurs from the floor at this point, and I too began to worry at his behaviour), '. . . since eating wood is not to the tastes of a roomful of insipid, spoilt children like yourselves . . .' (and by now The Machine was empty. I expected the worst), '. . . perhaps you require something a little more piquant?'

He began to unscrew the brass plaque. It was already dangling from its final screw when the first guffaw was heard, but even before he could turn around and face the audience a host of *Shhhhes* and *Quiets!* had silenced the guilty one.

The plaque dropped into his hands and he held it up for all to see: *Mulligan & Sons*.

'Sixth of an inch solid brass, my good men,' he said. 'I

would invite a member of the audience to verify the fact, but I doubt whether a single one of you pathetic mummy's boys has ever set foot inside a foundry, or indeed a workshop of any kind!'

It seemed that he was right, for the mumbling which followed his announcement was tinged with embarrassment. Then, at the back of the crowd, a dark-haired young man stood up, to the applause of those around him. A wave of surprised, rising intonations swept across the room, and Mulligan's authority seemed to dissipate at once. Towards the stage walked a tall, broad young man in a black suit far too small for him, his eyes cast down towards the carpet, and appearing not to enjoy his moment of celebrity in the least.

He arrived to great cheers, and Mulligan slapped him roundly on the shoulders, as if to confirm his acceptable solidity. The plaque was examined front and back, around the edges, and even through the screw holes. Finally, the young man nodded bashfully at the crowd and muttered something.

'Speak up!' someone shouted.

'It's brass,' he responded, but with the force of his nervous voice tailing away almost to nothing before the second word reached the front row of tables.

Mulligan took the plaque and dropped it into the funnel. I knew it was coming, but as it clattered down into the abyss, and with all eyes suddenly on The Machine, a curious, floating sense of panic seized me: it wouldn't work, it simply wouldn't, not a piece of solid brass. Yet there I was, poised with crank handle in my hands, the only person (I supposed) who had the faintest suspicion that the grinder had its physical limits, that whereas the occasional thin fragment of metal, a furniture tack towards the end of a performance or a stray hatpin from time to time, was one thing, a block of solid metal was quite another. I might add that as far as the *swallowing* of the brass itself was concerned I had not the least worry, for Mulligan still had three pints of liquid remaining from his aborted chair-eating, and in any case we would certainly be on our way soon after the last spoonful of brass filings had been swallowed . . . Nevertheless, I turned the handle with trepidation, as my arms became the centre of all interest.

The mincer caught the plaque in its greedy fingers. Groan of metal on metal. And then I could turn no more. Hard as I tried, jerking the handle backwards and forwards the loose inch of movement which it yielded, I couldn't make any progress, not with all the weight of my body pushing and straining against the damn thing. Something, I was sure, was going to give. Not the handle, for that was thick, cast iron. Nor, I guessed, the tough steel grinding teeth which lurked at the base of the funnel. What was about to give was my body, which twisted into one tense contortion after another as I struggled hopelessly, trying not to fail the great man, not to bring his final performance to a close on the pathetic note of an unfulfilled claim, a thing *not eaten*.

But the handle refused to move, as if it too had lost its appetite. And in truth I didn't blame it, after all the chairs, the plants, the walking sticks, coats and hats, shoes, boots, wallets, the toupee of an embarrassed and very drunk town clerk in Wallasey, any number of rugby balls, each carrying the fond memories of several dozen half-comatose old boys with it down Mulligan's gullet . . . Oh! how I winced as his life's work flashed before my eyes, all the stories and all the stuff I myself had ground for him. I wondered, indeed, whether The Machine was doing him one last favour.

Then I heard muted cheers, and I looked up from my pained hunch over the immobile crank handle to find myself being bustled by Mulligan and the large young man, one of them on each side of me, and both seizing the handle with such purpose that I was forced back between their bodies and clean out of the way. They set themselves against the iron handle, like two enormous ballet dancers at the practice barre waiting for instructions.

They didn't wait long, though, because between them the two men soon persuaded that stubborn arm to resume doing what it did best, and the room was suddenly full of the snap and thump of grinding metal. The Machine did perhaps begrudge the task a little, corners of the flattened travelling crate which formed its base rising clear off the floor and thwacking back down repeatedly as one and sometimes two of the contraption's legs veered up in strenuous complaint. But Mulligan and his new assistant stuck at it, despite the heavy labour it clearly cost them.

Eventually, a fine golden-brown powder began to trickle out, and the assembled audience broke into excited jabberings. As soon as I saw the familiar pyramid of dust begin to grow on the gold platter my anxiety lifted. Mulligan had only to wait for a convincing mound to build up and then flick the supply switch. Three spoonfuls of metal filings would hurt no one and, let's be honest, do *you* know how much powder a solid brass plaque makes?

A great deal. The plaque made a *great deal of powder*, because Mulligan did not turn off the supply. On the contrary, his grinding became increasingly spirited, until the unfortunate fellow at his side began to cast nervous glances at him, as if some strange mania had taken hold. In the end nothing more than the odd wisp of heavy dust dropped from the nozzle of the grinder, yet Mulligan went on and on, the handle flying round like the pedal of a speeding bicycle. Ominously, the platter boasted a substantial mound, and it seemed that only the great glutton himself was oblivious to the fact, for even the young man who had assisted him in the grinding had turned to stare at the curious product of his efforts.

Out came the spoon and, of course, you know the rest.

Only it wasn't quite the normal end to an evening with The Great 'Cast Iron' Mulligan. After the last of the plaque had been ingested, Mulligan found himself with a still-mesmerised bunch of drunken youngsters in front of him. Mesmerised, that is, but still a bunch of arrogant fools.

'Is that it, Mully?' someone shouted, to which a few equally intrepid souls added their dissatisfaction. Mulligan, for once entirely lost for words, stared at the offending stripling for a handful of seconds. He took up his Egyptian jug, which thanks to the unusually short programme still contained a full pint of the sticky orange liquid, stepped up to the lad and covered him in it, head to foot.

What followed I recall only as a series of blurred, fragmentary images. Two or three young men hanging on to Mulligan's shoulders ... a fist slapping into a surprised chin ... legs flying up like brandished hockey sticks ... contorted, grimacing faces shouting. Then a red-faced Mulligan was struggling to shake off half a dozen violent revellers and, once he had done so, launched his forearm with great precision towards the small, blond head of one unfortunate youngster, whose body immediately crumpled under the weight of the blow. He was laughing out loud as one by one his assailants flopped down to the carpet, or withdrew from the affray shaking their heads in confusion.

'The Machine!' he shouted over his shoulder. 'Pack The Machine!'

The crates were soon packed. Those few partygoers with any remaining belligerence looked around them and, finding nothing but pain and cowardice to back up their next assault, shrugged their shoulders and wandered off to the bar.

The young man who had helped with the grinding snuck out with us through the back of the stage to help load the crates into the Rolls. Then, opening one of the crates, Mulligan found the gold platter, wrapped it in a large, oily rag, and presented it to the young man.

'Here, my boy. I won't be needing this any more. Take it, with the gratitude of Michael Mulligan.'

The fellow appeared pleased enough with the gift, until he felt its weight and deduced its composition. His big, boyish face turned from surprise to disbelief, and he made some mime of protest, offering to return the valuable plate.

'Nonsense!' said Mulligan, brushing the idea away with his hand. 'No need of it now, you see. None at all. I have,' and here he cleared his throat rather dramatically, 'retired.'

We bade the young man goodnight, and off he went. He had only spoken two words to us all evening: *It's brass*.

The drive home that night was unusually tense. We said nothing, and we made no stop along the way.

The next morning he presented me with The Machine, and announced that he was going home to Ireland.

*

Some years later, Captain Gusto arrived in Poland. A tiny border town in the west of the country, all consonants and drizzle. Twice before I'd stopped off there, only a few miles from the point where Czechoslovakia, Poland and East Germany met. Whilst the money I made hardly paid for my transit to the next place, there was always enough interest in my act to draw a decent crowd.

When I got there it was midday, raining, and I set up in a muddy corner of the fairground. My stand consisted of an old Morris truck, the side of which opened out to create a small stage, on which The Machine stood. As I secured the little feet of the stage in the soft ground, I got the feeling that the fair was permanent, that it had been there for months, years, and the locals had lost interest. The faces of the other stallholders were as grey as the sky, and their solemn frowns warned me to expect slow, slow trade. As the afternoon progressed I saw why. The odd loner mooched dispiritedly around, tempted by nothing, reaching into his pocket only to pull out a crusty handkerchief. The manager of the fair, who as always had provided me with a handwritten sign explaining the nature of my act in Polish, assured me that things would improve. I handed him the site rent and hoped he was right, for I had not a zloty more to my name.

By early evening things had picked up a little. Groups of twos and threes wandered aimlessly about, still the crusty hankies, still no zlotys. Something had happened to the town, its former dour, humourless expression had turned to certain misery. A young man, eager to engage me in conversation to practise his English, explained that several local factories had been scaled down or closed altogether after a spat between the local administration and the central government. Times were hard and, as the young man said, with a curious boisterousness: 'Nobody love to give her sausage you now!'

I pondered my ill fortune. What would Mulligan have done? No sausage, no zloty. No zloty, no go anywhere. In the past I had always managed to wangle a tankful of petrol during my brief excursions behind the Iron Curtain. It was far cheaper there, and the fairmen seemed to have access to it. For that reason I had left German soil and meandered through northern Czechoslovakia with hardly enough fuel to get me halfway back to the safety of the West. I feared what might happen to The Machine if I couldn't make it quickly back over the border, for these Polish folk had always impressed me as harbouring an imprecise shadow of cruelty within their deep-throated laughter. Had I known then just how cruel, I most certainly would have left the Iron Curtain securely drawn across that particular place.

So, dreading the idea of what might become of me if insufficient raw material found its way into my stomach that evening, I threw Captain Gusto into a bold display of self-publicity. As you might imagine, drumming up business for an eat-all sideshow without the aid of *language* was as trying for the Captain as it was puzzling for those onlookers whose attention I managed to catch. Not quite sure of what exactly was written on my sign, I nevertheless did my best to reflect the description of my act in a comical mime. Everything within reach I pretended to eat, from my own shoes to the caps of half a dozen onlookers. Confused yet intrigued, people shuffled up closer, read the sign, and fell into disgruntled conversation with their shrugging companions before wandering off, apparently none the wiser. The boy was right, nobody loved to give me her sausage now.

The night closed in, and slowly the crowds grew. I persuaded a young couple to part with a bagful of toffee wrappers, but it was a vain gesture, and as I gobbled them down straight from the bag, without even bothering to grind them up, they looked on with expressions of pure bewilderment, as if to say, *Why would you do such a thing?* As they walked away, embarrassed I think, I wanted to chase after them and make them read my sign. But I was too shy. Mulligan would have marched up to the young man and broken the sign over his head, whereas Captain Gusto was simply left there looking ridiculous.

Drunks hobbled by, the odd group of teenagers stopped and giggled, and one or two small offerings were accepted, ground and ingested. For pitiful amounts. After several hours of this I had garnered barely enough coins to run my idle fingers through as I waited, hands in pockets, next to The Machine.

Then a straggle of men approached. They were all middle-aged, dressed in rough, old donkey jackets, and each one had a cigarette hanging from his bottom lip. They eyed up my sign mischievously, and from the way they bundled and shoved into one another I could tell they were interested in a bit of fun.

'At last!' I said to myself, breathing a long sigh of relief as I prepared to launch into the long ritual which Mulligan, on hearing of my fairground style, had once mockingly named *The Belly Auction*. Proudly, I strutted up and down in front of The Machine, stroking my stomach with feigned pride, and began to sip from a beaker of the orange liquid which

I always carried with me. Then I strode arrogantly up to them and held my sign in front of their noses. They were a dirty-looking bunch, and the smell which radiated from them I can recall still, a damp, earthy mixture of raw pastry and tobacco. But I knew how to get the best from a bunch of drunks. So, choosing the man with the shortest cigarette stub poking from his lips, I stepped up to him, plucked the smouldering butt from his mouth, snubbed it between thumb and forefinger too quickly to be seen, and popped it into my mouth. As usual, it provoked mild amusement, and also caused each of them to re-examine the extravagant claims which my sign announced. They went into conference and I, well accustomed to the inevitable course of the little drama, withdrew a couple of yards and resumed my boastful prowl.

At last one of them was pushed forward by the group, a look of confusion on his ugly face. In one hand he held a pencil, and in the other a single coin. I made as if to mock the item and, snatching both the pencil and the coin from him, returned to The Machine to commence grinding. In half a minute the thing was ground up and swallowed down, along with one or two drafts of my sweet, lubricating liquid.

By now a modest crowd had gathered, attracted by the noise which the drunken men made. I strutted more out-rageously, working hard at a look of contempt which, in truth, I never felt quite comfortable with. But it worked. Another impromptu conference, and one of them, having been pressed with sundry coins, offered his cap. The cap in question was not an inconsiderable thing in itself, and I began to think of large payments and early to bed. However, the palmful of coins which came with it was, even by my desperately low standards that night, insufficient. In any case, I thought I might be able to improve on it. So I took the cap and tossed it back in the chap's face, making my dissatisfaction with the money evident. The growing crowd around us burst into laughter, although my would-be clients themselves found the act rather less amusing. Instead of augmenting their offer, they seemed to lose interest.

As they were about to leave, I grabbed the cap again and, waving my arm around as if boasting about the size of a fish I had allegedly caught, tried to indicate that my appetite was altogether more substantial than anything the size of a mere cap would satisfy. The crowd seemed to get it, for a range of encouraging and humorous-sounding comments came from all directions.

The middle-aged men themselves suddenly burst into activity. Whilst two of them made exaggerated gestures that I was to stay where I was (as if I was about to move), the others rushed off.

'Oh, a couple of cabbages! Let it be vegetable!' I wailed inwardly, rejoicing in the easy way that I had ensnared the lot of them, and already thinking of leaving the miserable place. Or turnips! I would have settled for half a dozen turnips, in whatever condition. The pulp of a rotting turnip is far less trouble that one might imagine.

There were by now something approaching a hundred people gathered there watching me, and each one appeared to have an opinion as to what the men would bring for me to eat. I kept up the strut as best I could, but this was not a comfortable moment, for as the anticipation grew so too did the difficulty with which I might be able to refuse any item proffered.

Then a few of the men returned, empty-handed, and a murmur went around the crowd as they began to circulate, whispering in ears and grinning stupidly. From where I was stood I could just make out the furtive gestures of money changing hands, and I realised that the men were collecting a coin or two from everyone present. This went on for several minutes until, when the collection was complete, a hush fell over us.

The other men now returned. They pushed their way through the crowd and strode up to me, a dark tarpaulin suspended between them. They dropped it and stood back. One of the money collectors stepped forward and on the tarpaulin he placed a cap heavy with coins. I got to my knees and weighed the cap. It was *very* heavy. Keen to maintain the tenor of the performance, I admired the money extravagantly. Then I pulled back the top of the tarpaulin.

A dog. A dead, half-rotten mongrel. Something between a Yorkshire terrier and a Labrador pup. Eyes dull and sunken, its flanks matted with the dried blood and pus of recent decay. Just for a second I tried to believe that it was a fake, part of an elaborate joke. But I touched the carcass, and it was real enough. It had begun to stiffen, and odd patches of fur had fallen away, revealing grey-fawn skin already dry and tight around hardening flesh.

The men drew closer. Their faces twitched with pride as they smiled their satisfied smiles at me. I stood, sickened more at their grotesque faces than at the sight of the dog, and spoke out over their heads.

'You people are too foul and loathsome to throw me your cruel orders!'

An attempt at something Mulliganesque. But I was wrong.

I had heaped too much derision on these poor, dispossessed people. And derision cannot be withdrawn, especially not when one has no words with which to do it. I was condemned, in the plainest sense, to the consequences of my own actions.

So I ate the dog.

I ground wildly, watching the movement of the carcass in the funnel, not knowing which parts moved as a result of the grinding, and which under the power of unseen colonies of industrious parasites deep within the decomposing flesh. Bones cracked and juddered through The Machine, and hairy fragments finally began to drop on to my plate, accompanied by the nauseating stench of decay.

I flicked the supply switch as soon as it seemed credible, leaving half the animal hidden inside the mechanism. But there was already a sizeable pile waiting for me. And then one last trick taught to me by Mulligan, the very last resort, from the emergency first-aid cupboard of the eater. A pint bottle of Tabasco sauce, which I emptied straight into my jug of orange liquid, to the delight of the crowd. I kept back the final inch of sauce from the bottle, and used it to wash around my mouth until I was completely numb.

I ate energetically, maximum quantity, greatest speed, and drank my hot liquid greedily. Gasps followed cheers, then groans of horror. The bitter, ammonia-stink of dead-dog mince reached far into the crowd. One or two fainted, and others staggered off in disgust, holding their throats until at last they spilled their guts on to the ground. People rushed in to watch, and an equal number rushed away, not quite believing their eyes. Each spoonful was thick with a heavy, musty-tasting fat, which collected in a thick film on the roof of my mouth. In desperation I tried to remove it with my fingers, scraping manically at the build-up of dog grease, and finding that it was also full of matted, bristly hairs. Then another slug of the burning liquid. I refused to look closely at the plate, keeping my eyes half shut as more and more of the revolting pile disappeared down my throat.

At last I came to the scraps, which lay in a smear of oily black blood on the plate. I looked about me, at the drunken men themselves (many of whom were still grinning), and wondered if I could contrive to spill what was left. My jug was empty, and there was no more Tabasco . . .

They were still looking. In it went. But with nothing to help its swift journey down, that last spoonful lingered, unswallowable, on the tongue. Saliva oozed and mingled with the dog until acrid juices filled my trembling mouth and I feared that the whole lot might re-emerge. However, with a combination of physical effort and the strongest, almost serene act of will-power, I did eventually force that final mouthful down. Immediately, my whole body began to shiver out of control.

At that moment I spotted a clear bottle in the hand of one of the men close by. I grabbed it and filled my mouth with its pale yellow contents. Strong alcohol, although more than that I couldn't guess, nor did I care. I swilled out my mouth, spat it out, and then drank down a large measure of the burning liquid. From within a distorted, swirling haze of nausea and light-headedness, I peered out at the laughing faces which surrounded me. Through my creeping, tingling flesh I felt a series of hearty slaps on shoulders and back. I had done it, and I knew then, like Mulligan before me, that I was full.

But the men, whose capful of money I had managed to lock inside my van despite the hullabaloo, refused to let me go. The bottle was pressed repeatedly to my lips, and slowly, like a casual, upright rugby scrum, we moved off, away from the relative sanctity of The Machine and the fair, into the darkness of the night.

We came to a halt under a huge tree, the distant sound of the fair still in my ears. Out came two more bottles of the yellow alcohol, which since my first, desperate mouthful, I had deduced was some sort of rude, home-made spirit. Tiny, thick glasses emerged from coat pockets, and each was filled with the stuff. One man went through a very slow, exaggerated drinking ritual for my benefit, stopping at every move to make sure I understood. First, he uttered a brief invocation, then drank down the spirit in a single draught, but with the added intrigue of doing so with his eyes firmly closed. Next, he threw any remaining drops from his glass over his shoulder in one quick arm movement, whilst emitting more sounds, this time something which sounded like *zw-sh-ss-szhszh* . . . There he remained, his arm frozen aloft, glass tipped over his shoulder. His companions shouted their approval.

With a dead dog inside me, and strong, sickening acid rising in waves from my stomach, drinking home-made spirit in a dark field was not naturally part of my plans for the remainder of the evening. However, I saw in the men's faces no hint of an alternative.

One . . . Two . . . Three . . . Mumble . . . Eyes closed . . . Drink . . . *Zw-sh-ss-szhszh* . . .

I looked around, my mouth stinging with the cold, peppery liquid. We laughed heartily, like pantomime rustics. The glasses were refilled. Then they were refilled again. And again. Between shots there was boisterous conversation, and much backslapping (especially mine). My presence appeared to be particularly welcome, and they stared right at me with a combination of surprise and fascination as I kept up with their monstrous, hardened drinking. The second bottle came and went, and I noticed someone returning with a third. I hadn't seen him leave, I don't think, but by now my head was nodding involuntarily on a rubber neck, and I tried without success to clean my mind of the thought of what was going on inside me. The situation deteriorated, and with it the firmness of my legs. And all the time the animal lay patiently within. I imagined maggots and ticks, warmed into action by my own gastric juices, forming little exploration parties and wriggling outwards from my stomach, crawling along the bones of my legs and arms, nibbling at fingers from the inside and dribbling their unctuous goo over the very sinews of my body. I saw them planting their thousands of eggs in my reddened stomach lining and gnawing at my frightened liver until it gibbered out of action.

My body was giving up on me, yet the glasses were filled and refilled. I could hardly keep my eyes from closing and, conversely, could hardly hold them closed as I forced each excruciating glassful down my throat. Eventually, I gave up trying, and with the dull, echoing sound of the men's laughter booming relentlessly in my ears I brought the glass to my lips yet again.

Unable to close my eyes as I swallowed, my head drooping down on to my shoulder, I caught sight of the chap next to me throw his drink clear over his shoulder, never drinking a drop of it. Immediately, the *zw*s and the *szh*s were uttered around the group, and beneath the sound of ugly consonants I made out the patter of liquid falling on to the ground. I realised that I was the only one still drinking.

*

Mulligan never got to hear about the circumstances surrounding the retirement of Captain Gusto, for he was dead on my return home. Of natural causes.

Had it not been for the dog I would have been back in time to see him. I had left Poland, still leaking at both ends and desperate to put my ghostlike body in the hands of the very first West German doctor I could find, and news of his imminent departure was already several days old when I received it. By the time I made it across to Dublin he was gone. I hardly had time to stroke his pale, smiling face before an enormous lid was hoisted on to the coffin and screwed down.

Eight pall-bearers got him with some difficulty onto their shoulders, and the hearse creaked and groaned all the way to the church. As the priest droned on, reading without animation from a little black book, I tried to imagine the great man in his prime, dazzling maharajas and actresses in Paris, joking and cajoling tables of glittering New Yorkers, that nonchalant flick of thumb and forefinger as another tasty morsel was popped into the non-stop mouth. I remembered making that first batch of orange liquid, the one which cost me my job, and the majesty with which, night after night, I had watched him enrapture his audience with stories too far-fetched to believe and then confound them by repeating the feat right there in front of them. The coffin was lowered slowly into the ground. On it was a plaque, polished brass: *Michael 'Cast Iron' Mulligan.*

With some effort I managed to stem my tears and bring my foolish, quivering chin to order. I knew that I had never been a worthy successor, not really. Then again, times had changed, I told myself, and I had made the best of things. As handfuls of dry earth rattled down onto him, one idea refused to leave me. Again and again I asked myself, and couldn't quite find the answer: had he been there in place of me, would he have eaten the dog?

After that I retired Captain Gusto, along with his Marvellous Mouth, and packed the mincing machine away for the last time into its old wooden crates. And I never went back to Poland.

No, I had never truly dignified the name of Mulligan, just as on that first evening I was not quite big enough to wear his clothes with dignity. However, there will always be one place, dirty and perhaps forgotten to all but its inhabitants, deep in a dark corner of a dark country, where the name Captain Gusto will be remembered.

THE POSSESSION OF
THOMAS-BESSIE:

a Victorian melodrama

I

1888. A workhouse not far from the city of Leeds.

At dead of night I dropped out, on to a cold stone floor. She licked the slime from my head. But there were others to see to. Five of us in all. So I pulled myself up into a ball and waited. This was good. Wait, and you'll see things far beyond the imagination. Find yourself a quiet spot. And watch. That's where it'll happen. In front of your nose.

By the time Joseph Markham was ready for his early-morning tea, the new arrivals had been discovered, in a small closet room which gave on to the scullery. The workhouse's much loved ratting cat, never before pregnant, was given a plate of milk. *There on the bare stone floor!* people cried in pity, and did what they could to make her post-natal sprawl more comfortable. Rags were fetched to form a makeshift cushion. And numerous scraps of food were left on the rim of the plate. Eventually, she fell asleep, sated on bacon rind, milk-softened bread and sweet biscuit.

Meanwhile, her new ginger-and-white miniatures had become the centre of attention. Workhouse staff crowded

71

in, gripped suddenly by a desperate urge to pick one up and coddle it. But clamour, as with all things in that place, was determined by seniority. So it was Markham, the superintendent, who took his turn first. A single kitten was placed in his arms. It lay there, quite motionless, a tiny lump of fur about as big as a screwed-up handkerchief. But warm. It warmed him right through, until he lost his usual stiff severity, and those around him in the scullery chuckled to see it. Then, in a rare moment of gentleness which fell like a thread of gossamer on the air, so transitory that its memory began to fade instantly, he lowered his chin to the animal held against his chest and gave it a kiss on the top of the head, as fondly as a child seeing its newborn brother for the first time.

Next, it was the turn of the clerk. He had only poked his head into the scullery to see what all the fuss was about. But Markham, a glint of delight in his eye, beckoned the clerk in and pushed one of the kittens into his unsuspecting (and as it happened, asthmatic) breast. From the clerk they were passed to the overseer, to the cook, and thence to a groom who happened to be there on an errand from a local benefactor's house, but who took his rightful place in the hierarchy.

With great care all four of the animals were now lifted from the floor, one at a time, as if at any second these small, living things might shatter into a thousand pieces. They were held up proudly like fragile prizes, to a chorus of cooing and breathy sighs of amazement. Then, as they were passed around from one pair of anxious hands to the next, wonder turned slowly to amusement; with growing confidence people began to handle them two at a time, laughing out loud as they struggled with their delicate haul. For the men in the kitchen the feat of holding two kittens in *one* hand seemed to have an added significance, and each of them had a go, grinning with pride, their brace of kittens hanging from a single arm.

Around the animals went, back and forth in all combinations. A clumsy first-timer would take one, holding it up for all to see as if the warm little mystery packet had only at that moment been discovered; with growing confidence, he would beg for more to be piled into his arms, until cries of caution were raised. The kitchen's two scullery maids, knowing that their turns were still some time off, clucked and gasped the loudest of all, and in the end they too found themselves holding a pair of kittens each. But this was not enough and they did desperate, squabbling battle to hold all four at once.

Tea was poured, as if in celebration of the new arrivals, but also to bring these unusual festivities to a close. A general mood of reflection fell about the place. They'd have to be drowned, someone whispered, and others, unable to refute the idea absolutely, looked down at their tea. As the horror of the thought set in, they began talking of who might take one.

'Mrs Thacker's a widow now,' said Cook, and almost immediately it was agreed that Mrs T would have at least one. Of course she would, a bit of company for her. Eyes were drawn inevitably back to those four vulnerable mounds of white and ginger, to their helpless yet quizzical one-day-old faces, and it seemed impossible that homes would not be found. At the back of their mind, though, each person knew that later the same morning an old flour sack would be filled with rocks from the workhouse grounds.

The superintendent drained his cup. Each of those around him took the hint and had their own final sip. Only the two scullery maids, who had endured the longest wait, continued fussing with the kittens.

Markham's fondness for cats had previously been limited to the satisfaction of finding his workhouse free of vermin. He would eye his big ginger ratter with pride each time she dragged in another slain rodent, perhaps thinking that he himself deserved some credit for the kill. But now he was full of admiration for the poor thing, who had carried four kittens to term without anyone noticing, and had delivered them alone on the stone floor. He stole back into the closet where she slept, resolved to give her an affectionate stroke. And there he made a discovery. A fifth, dead kitten. He stood in the doorway, looking first at the mother, sound asleep on a heap of old cloths, and then at the small lump of fur in the corner, obscured almost to black invisibility by the dark shadows in the windowless room. How much better it would be, he thought, to take the little carcass out now, an act of kindness to the mother, who would thus never have to see her own dead child. Quietly, he crouched down and pulled at one of the rags, drawing it slowly from under her, his eyes never leaving the dead kitten. As he prepared to stride across to scoop up the dead body and wrap it in rag, one of the maids bustled into the room, all four of the new kittens in her arms, and a pout on her face. She deposited them on the floor like a child with a new toy which is suddenly no longer amusing. She turned and left without a word, ignoring Markham entirely, a small insubordination which he hardly noticed. But the interruption had stopped him in his tracks.

Markham returned to the scullery. He noticed that even at this early hour there was a sense of unease, as people prepared to get on with the day's work. An old sack had been brought in from somewhere.

'John,' he said to his overseer, 'there's a dead kitten in there. Must have died last night. She had five, not four. Go and clear it up, will you?'

The sound of his voice was a sort of announcement. Markham it was who must order the drowning. *There*, his tone seemed to say, *the truth is we'll kill 'em.* So no one was saddened at the discovery of a fifth, dead kitten; that was the lucky one.

The overseer disappeared whilst Markham fidgeted with the length of rag, which he found was still in his hands. Those who remained now almost craved a sharp word from him: *Go on then! What're you all staring at?* they wanted to hear him shout, as a kind of release, an admission of guilt. But he said nothing, and continued toying with the cloth. People began to slip away.

Then John returned.

'It in't dead, sir,' he said, 'an' it in't a kitten!'

Markham stood for a moment, mouth pushed out in a moue of concentration.

'What do you mean? It was dead when *I* saw it.'

'Well, it in't now!'

What was the point, though? Dead or alive, it made no difference.

'Oh, let's keep it!' cried one of the maids. She had worked out what the sack was for, and now spoke as if the other kittens were already dead and gone, although they were at that moment only three strides away, enjoying their first taste of life.

John stuttered, shaking his head. 'I . . . w . . . w . . . wouldn't . . .' but could make no more progress than that.

'Spit it out!' Markham said, but hadn't the patience to wait for a reply. He marched straight to the door, John jumping clear out of his way, and stepped again into the small room.

There he saw it, still in the shadows, but moving, nuzzling against its mother's side. A kitten it was, and alive. But it had wings. Two extra limbs stood proud of its body in the space between head and shoulder. They were thin and clawless, and shorter than legs, as if the paws had been cut away and the fur pulled tight over the stubs. From each of these little limbs, attaching itself to the side of the kitten's back, grew a triangle of skin. And whereas the limbs were heavily furred in white and ginger, the wings themselves were more sparsely covered, the fleshy hue of fawn-pink skin discernible underneath.

Markham's eyes glazed over, fixed so intently towards the corner of the room that for some time he was unable to move them. His mind began playing tricks. He blinked, and when again the kitten came into focus he felt a flicker of familiarity. For an instant he saw nothing unusual, and, somewhat disoriented, asked himself why he was in the scullery looking at a kitten. But then something unnerved him and again he saw that the little thing, alone amongst its siblings, had two fully formed wings on its back.

Its mother stirred, and at that moment Markham's mind span three ways at once, leaving only twisted confusion where sober logic had once reigned. He saw himself in the presence of the animal which had given birth to an abomination. A fine ratter she may have been, but surely possessed by the Devil. The wicked mutant kitten that she had secreted within her evil womb was an offence in the eyes of God. No doubt about it. An *a-bo-mi-na-tion*, he repeated to himself, breaking it down into syllables, as if in this way the word was compounded and multiplied until its damning resonance became unequivocal. A-bo-mi-na-tion.

But then a small shadow of doubt. Cats have no souls. Do they? Surely not. So what part might the Devil have played in this? A soulless cat? In what way might . . . how might the Lord . . . ? But even now the superintendent's mind had become wrapped up tight in the matter, and his thoughts span and twisted by reflex alone, without any reason or sanity. On the fifth day (or was it the sixth?) didn't He create animals? The exact day was unimportant. What mattered was the question of whether this could be the Devil's work. The Bible. The Bible! What did it say? Markham, like everyone else, had heard of *mutants*, such as that five-legged calf born at a nearby farm a few years back. The mere description of it, he recalled, had been horrific, and the poor animal soon found its throat cut by a farmer too unworldly to know that people in towns and cities pay good money to see such things. Mutations were one thing. Deformities of one sort or another were no rarity. But this could hardly be counted as an accident of birth. The wings were so perfectly formed that they seemed to bring with them the sardonic cackle of witchcraft. He closed his eyes and tried to imagine a cat in flight. The wings were the same, the way that the animal drew itself smoothly through the air was utterly natural.

No; by some dark, evil design had this admixture of beings evolved, concocted by who knew what malignant spirit, sent to haunt Man on Earth. And by whatever cruel plan, for whatever reason, it had been visited on the workhouse.

There he remained, until his silence attracted the interest of those who were still in the kitchen. Each person gave out a little gasp of astonishment as, one by one, they crowded into the doorway and stared with disbelief at the winged kitten, which was now more animated and had even begun to move its wings fractionally as it stretched its four legs. Behind Markham people pushed nervously, eager not to set foot in the room, but with an equal desire to see the profane and horrible sight within. As they pushed, Markham himself had no choice but to move forward, so that in the end there came a point when the whole body of dumbfounded onlookers moved en bloc through the doorway. The ratter, still indolent after her ordeal, but now taking care of her litter with what energy she could muster, jumped up suddenly, jaws spread wide, hissing furiously. She moved back, shoulders dipped, until the object of interest was hidden beneath her, the kitten's little wings brushing its mother's underbelly, its tiny head between her two front legs.

With shivery screams and whoops of fear, the crowd retreated to the far end of the scullery, where they flapped and winced in a kind of jittery, light-headed panic. The maids had to be sent out into the yard to calm down. Poor John the Overseer could say nothing more than *It's t' Divil come!* over and over, until even the less susceptible amongst them began to believe it. Why had they been chosen? Why had the coarse hands of demons touched them, why this beast in their midst, in their scullery? But also, as their comprehension failed to find even the most transitory moorings, another thought crossed their minds, though it remained unsaid; as the morning progressed, and the existence of the little mutant kitten slowly became a reality, the question spoke louder and louder to each of them: would it fly?

Only Markham remained, looking straight back at the ferocious ratter, and from time to time catching sight of the kitten's quick little eyes which – could it be true? – had begun to open. The other four kittens crawled aimlessly about, unnoticed by their mother, whose whole attention was taken up in the protection of this one offspring. In her body there was a warning, visceral and persuasive, something which he had never seen before in an animal; were the kitten to die, then its mother would die first.

Markham withdrew to the scullery in search of milk. He went almost unnoticed, since the hullabaloo was now at its height, and the two maids seemed to be in danger of becoming hysterical. Returning to the cats he crouched down in front of the ratter, whose defensive stance had not changed, and drew the now empty plate towards him. He poured more milk, whilst the ratter looked on with interest. And then, the plate once again full, he pushed it very slowly in their direction. The mother, seeing him get too close, began to hiss, her voice curdling to a low groan, and as he got right up to them he felt her hot, metallic breath touch his face. Though only inches separated them, and every hair on her body stood up from the skin, he finally delivered the milk to the kitten, letting the plate come to a rest with its rim touching the ratter's forelegs. A little of the milk spilled, and immediately the kitten sniffed at it with an alertness far beyond its few hours of life. Above, its mother hardly moved,

her voice still audible, her body calm but tense, waiting for
the inevitable: when Markham made his grab for the kitten,
at that very moment she would sink her front claws into his
eyes and her back ones would tear at the soft, wobbly pads of
flesh on his cheeks. She watched his pupils flutter from side
to side. She had picked the spot. She was ready for him.

Markham didn't grab the kitten, though. He just looked.

*My four brothers and sisters disappeared. Not me, though.
No one would have dared to, I suppose. So there I stayed,
and my mother took me as her own, which I almost was.*

Markham gave orders that if possible homes were to be found
for the four kittens. Alice, the younger of the two scullery
maids, was dispatched to go about the district knocking on
doors and offering them for adoption. But she had no luck.
Even since their discovery word had got around: the workhouse had mutant kittens to give away, and people had their
excuses ready when she called with the offer of free pets. Late
that afternoon Markham collected the four healthy animals,
he being the only person who the mother cat allowed into
the closet room. He took the kittens without looking at their
mother, and showed them the darkest kind of death. After
that he could hardly look at his ratter again, since guilt ran
through him like the shingles. And the sadness of watching
that heavy sack drop below the water's surface, the confused
movement of drowning bodies discernible as with a flourish
of bubbles the sack disappeared from view, returned to haunt
him for years afterwards.

The question of the flying cat caused no end of ill feeling,
and even prompted a rare complaint from the inmates of the

workhouse. But Markham gave strict instructions that the poor thing was one of God's creatures and was to be put up with out of compassion. On this point of theology not all were in agreement, and soon afterwards the pastor of a local Baptist congregation (of which John the Overseer was a member) came calling to establish once and for all whether the kitten was indeed one of God's creatures. However, although he stayed half the afternoon, and ate his fill in the kitchen, the winged cat and its mother never made an appearance. In the end he left, his time wasted, and perhaps believing that the whole thing was a hoax. Markham expressed his regret, and explained that though the kitten was only a few days old, it was already strong and alert enough to accompany its mother on her ratting duties, which extended to all parts of the workhouse and its outbuildings.

It was in one of these buildings that the two outcasts lay hidden for those first few weeks. Markham, fearful of the actions of his staff, had sought some kind of sanctuary for the kitten and its mother. He had finally managed to coax them out from the scullery, waiting until the evening of the second day, by which time people had got somewhat used to the kitten, everyone having stolen enough glances now that the initial shock had worn off; some people even managed a wry smile at the sight of those perfectly formed wings – they were certainly original, however devilish. After dusk, with great patience and understanding, Markham led the cats to the outbuildings in the grounds. They were old stables, already there when the land for the workhouse had been bought, and were now used only for the storage of that special class of object: things beyond repair but which no one wants to throw away. Inside were rotten cartwheels and rusted, decaying ploughheads; tossed into the back corner of one stable was a heap of ragged tarpaulin which seemed to be there for the sole purpose of attracting vermin, and indeed had long been the ratter's most productive hunting ground; old iron buckets lay about like fallen soldiers, some of them more holes than bucket, and there were odd fragments of farm machinery and stabling equipment that had perished beyond recognition, now little more than strands of sinewy dust and brass buckles gone black with tarnish.

Mother and baby were installed in the stable furthest from the workhouse, where almost no one ever went other than to deposit for all time a cracked demijohn or a chair carrying irreversible injuries. And though it was also the stable with the rat-infested tarpaulin in one corner, any place where not one but two cats live (and one of those with wings) might reliably be said to be vermin-free.

However, this was not quite the case. At first the rats were curious, and would come close, perhaps thinking that wings put an animal at a disadvantage. The kitten would stand there, shivering with fright as the rats crept gradually closer, sniffing the air to see whether it might be edible, or a figment of their imaginations, their brown-grey bodies twitching, fleshy bulbs of muscle and at the back a tail dragging like rope. But the old ratter taught its young kitten how to be bold and cautious, a good combination. It soon discovered how easily a rat's neck would snap under its paws, and how, though the rats were quick and often got away, by stealth and timing it could make a kill.

For the next four years the two of them lived there in relative peace. Markham would make sure that although the winged cat was never loved, nor in that time did it ever feel the caress of a human hand, nor hear a single fond or affectionate word, there was always some scrap of food left for it and its mother in the little windowless room off the scullery. And between them the two cats repaid their debt to Markham in regular instalments.

Then my mother died. One day she was alive, mauling a family of mice until their heads came away from their bodies, and the next she was dead. And death eats into life, destroying and rearranging whatever it likes; afterwards the world is a slightly different place. And a crueller one.

Markham dragged the dead ratter by its tail all the way to the furnace room in the basement of the workhouse. Preferring not to handle her big body more than that, he used a coal shovel to throw her in. There he stood, watching the white-and-ginger fur blacken and turn to smoke. The heat of the yellow coals ate into her body and she twisted so grotesquely in the flames that he panicked, thinking she might still have been alive. Then, the fire having taken her completely, he turned from the furnace with a sense of foreboding, as if in those flames the truth about the cat was finally revealing itself.

He turned. And there it was. Far against the wall, illuminated by the flickering red light of the furnace. The winged cat, looking on as its mother burned. Flecks of light from the fire danced in its wide, terrified eyes, and behind it the exaggerated shadows of its two wings cavorted on the wall, as if playing out some announcement of horrible intent. Such was the aspect of death there in the shadows that

Markham was suddenly in no doubt; he had harboured a devil-creature, misled in his own weakness, beguiled by the quiet, unassuming face of evil itself. And now, with the flames of the furnace on his back and that thing between him and the door he understood the fearful gravity of what he had to do.

For the next few days the strange, mutant orphan had no choice but to hide in the darkest corners it could find, shivering at the sound of every footstep, pulling its deformed body ever further from sight. Markham was resolved to be rid of the demons which had seized him, to rid the world of the abomination he had tolerated those four years. With a purposefulness which bordered on insanity he patrolled the workhouse and its grounds for three days solid, a loaded shotgun in his hands. He turned up barrows and buckets, and poked the newly oiled barrel of his gun into every last inch of the place, ready to blast the cat into a thousand pieces, ready even to have its evil presence smeared on to the walls of his workhouse, its wings torn apart with lead, there to be scraped away like caked-on bird droppings. For three days he did nothing else, from first to last light. And those around him seemed to understand, because they also became uncomfortable with the idea of having that monstrous cat about the place without its mother, as if it was only the old ginger ratter that had kept the evil spirits of her malformed child at bay. Even the more charitable of them accepted that there was no alternative but to kill the thing, and on that basis they preferred to mourn the mother rather than the child. What none of them knew, though, was that as Markham stalked the cat in every last spot he could find, in his jacket pockets he carried with him a Bible, a small cross and an entire head of garlic.

Try as he might, though, he could not find the creature. After three long days of unsuccessful hunting it was assumed that the winged cat had perished, lost and defenceless without its mother's protection. Slowly, as more days passed, Markham perceived a certain lifting of spirits around the place, a lightening, a freeing-up which culminated, not more than three weeks later, in the news that Alice, by now a young woman of twenty, was engaged to be married to Tom, a groom from a nearby estate, the very same groom indeed who had been present at the discovery of the mysterious litter of kittens four years earlier. In those four years he had persisted in a campaign to woo Alice which had recently come so close to full fruition that he now believed an offer of marriage was his only hope.

*

Alice has discovered a new sense of adventure. The engagement has been announced, and memories of the cat are already fading. It is a strange feeling, as if she has stepped across an invisible line, and now needs some means of proving to herself that she will never step back. Since it is the height of summer, the old outbuildings are dry and habitable, if not for regular living, then at least for the use of courting couples. The most comfortable of these has the remains of an upper level, like a hay loft but smaller, perhaps a stable lad's quarters in earlier times. Tom and Alice have been using this place for secret half-hour trysts, unaware that every last member of staff knows not only where and when their visits take place, but, through the automatic transmission of confidences which pass between Alice and a younger maid in service, the full extent and detail of everything they get up to.

On the very first of these meetings after the engagement is announced, the two of them find the loft hotter than usual, the air stiller and more compelling, and even a little difficult to breathe. In the heat they are soon half naked. And at this point Alice quite calmly decides that since on the last few occasions her lover had seemed unable to wait any longer, then she might as well be unable to wait as well. What with the wedding just around the corner, she reasons, a single transgression is almost a rightful kind of anticipation. She resolves in her mind to keep the whole thing secret, though all the time knowing that it will be the very first thing she tells her friend. There on the wooden planks her body now yields an extra measure, and she draws him on to her a fraction more than normal. He stiffens, pushing himself against her thigh through their remaining layers of clothing. Then she surprises both of them by reaching beneath herself and pulling down her drawers. The air throbs with the frantic beat of his heart as it throws itself almost clear out of his chest, and his breath is quick and irregular against her neck as he fidgets to free himself of his trousers. There is little ceremony between them, both too tense to stop and look at each other, more desperate, indeed, to avoid looking, as their bodies meet and rub together for the first time, wet and tingling for that magical dream-second before the enormity of expectation overpowers sensation.

He enters her slowly, careful not to put all his weight on to her. She feels some pain, and he is ready to withdraw. But she shifts her legs and holds him there and finally he lowers himself all the way down until their hips touch. And they lie quite still, hardly breathing, as if they can remain like this for ever.

Then her body tightens, and as she shifts beneath him he feels himself move inside her.

'Listen!' she whispers, her attention taken by a sound nearby. He doesn't hear, and begins moving in and out of her, drawing himself up on his arms, his face now towards the ceiling, his eyes closed.

'Listen!' she cries again, more insistent, tears welling in the corners of her eyes. She twists her torso desperately to shake him off her. But he pins her down so hard that she can hardly move. Someone is there, and she begins to sob at the thought of being discovered, that dreadful fear in her stomach of something long waited for going irretrievably wrong. The sound again, to her left this time, more distinct, louder, closer to the ear. She throws her head sideways and there, not a foot from her face, is the cat, wings at full stretch, eyes big and burning behind a skeletal face, its body withered from hunger, the skin drawn close to the bones on its cheeks and pulled tight down its neck, its fur thin and matted.

She screams, drawing in her arms to cover her chest, her legs kicking out as if in the throes of a fit. Tom also cries out, but from ecstasy not fear; his eyelids flutter and instinctively he covers her mouth with his hand as he thrusts again and again into her, unable to stop.

After he has finished he notices that, though she has turned silent, she is whimpering beneath him. Then he too sees the cat, which is still there, its head slightly to one side, purring quietly. Alice shakes like an epileptic. But Tom in his confusion finds it impossible to blame the cat, for he sees no connection, no culpability. Unlike Alice, who will never recover from that horrendous sight, the horrible vision of wickedness that greeted her as she stepped finally out of childhood; unlike Alice, then, he at first does not understand. But as he grows small inside her, then pulls himself out, he realises why she is hysterical, their precious moment turned evil.

He swipes out at the cat. Through tear-filled eyes he misjudges his swing, smashing a hand into a wooden pillar with enough force to crack two knuckles. He rolls off his fiancée and into a ball of self-pity on the wooden floor.

Within a week Alice has been admitted to an asylum, her descent into madness as sudden as it is inexplicable. She is cared for at the expense of a trustee of the workhouse, whose generosity in the case owes more to pragmatism than compassion: Tom works for him and it is feared that unless his fiancée is got rid of soon, then the boy might also turn mad. Later, when Alice miscarries, she understands nothing of what has happened to her.

Tom is never told.

II

The platform was the only refuge I had. After my mother was gone I discovered that it was the best place to be. Half dead with hunger and grief and fear, I was. But if I'd known that they were going to be there, so whispery-quiet that at first I didn't hear them . . . They were irresistible, the tenderness, the two of them so full of kindness, hiding there.

That afternoon the cat managed to escape Tom's hand. And although Alice was never seen there again, Tom was back soon enough. But not so tender now. He returned the next day, at dusk, drunk, on a bicycle which he hid behind the outbuildings. He came stealthily and stayed half the night. And the next. Hours together, night after night, to kill the winged cat. Up and down the rotten ladder he went, up to the little platform, heedless of the rats which at that time of night scurried about with little regard for him. Sometimes he had a knife in his hand, sometimes a cudgel, and sometimes also a lady's handkerchief, which from time to time he would kiss as if to give himself strength, although it provoked in him only a childlike stream of tears, and there he'd sit, alone in the dark, sobbing.

What with one thing and another, then, the cat had to escape. One night, after the poor boy had given up hope of making a kill and had gone home, it abandoned the workhouse. Fearing that dawn would bring a host of new difficulties, not least the problem of visibility, it went immediately in search of a place where it could curl up and sleep in safety. By now it was so frail that it managed to cover little more than two or three miles, struggling on hunger-weakened legs, incapable of scaling walls or exploring its new terrain with any real energy, simply moving onwards, knowing that something would turn up.

Finally, it crept through a hole in a pair of wooden gates and found itself in an old courtyard. The sun's first breath of life was just then making its way into the sky. Grass, which grew freely in the yard, turned from black to indigo, to a dark marine blue and, with an eerie, rippling haste, through shades of deep green and turquoise. In the far corner lay an old ceramic sink, tipped on its side; and now that too began to catch the light, a big, rounded-off square of luminous blue-grey, but changing slowly against the surrounding darkness, its edges gradually sharper, its emerging whiteness more and more vivid. The cat went straight to the sink and dipped from view, its weary body falling somewhere between sleep and exhaustion. From trees that were still little more than inky stains against the sky, birds now began to chatter and shout in earnest, like a thousand high-pitched caricatures competing to be the funniest, desperate to earn favour with the new sun. But despite all this, the cat fell straight asleep.

The courtyard was overgrown with grass, lush and heavy. There was the insinuation of cart tracks leading from gate to stables, but even these were no more than old scars, just the outline of former wounds that would never disappear completely. To one side of the stable doors was an old horse cart. A man stood, leaning against it. His face was inclined upwards, to the multicoloured strata of the sky in the east. As he watched, his lips moved fractionally, putting a word to each subtle shift of hue in the sky: *navy, magenta, sapphire, puce*. He invented words – *pucetta* for a vague purple on the very edge of burnt yellow – and amused himself with more elaborate descriptions – *lightish darker blue* and *quickly fading red-tinged blue-yellow* – mouthing each word silently into the air, his eyes wide open, the noise of the birds chaotic and deafening. He had been there half the night, patiently waiting in pitch darkness to see the sun rise for the first time on his new home. There he had been, unwilling to miss a second of it, when the cat crossed right in front of him. But neither he nor the cat noticed the other.

The sun came up, and I was over the worst of my weariness. A fresh, good feeling soaked into my fur, and the heat of the new day was quickly in my bones. I felt as if I had been rolled up tight and was now opening again.

The cat stuck its head up above the top of the sink. And there he was, not more than three or four feet away. A man, in a baggy old suit that was well worn and darker than normal, almost black, though it was hard to tell, since it was shiny with grime. He stood against an old horse cart. In his hands was something small. He held it close to his face, turning it in his fingers. But apart from this not a muscle of his body moved, and when the breeze caught the hem of his jacket, the whole of him seemed to sway.

Finally, he placed the cigarette carefully between his lips, as if there was one ideal way of doing it that he had nearly perfected. Even without lighting it he took satisfaction from it, slowly drawing the air in through the sides of his mouth, inhaling imagined fumes. When he did light it the little ceremony was brief but exact. Afterwards, he shook the match with a sweep of the arm so expansive and natural that there could be no other interpretation but that here was a man at last in his own world.

He stood quite still, a cloud of smoke falling around him. Then he turned, and his eyes fell straight on the cat, eyes that were dark inside and out, eyes that frighten people. Though not cats.

John Longstaff felt betrayed by the silence of the morning, tricked in the belief that he had been alone as the sun rose. How long had the cat been there, a trespasser, watching? He stared at its small ginger head. And to his surprise it stared back, straight into his eyes. There they remained, man and cat, their gaze steady and unhurried, the early sun growing stronger and more insistent, heating up the tops of their heads until they prickled. Both were thinking of their next move.

In the end Longstaff took a step forward. The cat immediately disappeared, dropping down as far as it could, its face squashed flat against the bottom of the sink. Longstaff came over and crouched down. He stayed there a long time looking at the animal, which lay as if dead on the white ceramic. Then it pulled its face off the hard surface and looked up. Longstaff's eyes were close, unnerving, the kind of eyes that stare right through you, hinting at the vastness of their own light and darkness. He extended a hand and stroked the cat's head. His hand was small, and he turned tufts of fur one way then the other, exploring it with the ends of his fingers. The cat, with its workhouse caution, prepared for the worst. Longstaff ran his fingers across its head and on to its back. He followed the ridge between the two wings and, sensing something unusual, traced the outline of one of the wings, right along its edge. The animal froze rigid, and then, just as Longstaff's curiosity was such that he knelt down on the ground, shuffling in as close as he could, almost crawling inside the sink, the cat bolted with a frenzied burst of panic-energy, leaping right over Longstaff and darting off into the stables behind him.

Longstaff sat on the sink and smoked another cigarette, watching the stable doors. After he'd finished it he ground the quarter-inch butt into the grass with his boot. Then he stole over and gently pushed the stable doors shut. But straight afterwards he opened one of them again, at first just enough to peep inside, then, on an impulse, throwing both doors wide open. Yellow light broke in through the doorway. The dust in the air seemed to shimmer with heat. And the cat was caught there in the sun. It had been about to ascend an old ladder which led to a raised platform high up in the stable. But now it stopped, its front feet on the lowest rung, its head looking back over its shoulder. Then it opened its wings, stretching them out to their fullest extent, the little limbs vertical in the air and the skin pulled tight, the sun warming them through.

Something like a cough rose from Longstaff's throat. A wheeze, followed by more rasping breaths, the noise getting louder until his laughter seemed to pour from his throat in vomit-like gushes; it filled the stable, each terse echo met by another, more powerful roar, his body pivoting at the waist, his torso swaying so wildly that it looked ready to snap off. He flung his arms out, fingers spread, and felt the raw power of the sun on his back. The cat climbed the ladder and found itself a place on the platform, from where it looked down and watched him rejoice.

He went to fetch his wife and their two young daughters. They stood, huddled together at the stable door, their eyes following the direction of his outstretched arm. They gazed up at the winged cat, wonder in their faces.

At first I wanted to run straight to them, to let them fuss over me. How I longed to feel their hands against my fur, tickling the skin behind my ears, and hear them laugh each time I sneezed. But I kept my distance, resisting the temptation, watching.

After a while the more intrepid of the girls edged into the stable. Looking around to see her father's beaming approval, she went over to the ladder and tried coaxing the cat down. It held back, and seemed to look across to the girl's mother, who stood at the stable doors. Seeing that it was not going to move from its spot up on the platform, the girl finally decided to climb the ladder herself. Words of caution came from the mother, who looked as if she were about to rescue her little child. But Longstaff held up an arm as if to restrain his wife, all the time transfixed by the sight of his fearless daughter as she began to climb the ladder alone.

She made slow progress, her eight-year-old legs straining

with each oversized step, and the further from the ground she went the more nervously she glanced back down to it. When her head did at last poke up above the platform she stopped, a smile of pride breaking out across her face. Then, holding the ladder with one white hand, her legs quivering beneath her, she reached out and stroked the cat's head, the palm of her hand flat and clumsy. The smile intensified, and she ruffled its fur with that beautiful combination of innocent pleasure and curiosity. Then, as her hand moved down its back, she froze suddenly, terrified, and could not even pull the hand away; there it remained, resting lightly on a wing until her face had turned to a dumb scowl, tears filling her child's eyes.

Longstaff exploded with laughter. His daughter turned, helpless and terrified. Even as she did so her father was there on the ladder to catch her loose, frightened body in his arms, pulling her face to him until it was squashed hard against his ribs.

'Look!' he whispered in her ear. 'Don't you wish you could fly? Look!' And he nudged her chin upwards until she could watch him run his fingers over those ginger-white wings. 'A magical cat, come to us!'

And after she had become accustomed to the sight of the animal he took her in one arm and the cat in the other, and the three of them made their way down the ladder.

*

'The censors can't catch me!' Longstaff would shout in those early days, intoxicated by the solid reality of his own success, there with his family, in their new house.

He had arrived in the city just in time to be listed on the 1880 census. He was eighteen and had left the small

Yorkshire farming village of his childhood with no trade and no schooling beyond reading and writing, which even as a young boy he had taken to without effort, along with arithmetic, in which he seemed to need no instruction at all. Both his parents were dead, his mother having died that same year. On the 1880 census the word 'labourer' had been recorded as his profession, for at that time he had no trade at all. Ten years later it had become 'coal leader and remover', though this was too modest even then. Two years after that and John Longstaff took possession of his own premises: stables, storehouse and private dwellings. His wife Flora and their young daughters could hardly believe what had happened, even after they finally told themselves that their new home, with its parlour and separate kitchen and a big fireplace in every room, was not in fact the setting for a long, ecstatic sequence of dreams. Incredibly, he bought the place with cash, getting it cheap from a widow who had let it stand empty for so long that people assumed it was no longer for sale. More than incredible, though, something almost miraculous to Longstaff, was that it had a name: *New Court*.

'The census'll not get me right, not one year to the next, never mind every ten! There's not words to describe John Longstaff,' he shouted, a daughter in each arm, and swung them around so fast that their legs flew out horizontal and bumped into the enormous oak dresser which filled one side of their new dining room. 'Where'll we fly to, eh?' he asked them, his rough voice like a teenager's, mid-range and torn through with unresolved hoarseness. 'Anywhere!' he cried, and piled both girls on to the table in the middle of the room, which was so robust that it could have taken a hundred more. There they lay, collapsed, breathless with excitement, flopping hopelessly on to each other, their father looking on, hands on hips, his eyes wet and giddy.

Since arriving in the city, twelve years earlier, Longstaff had worked every waking hour. When his body was not actually employed for gain, in those rare moments of physical inaction, he was still at work, thinking things through, always several steps ahead of himself, planning, building his future on foundations which themselves were still to be built. From labourer he found work as a coal leader, and then into the delivery business generally, working for a host of employers, never stopping too long at any one job, but always making sure that he had learned all there was to learn about the job before shifting quickly on to whatever was more lucrative.

Also, he kept hens. He bought a dozen to start with, housing them in an old shed in the corner of a field that he rented for next to nothing. At the end of every day he'd rush off to feed and water them. Workmates would laugh, shaking their heads at his unremitting energy, as if the very idea of a dozen hens was a joke, neither pets nor a business. However, the dozen began to multiply. Each time someone asked, it seemed, there were more of them, until in the end he had to rent half the field and erect several long huts, which he did himself, using wood from a disused barn that he got free from a farmer in exchange for an agreement to buy grain for a year. He rarely had problems with thieves, after a couple of boys who were stealing eggs one night were so badly beaten that although they could not say who had assaulted them in the dark, their bruises served as a warning to others.

He delivered the eggs on Saturdays after work, door to

door, returning home only when his week's stock had all been bought, no matter how long it took. And if he ran out of houses to call on, he would stand outside pubs, waiting with his last half-dozen in the freezing rain until someone, perhaps drunk and eager to make amends by returning home with at least something to show for the week's money, bought them from him. In the end he needed a horse and cart to make the deliveries; his round took in bakeries, hotels, market stalls, and even the workhouse. Bakeries in particular bought from him eagerly, because he had a reputation for reliability, and without eggs a bakery is nothing. He would deliver to them on a Monday morning, loading his cart up at 4 a.m., and driving his horse hard to make his rounds before work began. The bakers, though they took his eggs, thought him quite mad. There was something in his short, meatless body, a jumpy itch of nerves, that put you immediately on edge; and there was a sense with him that whatever was going on, whether he was negotiating a price or just passing the time of day, everything had a purpose. In the end even his cough, or a flick of the wrist, seemed to mark a significant victory for him.

For twelve years he kept the hens, stealthily putting the profits aside, and each year increasing the flock, though he always made a joke of the eggs to his workmates, as if the whole thing were of little importance. Finally, he was delivering over seventy dozen a week from three hundred birds, and had about a hundred boiling fowl to sell each year on top of that. Only he, it seemed, could see the true beauty in a hen: it cost nothing to bring into the world, it gave you three or four eggs a week to sell, and when it was three years old it could be sold for the pot. The very mathematics of the animal's existence sent Longstaff into a kind of rapture, and more than once he shook his head in utter bewilderment, quite incapable of understanding why the whole world was not keeping hens. After twelve years he had accumulated more money from his flock than anyone he knew had earned in twenty.

By the time of the 1890 census Longstaff, though just a 'coal leader and remover', was on his way to becoming one of the richest in the district. Two years after that he sold the hen farm and bought New Court, filling it with grand, oak furniture from the house sales of bankrupts and the deceased which his new removal and haulage company organised. On his first morning there, as he watched the sun rise above solid stone that belonged entirely to him, a flying cat appeared, to complete the miracle.

So the winged cat was introduced to its new family, who petted it that morning, there on the stable floor, until it seemed as if they might pet away the fur on its body. That night it fell soundly asleep on a blanket in the scullery of its new home. The following morning it had to be persuaded from its slumber with a dish of milk, and was fed so much bread from the girls' breakfast plates that in the end their mother had to put a stop to it.

The Longstaffs had just arrived at New Court, and the appearance of a winged cat turned their natural high spirits into a kind of boundless excitement. Each day ended with the thrilling promise of the next, and for many weeks they all, parents and children alike, had difficulty closing their eyes at night, such was their desire simply to open them again on a new morning. Night after night Longstaff himself did little more than drift in and out of a light, delirious sleep, and by dawn would be wide awake, listening out for the sound of his daughters, as punctual as the sun, as they fidgeted and wriggled with impatience for the start of the new day. Eventually, he would allow them to get up, even if there were still two hours until breakfast, just so he could watch their limitless delight at everything around them.

The cat, which was christened 'Catty' without anyone having thought much about it, padded inquisitively around the house, and seemed to lend each room a sense of magical possibility; it allowed Longstaff and Flora to dream deeper and wilder dreams of their future, and as for the girls, from the moment they first stroked those soft wings, the difference between make-believe and reality evaporated, because now they existed in a place where the imaginary was no stranger than the song of a thrush at day break or the braying of a horse late at night. In short, the cat was a good thing.

During those first weeks at New Court, when they were still deciding where all the furniture should go, Longstaff's haulage business began to grow at a rate which even he found surprising. For many years his credo had been one of a simple faith in hard work and hard cash, but now he ceded that a kind of charm must have been spun over him and his family. And though in his whole life he had never once invoked the help of any being, he nevertheless saw in the confluence of events on that first morning at New Court a blessing and a providence; later in his life, when it was all over, he would look back on it and weep.

One evening he arrived home after a tiring but profitable day's work, to find wife and children grinning like fools. Flora was laying the table, and the girls sat in a corner, petting Catty with careful attention, as if the animal had fallen ill. But they were not sad. He stood there for a while in bemusement until the other three burst out laughing; then he too laughed, though without knowing why.

'Show him, then!' Flora told the girls, as if her husband had been kept waiting long enough. The two girls, after giving the cat one final, indulgent stroke each, approached the great dining table. They both reached into their pockets, then let a handful of coins fall on to the tablecloth in front of them. There were no more than five or six in all, but they fell noisily from the girls' hands like a cascade of treasure.

'It's Catty's,' one of them said.

Then the other: 'We're going to buy a cathouse, with windows and a door!'

Longstaff looked at the coins and then at his daughters. Long years of chasing and hoarding money had left him unable to resist its base allure. But this first sight of his own children handling money, their own money, and their obvious pleasure in possessing it, induced in him peculiar and contradictory emotions.

'But how . . .' he said, almost fearing an answer, '. . . how did you get it?'

The girls turned to one another and giggled, and it was their mother who finally explained.

'They've been charging folk to see Catty, that's what they've been doing. A farthing a time, right here in the yard, an' all,' and she nodded towards the window as she continued arranging things on the table.

'Well,' Longstaff said at last, eyeing the paltry sum scattered on the tablecloth, 'you'll be needing more than that to buy a cathouse. Why not let me buy it? We can . . .'

His suggestion was drowned out by such loud and incoherent protests that he soon gave up hope of doing any persuading at all. Instead, he turned to his wife for support, who felt compelled to continue the story.

'First, Mr Heath came to pay his bill,' she said, 'and they got him to pay a farthing.'

'Each!' one of the girls boasted, holding up her farthing.

'Each?'

'Each!' said Flora. 'And then his wife came round to see if it was true, and that made four farthings.'

'And then Mrs Heath told Mrs Barker,' one of the girls continued, breathless with pride, a little pant for air between each word, 'and she brought someone who we don't know. But they only paid one farthing each. That makes six, Daddy!'

And word got out. Each night Longstaff would return home with his crew, and whilst the horses were being stabled for the night he would sneak into the house and look for his daughters, who would be hidden away in some corner or other counting and recounting their day's takings, or making stacks of coins with all the money they had earned so far. They chattered endlessly about the cathouse, where it would go, what colour the door would be, whether it really needed a sink in the scullery . . . And if there had been no visitors that day, then their father would give them a single farthing just to keep things ticking over, and also in order that he be allowed to stay for a minute or two, cross-legged on the floor with them, and listen to the elaborate discussion about the cathouse, which he still found difficult to imagine, although the two girls seemed to understand perfectly.

One Saturday afternoon an open-topped charabanc turned up at New Court with eleven passengers aboard. Flora and the girls were out shopping, and Longstaff, having just then returned from a job, was milling about in the yard alone. The visitors wanted to see Catty, and had come all the way from Dewsbury. He made a quick calculation: ten miles in a charabanc, on a Saturday afternoon, multiplied by eleven. The mathematics seemed to suggest that a farthing was not enough. Who would set out on such a trip without a certain kind of expectation, and money in their pocket to back it up? Would people travel such distances for a mere farthing's worth of entertainment? He decided on tuppence each, which they all agreed to eagerly, although several added the proviso that they wanted to see the animal in flight for the price.

'Can't promise that!' he scolded them. 'It's not a dog doing tricks, you know. Flies when it feels like it. Takes orders from no one.'

In the end they agreed to take their chances, and Longstaff went off to find Catty. He found the cat nibbling from a slice of sweet cake which its two young keepers had secreted inside the thick pile of blankets which served as its bed. It looked up at Longstaff with that guilty little snap of the neck which tells you all you need to know. He left the cat with its sweet secret and closed the doors on his way back out to the yard. Returning to the group, he shook his head as if in exasperation.

'I told you. Got a mind of its own, that cat. It'll be off on a fly.'

The visitors gasped in amazement, unashamedly.

'I know!' he said, relishing the effect of his extemporisation. 'It's most likely up at the Towers! That's where it goes. Flies around up there. Sometimes it sits up in a tree, or on the roof of the house. You'll most likely see it up there. If you don't, come back here later on. It's always back at teatime. You can count on that.'

The crowd bustled with excitement, bumping into one another as they scrambled to get back up on the charabanc. Longstaff gave them directions to the Towers, which was a large Gothic house about a mile away, the kind of place that is always said to be haunted, just because a few bats live there.

They left in a state of high agitation, already looking up to the sky in search of the cat having a fly. Longstaff stood by the gates of New Court and watched them disappear up the road.

Sure enough, the charabanc returned about an hour later, and this time its occupants not only had their tuppences ready, but would have paid more. The cat had indeed been spotted, but far off in the distance, perched so high in a tree that only its outline could be seen. Several of them thought they'd seen it take off and land in another tree, but there was some doubt about this. They were now so desperate to see the cat up close that Longstaff could have charged them a shilling each. But he stuck to the original price, and as he took their money he explained about his little daughters and their plans for a cathouse; people were so delighted with the story that a few gave an extra farthing or a halfpenny, just for the girls, and Longstaff bit the insides of his cheeks as he dropped the coins into his trouser pocket.

Catty had by now polished off the sweet cake, and also half of a second piece that Longstaff had left on the blanket. What with all that sugary food and as much milk as it could drink (Longstaff made sure of that, too), the animal now dozed in an idle, over-indulged way which one might almost have called decadent. It hardly moved its head when he came to fetch it, and had to be carried as far as the doorstep, where it did finally manage to support itself on four legs as it made its way out to the yard.

The visitors bleated with rapture. There was something instinctive in Catty, who immediately sensed the crowd and took on that erect swagger of the natural performer, wings spread to their fullest extent. And although the cat padded about pretty slowly, those ginger wings nevertheless dazzled all who saw them.

'It's only just got back. Been out on a fly all afternoon. All afternoon!' said Longstaff, now wondering how far he should take the joke. 'Are you sure you didn't see anything up at the Towers?' He knelt down and stroked Catty's head. 'I sometimes see you there myself, don't I?' And then, returning to address his public: 'Many's a time we see Catty up there if we're out on a job that way.'

After ten minutes of Longstaff's patter, tuppence seemed like good value to all concerned. The visitors were dumb-struck, and peered down at the cat as if it confounded all the laws of the natural world, not just those of zoology. And Longstaff, though somewhat regretting that he had not set a higher price, had found himself a new vocation. With each additional description of Catty's prowess in the air – the distances travelled and the speed and agility in flight – as these stories mounted up, one on top of the other, taller and taller, each a little more fabulous than the last, the audience almost begged him not to make the poor animal take to the air again. *Why, no wonder it won't fly now!* they cried. *The thing's exhausted!* The animal was indeed exhausted, from a bellyful of sweet cake. Eleven visitors, though, went back to Dewsbury to spread the word. A flying cat.

That evening Longstaff narrated the episode to his wife and children, guffawing at the idea of the charabanc circling around outside the Towers with those on board thrown into a fluster every time a crow flew overhead.

'But it's true!' his daughters told him, jumping and shaking with a manic insistence, as if the matter was of desperate importance. Catty, it seemed, really could fly.

Both parents threw up their arms as if this were startling news. The girls continued, claiming that they had seen Catty swoop right down across the stables, one side to the other, from high up in the roof, and that it would sometimes jump right off the platform and glide down to the floor, flapping its wings to break its landing, hovering above the ground for a moment or two before dropping on to its feet. The girls pleaded to be allowed to go to the Towers the next day, since they also wanted to see Catty flying there.

Longstaff saw no way out. He couldn't make the cat fly, but neither could he take them to the Towers only to be disappointed, to discover that their father had been lying. So he announced a game of table-jumping, and to his relief this put paid to any further talk on the subject of flying cats.

Flora cleared the table, and then removed its thick velvet tablecloth, revealing the big, heavy wooden structure. Whilst the girls squealed with anticipation, both mother and father prepared to play, he by tucking his trousers into his sock garters and removing his jacket, she by tucking her skirts into the bottom of her long johns. The two of them stood side by side, facing the table. Then, as the girls counted to three, they crouched down, knees springy, their bodies taut and ready. On three they both sprang into the air, and he cried out so loud that had anyone been listening from the next room they might have suspected murder. As they jumped they brought their legs up under them, and with great adeptness landed with their feet on the table, which even as they performed it seemed close to impossible. The girls applauded wildly, and Longstaff, looking sideways at his wife, smiled as if in making one clean jump she had issued a challenge which he meant to fight to the death.

After a few seconds' rest they both dropped back down to the ground. Then again: one, two three . . . *up*, to another scream of approval from the girls. This time Longstaff dropped back down almost immediately, but Flora took her time, reckoning that he would tire himself out and in this way she might outwit her husband. She too dropped back down to the floor, and then they were off again, up and down. The thud of their shoes on the table echoed around the house, accompanied by squeals of encouragement from the girls. One, two, three . . . *up*, each time a little less energetically, and each time Flora struggling a little more to make sure her feet reached the level of the table. But not Longstaff. After six or seven jumps he was throwing himself up and down like a chimpanzee, mindless of his wife, and humming to himself, his eyes staring straight in front of him as if only the jumping mattered.

Flora gave in. Shaking her hands in surrender, she flopped down on to a chair and Longstaff had won. He didn't stop, though. He wouldn't. Not even when, after several more jumps, the others shouted out to him. On he went, up and down, panting heavily and uttering a strangled grunt with each new explosion of energy. Up and down, without pausing, sweat soaking through his shirt and running down his face and neck.

'Look . . . here!' he shouted, one word on the up, the next on the way down.

His daughters did look – in confusion. Flora came as close as she dared to the table, but was powerless to stop him.

'. . . I . . . can . . . fly!'

III

Tall and thin, and a face like a rat. Silent, sniffing around, dragging his tail after him. Then, just as I expected him to leave, there was movement behind me. Rat-man froze. I heard a single footstep. Then the world went black.

One morning a young man came calling at New Court. He was gangly and had a thin face with a scrap of dark moustache on his lip, which gave him the look of a half-handsome rodent. He entered the yard without a sound, and stalked around as if trying to find someone. Longstaff and his men were all out on jobs, and Flora and the girls were gone as well. Everything was locked up, and the place was quiet. Then he saw what he wanted, perched on the top of an old sink, letting the sun bake its back. His eyes fell on it, and his whippy, rat-like body froze suddenly. Too suddenly, perhaps. The cat sensed that something was wrong. In that same instant a sack was thrown over it, and someone whipped Catty up into the air and out of the yard.

Inside the sack the cat screwed itself up so tight that its wings were pulled right over its head, eyes shut against the pinpricks of light which permeated the weave of the cloth.

The two gypsies made off on horses that had been tethered just behind New Court. And gypsies they surely were, from their dark, weather-worn complexions to their thin, unreliable moustaches. They made their way swiftly out of the city, through its latticework of closely packed streets. Mothers at open doors pointed them out to their children, as if there was something mysterious and foreign about them; they kept protective arms on their children's chests, curious at the sight of the men but glad to see them departing, as if this were, all things considered, the best way to see a gypsy.

The hot sackful of cat was held firm by one of the men, close up into his armpit but not too strongly, so that the animal was in no discomfort. They rode on until the dense, urban clutter relaxed, then houses themselves became sparse, with whole stretches of green separating single dwellings. Eventually, they came to a wood, and scattered about under trees on the edge of it were some dozen caravans. Several were recently painted in dark blues and maroons. Others were older and duller, whilst one or two were dropping to bits and looked as if bucketfuls of filth had been emptied onto them regularly for years on end; anyone would have thought they were abandoned had it not been for the lines of thin blue smoke which rose from their little tin chimneys. A couple of thinnish dogs sniffed about here and there, and pissed on the wheels of the caravans.

The two men dismounted, and whilst one dealt with the horses the one with the sack went straight to a caravan (one of the more elegant ones) and, mounting its steps with great care, entered.

Inside, sitting in an armchair which seemed to occupy

the whole of the far end of the caravan, was an enormous woman.

'Well! Come on! Let's have a look!' she said, bursting into life and hauling herself some inches up from her seat. But she flopped straight back down; the idea of getting up had been a bad one. So there she sat. And there seemed to be no end to her. Instead, there was a general movement of things which must have belonged to her body in some way. She spilled over the arms of the chair and out on to the floor in rolls and odd-shaped dollops of woman, and spread up behind her own shoulders, upwards and outwards, in all directions. She seemed to be nothing more than a big fat face grafted on to the back half of the caravan's chintz interior, her flabby mouth speaking not for a human being but as a mouthpiece for the whole dwelling.

The effect was not without some design, for it was her custom to wear gowns which were so vast and to arrange them in such a way that when she moved there was no knowing where she began or ended.

The young man closed the door behind him and laid the sack on the floor. Without saying a word he pulled away the cloth to reveal the cowering animal, then stepped back. The cat was huddled into a ball and at first it looked like any other cat.

The woman leaned forward and made little kissing noises to try and coax the thing out of its fright. And gradually it did raise its head to look around. Seeing no obvious danger it eventually relaxed enough so that its wings, which had been pulled in close to its body, spread themselves a little.

From the great expanse of woman there now came a low, gravelly sound, which could have been the beginnings of a growl in a normal person but was in fact a laugh. It grew steadily in volume, and with such warmth and joy in it that the cat, rather than take alarm, actually crept over to her and pushed its head against her legs.

'Oh, Max! Maximilian! What have you brought me!' and as she spoke she caressed the cat as if it were an object of exquisite beauty, the tips of her fingers tingling with delight as they brushed those furry wings.

Maximilian is not much of a name for a gypsy. And Maximilian was not a gypsy at all. That he cultivated a thin moustache could not be denied, but this counts for nothing, and his dark, weather-beaten skin was simply the result of being out of doors so much. Other than that there was not a drop of Romany in him.

His aunt, on the other hand, was all gypsy, from the famous Petronella family, who for generations had been fortune tellers. But then again, she was not his aunt. Max was an orphan, and at the age of eight or nine he had turned up at the fair where Petronella was at that time working. He somehow attached himself to the great woman, and she, unable to get rid of him or find out anything much about where he had come from, finally took him in. No one else wanted the wretch, and no one came looking for him either. It had been a matter of either taking him, or leaving him to fend for himself, which at the time he showed very little capacity to do.

Since then Max had skulked around whichever fair Gypsy Petronella was at, until by the time he began to cultivate the moustache he was well known at most of the fairgrounds of England. She had made sure he got an education of sorts, and he had shown a great interest in reading, accumulating old books and ragged magazines from wherever he could, hoarding them in every spare inch of space in the caravan.

It was Petronella who first heard about the cat with wings. The story had come to her bit by bit from customers who were eager to know whether laying eyes on a winged cat was a good sign or a bad one. Petronella said it was hard to tell unless every last detail of the sighting was described to her, including the precise whereabouts of the cat. It had not taken her long to get the address of New Court.

Her adoptive nephew was now eighteen and it was about time he started making a living for himself, instead of mooching about at fairs and feasts doing whatever odd jobs people threw at him. He needed a stall, an attraction. So Petronella decided to acquire the cat. Another young man without much in the way of fairground prospects was persuaded to assist in the theft. The two boys would each get a quarter share in the attraction, and would work it between them. Petronella, having paid for a new tent and taken care of all other expenses, would own the other half share. She was no fool. If the second boy proved unreliable, then she and Max together could force him out. But if the two boys turned against her, then she still had claim on 50 per cent of the attraction and could invoke the judgement of Solomon to demand the return of her half; it would be no skin off her nose, and what would the boys do with half a cat and one wing between them?

That's how the cat came to be brought to Petronella's caravan. She fell head over heels in love with the animal and indulged it so extravagantly that after only a few days Max began to tire of being sent out to buy cream or cuts of fresh meat for the precious cat. On one occasion his aunt ordered him out to see if he could get hold of a live mouse, since she was worried that the cat lacked amusement. But at this point Max put his foot down, and the matter was not brought up again.

Within a week of its arrival a tent had been made for the cat attraction, and inside it a cage had been constructed, all at great expense. Max himself designed the large painted hoarding which would announce the wondrous flying cat to the world. He pored endlessly over his collection of books for inspiration, sensing that it was no ordinary exhibit and that a simple sign would just not do; this was not a common thing, not a tattooed woman or a strongman, not a senseless diversion, like the coconut shy or the bran tub. No, a flying cat was different. It spoke of the grand histories of the ancient world, of myth and magic. Long and hard he looked, searching for the right allusion, the appropriate words and references, that perfect expression of what was, after all, a magical thing. And then it came to him, and immediately the sign was painted: *The Cat-Icarus.*

*

Longstaff had been out all day overseeing the removal of a company of wool merchants to new, larger premises. The company had expanded rapidly and was in need of more office space, and Longstaff, in addition to the removal, managed to sell them a number of desks and chairs that he had picked up cheap the previous week. All in all the day had been a success.

But then a problem. His price for the job did not correspond with theirs, and since the whole agreement had been verbal, there was no way of proving it either way. He argued as best he could, but what did he have to bargain with? The job was done and his men were ready to leave. Eventually, the company clerk appeared from the new offices. He listened to the debate without interrupting, nodding here and shrugging there, and Longstaff's arguments were so well put that several of the merchants' own men seemed convinced. The clerk, though, was less impressed. He pursed his lips and smiled at Longstaff, whose blood rose at the mere sight of this chubby little functionary with his gold watch chain and his well-oiled hair. The clerk explained that the extra money would not be paid, and that Longstaff could either accept what was on offer, or he could refuse payment and take his complaint to the Quarter Sessions. The decision, he said with a smile, 'is entirely your own, Mr Longstaff'.

When they got back to New Court it was already dark, and both Longstaff and his men were tired from such a long and dispiriting day. None of the men had dared say anything to their boss after the humiliation of the money, and once inside the courtyard they fell to work in silence.

Longstaff marched straight over to the house, determined to put the wool merchants out of his mind. Inside there was no one. Supper had not been prepared, and in every room there was an unusual calm, as if things had been recently abandoned. Then he heard Flora's voice coming from somewhere upstairs. She was comforting a child. He raced up the stairs three at a time, but even before he reached the top he could hear that in fact both his girls were crying and that his wife was having a hard time consoling them, such was the depth of sorrow in their voices.

He opened the bedroom door. All three of them looked up, startled by his sudden appearance. For a second there was quiet. Then the sight of their father seemed to set the girls off again, only now they sounded even more inconsolable.

'What's this?' he said, kissing first one and then the other child on their bloated, salty faces. Much as they tried, though, they couldn't get out a single word between the spluttering and the sobs.

'Someone's stolen Catty,' Flora said, and even she was close to tears.

'Stolen?'

'Yes. They've been in here, when we were out.'

The girls now threw themselves into a louder and more desperate lament, and their parents had to shout to make themselves understood.

'There were two gypsies here this afternoon. Someone saw 'em hanging around. And then someone saw 'em ride off, and they had a sack—'

'With Catty in it!' one of the girls cried out, hysterical.

Then the girls began to howl at the top of their voices, the very thought of Catty in a sack frightening them half to death. Their mother pulled them to her breast, partly from compassion but also to muffle their deafening cries.

Longstaff, seeing that he was of little use there in the bedroom, made his way back down to the courtyard, already breathing heavily, and with each breath the sound of blood stronger in his ears.

The men in the court had by this time deduced that something was wrong, and they hung around whispering, speculating as to what it might be. The horses had still not been stabled, and when Longstaff came back out of the house and saw them there in the courtyard he flew into a rage and took both of the horses himself, telling his men to go home and leave him in peace. He pulled the animals into the stables, ranting and mumbling like a madman, kicking and slapping them and yanking on their bits so hard that they whinnied with pain. This only incensed him further, and he took a long crop and beat them on their faces. They bucked and twisted, trying to avoid the blows, their shrieks echoing around the walls of the stables. The men tried to intervene but Longstaff beat them too whenever they came close, and really there was something in his eyes which was enough to warn anyone off. Soon the horses were jumping and cavorting so wildly that it was too dangerous to enter the stable.

In the end one of the animals spun around and caught Longstaff with its rump. The blow threw him into the wall, winded and dazed. He staggered to keep on his feet, his fingers scraping against bare brick, his legs wobbling beneath him. Regaining his strength, he grunted with anger and, seeing an old table in the corner, he kicked at it in a frenzy until one of the legs was broken clean off. He took the heavy wooden leg in his hand and brought it up from behind him in one long swing of the arm. It came down with such force on to the horse's head that the sound of the skull splitting was as clear as a whipcrack.

'There!' he said, his eyes bloodshot and his whole body shaking violently, his voice coming out in tremulous beats. He set to, battering the horse so savagely that within a matter of seconds it was senseless, and stood there, its neck drooping more and more, thick purple blood running from its head. The other horse cowered in the opposite corner of the stables, and the men stood at the doors.

On it went, until the top of the horse's head became

misshapen beneath the relentless pounding. Longstaff was covered in blood, which mixed with the tears that ran down his face, turning his cheeks bright pink. From his lips came a hideous, guttural sound and had his men not been transfixed with amazement they would have stood further back still.

The horse stumbled forward and crashed to the ground. Longstaff didn't let up. Again and again he brought the club down, until the animal's jaw was smashed clean off and its eyes were nothing more than pulp. Again and again, cursing so heavily that saliva bubbled out of his mouth and ran down his chin. Then, with his last ounce of energy, he pummelled the dying thing one final time, and collapsed on to the ground next to it. His face lay in a pool of blackening blood, which was drawn in and out of his mouth as he gasped for air.

*

The Cat-Icarus tent was big enough for a dozen people, fifteen at a squeeze. The audience would stand in one half of the space, crowded together in a little group. A cage filled the other half; it was taller than a man and as broad as the tent itself. A purple velvet curtain was draped over it, and when this was drawn back it revealed a sand floor on which two boxes of differing heights had been placed. These boxes were painted as if they were made of yellow stone.

To begin with the cage looked empty, for the cat was hiding high up on a ledge in the corner of the cage, obscured by the drawn-back curtain. After opening the curtains in a great flourish, Max recounted the story of how the winged cat had been a gift to his old gypsy family from the great Egyptian Sultan Kaliban, and how his own father had fought off bedouins and bushmen to get it to England in safety. At this point he gave the animal a prod with a stick.

I leapt down, wings at full stretch, down through the air, bearing my teeth and hissing. And when I landed I growled until I could smell the fear rise from their bodies.

The audience backed off in an instinctive, communal jump, a breathy, wordless sound falling from their mouths. Then, as their courage returned, they inched forward until their noses poked through the bars of the cage. Then the cat hissed once again, and sprang from one box to the other. The Cat-Icarus was a success.

*

Dewsbury Feast was an important date in the diary of fairground travellers. It took place on a large tract of grassland, in easy reach of the thousands of souls who worked in the wool-processing mills thereabouts. Sideshows, fairground rides and performers came from all parts of the country with the sure knowledge that in Dewsbury money was to be had.

On the second day of the feast the rain blew in from the west and sent the crowds in search of shelter. From tent to tent they scurried, coming to a halt in front of each sign for a second or two, counting their money and deciding between getting wet for free and paying a penny to witness a bearded woman, or the world's fattest woman, or to have one's fortune told by yet another woman, who from inside her tiny tent looked like she might also be the world's fattest woman.

Longstaff strode through the rain and didn't notice that it ran down his face and neck and soaked into his collar. He went quickly past each attraction, reading its advertisement as he walked. At one tent, larger than the rest, he stopped momentarily, and was almost tempted.

Try Your LUCK! in the Boxing Ring with PEDRO 'THE ROCK' ROCCA: ONE POUND 'STERLING' if you knock him down! FIVE POUNDS if you knock him out!

Longstaff stood, hands on hips, and only resisted because he needed all his energy for someone else.

He passed other attractions: toffee-apple sellers and hairy women; hot-nut stalls, barrel organs and strongmen looking bored. He came to:

GYSPY PETRONELLA, 'QUEEN of the ROMANIES' – Spiritualist to Royalty and FAMED throughout the World . . .

Then, at the next tent, he stopped. The attraction boasted an extra large advertising board painted shiny black with gold lettering. It looked brand new.

THE CAT-ICARUS
Born in the Shadows of the 'Egyptian PYRAMIDS'; Last Remaining Descendant of the Godlike FLYING CATS Famed Through ALL ARABY; With MAGICAL PROP-ERTIES, fully formed and Alive! With REAL WINGS; feared and praised throughout the Orient for its MYS-TICAL AND MOST DISCONCERTING EFFECT on all who witness it! 'The only true CAT-ICARUS at this fair and ON ALL THIS EARTH!'

A small crowd milled about near the tent whilst Max, its young, rat-faced owner, tried to drum up custom through the rain. He stood next to his elegant sign and swung an arm out as if to draw people inside. But he was new to the art, and his presence did little to persuade people that a cat famed through all Araby was worth a penny, even in a dry tent.

Longstaff took a shilling from his pocket and handed it to Max. He recognised the thin face and wispy moustache from the descriptions of two men seen riding away from New Court the morning the cat disappeared.

'Is it a black 'un?' he asked sarcastically as the young man fished for change in a pouch which hung from his waistband.

'No, no . . . it's a . . .' he answered, but even as he stammered he could see that Longstaff meant trouble.

'Never mind that,' Longstaff said, 'let's have a look at it.'

With that he shoved his rat-man into the tent. Coins spilled from Max's hand, and as he stooped to pick them up a couple who had been considering the Cat-Icarus finally made up their minds and entered. Longstaff looked at them, his eyes blazing now with a fury which was evidently not going to be contained much longer. Having retrieved the coins from the ground, Max offered them to Longstaff, who knocked his hand away.

'Get on with it!' he snarled, and the couple turned to leave, sensing violence in the air. But just then it began to rain more heavily, and others now pushed into the tent in twos and threes, holding out their pennies, and both Longstaff and the couple had no choice but to shuffle further inside to allow the rest of the audience a comfortable place to stand.

The rain was coming down hard. Crowds had gathered

outside many of the tents, and people huddled together, leaning in close to anyone with an umbrella. Some talked of going home, but most were keen to prolong even a wet feast day.

To the edge of one of these groups, right outside Gypsy Petronella's, stood a young couple. He held a large black umbrella above her, so courteously that only half of his own body was kept dry. Rain poured off the side of the umbrella, soaking into his shoulder and running down the back of his coat. For her part, the rain seemed to send her into a shiver, and she turned her nose up at the skies as if the afternoon had become a severe disappointment.

'Shall you have your fortune told, Miss?' he said, nodding in the direction of the gypsy's tent behind them.

'No,' she said, sighing with boredom and regretting the whole idea of coming to the feast with only her father's groom for company. She also knew that it would be another half an hour before the trap was sent to collect them.

'Tom!' she said. 'Look how wet you've got!' With that she pulled him under the umbrella and there they stood, their arms touching and he blushing with shame.

'You could try something else,' he suggested, desperate to escape the surprising warmth of her body.

'I suppose so,' she said, a look of lazy disappointment on her young face. Then she giggled. 'Look, Tom! There's a Cat-Icarus!' Only she pronounced it *Catty Carus* as if this was very clever of her. 'Oh yes! Let's both of us go and see it. It's only a penny. Come on, I'll pay.'

'Catty Carus?' he said.

'You know. *Icarus!*'

He looked down at his sodden boots.

'Icarus flew too near to the sun, silly!' she said with a tease. 'It must be a flying cat. Come on!'

With that she dashed across and stood in front of the black-and-gold sign, forgetting the rain, laughing out loud as she read the description of the flying cat. Tom came up after her and held the umbrella, but whatever it was she was saying, he couldn't hear it; as he read the sign he was gripped with a sudden hatred, his body trembling, and could have dragged that laugh from her stupid throat with his fingers.

She paid tuppence and in they went. Tom took down the umbrella and now held it in both hands to disguise his shaking. She mistook this as innocent fear of what lay behind the curtain.

'Don't be silly!' she whispered in his ear. 'It's only a cat!' But she saw how his eyes stared straight ahead at the curtains and she turned away, thinking him an imbecile and remembering that people did say he was a strange one, especially after that trouble at the workhouse.

The tall, moustachioed catnapper-cum-impresario pulled the tent's canvas doors together and secured them with a rope fastening. It was a needless precaution; the smell of steaming overcoats and oniony sweat rose to fill the tent, and the place was so full that not another ounce of humanity could have got itself inside without some other bit being squeezed out. He pushed his way through to the front of the intimate little crowd and cleared his throat. He stood in front of the curtains, looking more than ever like a rat, his face twitching, his eyes darting around nervously. The damp crowd awaited the appearance of the Cat-Icarus quietly, many of them wearing knowing smiles, willing to be taken in, anticipating no more than some ingenious deceit for their penny and, having escaped the rain, hardly expecting more than a wooden cut-out of a flying cat; they would almost have been content with that as long as they stayed dry for ten minutes.

His introduction was not grandiloquent. Pressing his back right up against the curtains he began, and with each hesitant word he looked more and more likely to disappear behind them. He did his best to concoct a decent story, of dervishes and banshees in faraway places, a witless blend of old history and rootless geography even more extravagant than the text painted in gold on his advertising hoarding outside; at one point he claimed that the Cat-Icarus had been the prized possession of the Chief of the Old Incas of deepest Persia, to the delighted scorn of one or two in the audience, including the fine young lady, who held a hand to her mouth to stifle a giggle.

But the real reason for this nervy, unconvincing performance was that at one edge of the audience stood Longstaff, whose eyes never once left those of his rat-man, pinning Max back with such dark accusation that even before the cat itself made an appearance, he was in little doubt that something fateful was about to happen. Then there was the young man at the other side, brandishing an umbrella with an intent that seemed to threaten not violence but rather some physical form of madness: his mouth was pressed tight shut, his nostrils flared, and he stared with a manic intensity into the curtains as if behind them lay the Devil itself and he, with his Umbrella of Destiny, was ready to slay it once and for all.

Max rambled on, half out of fear of opening the curtain

and half because he couldn't think of what else to do. On and on, pulling and scraping facts from the rapidly emptying encyclopaedia of his mind; he claimed that a great-great-uncle of his had done battle on horseback with the evil aborigines of Abyssinia for this very cat, oblivious now to the comic effect of his outpourings. Some wag at the back whispered, rather loudly: 'Then it must be the world's oldest cat!' and he was answered with a round of *shush*es and stern glances. More than once he regretted having secured the canvas doors of the tent so firmly, because he sensed that it was through these doors that his best chance of escape lay. He did not know exactly what the danger was, but felt the imminence of a strange disorder, and that in one way or another it was to do with the cat. However, this also intrigued him; it was something he wanted to witness, like an accident or some other mishap in the street. You're willing to run a small risk in order to see it. Of course, you don't want to be a part of it. But then, you don't want to have been nearby and yet have missed it by a matter of seconds. So now, despite perhaps his better instincts, Max made the decision that whatever else, the Cat-Icarus must be shown.

He threw open the curtains and announced the eighth wonder of the living world. But his voice, split through with apprehension, sounded like a cry for help. The cat, which had waited longer that usual on its high perch, leapt immediately down and came to rest on one of the boxes. Shrieks of horror greeted its arrival, and even as it landed, wings outstretched and a toothy scowl on its ginger face, the whole tent seemed to take a step backwards.

'Right!' said Longstaff, in a matter-of-fact way. He took his rat-man by the neck, and at the same time began kicking at the iron bars of the cage with his foot. This unexpected violence provoked even louder cries of alarm, and in the general panic people turned in all directions, holding their arms up in fright, at first not quite sure what was more distressing to them, the cat or the men fighting.

One voice amongst the crowd was louder than the others. As Longstaff continued to strangle Max and simultaneously try and break down the cage (a feat so impressive in its pure physical ambition that others in the tent were discouraged from intervening on Max's behalf), Tom fell like a madman against the bars of the cage. He took them in both hands, lifting himself clear off the ground like an angry gorilla, beating his head against the bars and moaning in a voice so full of loathing that the crowd was thrown further into disarray at the sound of it.

The tent began to strain under the crush of frightened bodies, and on the outside a few bystanders now looked on with interest, despite the steady rain. Gypsy Petronella heard the commotion and waddled out of her den to see what was going on, leaving a young woman inside with only half her destiny foretold, though, as it happened, it was the better half. The Cat-Icarus tent seemed to be alive, shaking and moving, pulsating as if it were an enormous, animal heart laid out on the ground and still beating. Pulling her shawl around her shoulders and taking a huge draught of fresh air, she strode over and prepared to do battle.

By this time things inside were getting out of hand. Longstaff's fingers, wrapped like solid iron around Max's throat, had now cut off the air supply entirely; he flopped about like a rag doll at the end of Longstaff's arm, who shook him mercilessly whilst still trying to kick down the bars of the cage. Tom, in an attempt to climb through the same bars, had become stuck fast between two of them, and could do no more than brandish his umbrella in the direction of the cat, which sat impassively at the back, watching.

Eventually, the doors of the tent were loosened, but instead of a great rush outwards, the elephantine bulk of Gypsy Petronella pushed its way in. What with the general commotion and the crush inside, the tent split at the seams in several places and within seconds had collapsed. A new, louder screaming arose; what with the destabilising addition of Gypsy Petronella, and the collapse of the tent, all those inside now fell forwards in the darkness and it seemed that the world, after some unnerving preliminaries, was finally coming to an end. The young lady, utterly without the protection of Tom the groom, fainted in a swoon and was taken up in the push of hysterical bodies against the cage, which began to strain and creak, because despite having an iron frontage, on all other sides it was made of boxwood. Pressure from the mass of bodies soon caused the destruction of the cage and, as its front fell inwards, many people followed. These included Tom, now in a apoplexy of unharnessed rage, and his young, unconscious charge, fine petticoats and all, her delicate body in a senseless flop which provided a soft landing for those who tumbled on top of her in the great human deluge.

Meanwhile, Longstaff, not one to let such things deter him, kept his grip, but he and Max eventually fell to the ground along with everyone else. Longstaff now took his free hand and used it to smash his victim's head repeatedly into the earth, stopping short of murder only because the soft, muddy ground yielded up a life-saving inch or two each time the poor boy's skull crashed into it.

Outside, a sizeable crowd had now gathered, impervious to the rain and happy to have found so entertaining a spectacle for free. Attendants from adjacent sideshows came to look, one of whom was the second catnapper himself, who owned a quarter share in the Cat-Icarus and saw that his investment was under threat. At first it appeared that the tent had simply given way with a full crowd inside. But word had it that Gypsy Petronella had gone in there to sort things out, and that sounded like trouble. Also, the level of noise coming from beneath the seething mound told of something more extraordinary. From the edges of the canvas people began emerging, crawling slowly out from under the tent, which now resembled an enormous crushed beetle spilling its guts. But inside, the activity seemed only to intensify. The cries got louder, and eventually two distinct voices could be heard above the rest. A very desperate plea for help came again and again from Max, who by now must have got free of Longstaff's hands. And another voice: 'I'll murder . . . fucking . . . damn bastard . . . cat . . . I shall . . .' a ceaseless string of foul curses and oaths, all rendered strangely inappropriate by the tearful, contralto whine of their speaker.

Despite the sight of the collapsed tent, which was so pleasing to watch that one felt inclined to leave it as it was, despite this, then, the canvas was eventually pulled away by a handful of fairground workers and the pandemonium laid bare.

As a heavy drizzle fell across the fairground, the remains of the Cat-Icarus attraction were enough to silence all those who looked on, even those who had just dragged themselves out from under it. For there on the ground was Longstaff, lying exhausted in his black suit, and who with the last drops of energy in his body struggled with both hands to lift the head of the young man next to him off the ground and then let it drop again. The owner of this head was hardly conscious, his tongue drooping from a gaping mouth, his eyes half open but entirely dead. Not far from them was a young man, shaking with heavy, distressing sobs, his body caught at an angle in the wreckage of the destroyed cage, his face red and puffy like a baby who has not stopped bawling since breakfast. In one hand he had an umbrella, which from time to time he used to swat the air, but like an automaton, with no sense or purpose. By his feet was a young girl in a fine overcoat, and under it a pretty dress soaked with mud. She lay curled up as if in peaceful slumber.

Then, further back, amid the ruins of the cage, something moved. From beneath the debris a huge, amorphous lump seemed to shuffle, then slowly it grew in little jerks and starts, bits of wood dropping from it until after a minute or two a dazed Gypsy Petronella emerged from the catastrophe, blinking and breathing heavily, yet with a slow gracefulness, and had Max been able to provide a commentary he might well have said that she rose like the proverbial phoenix from the sacking of Troy. She eventually got to her feet and dusted herself off. Under one arm, almost hidden from view beneath the vastness of her gown, she had the cat, which purred and rubbed its head against her bosom.

A constable was eventually brought to the scene, which had by that time attracted most of the visitors to the fair as well as many of its workers, who saw little point in manning their empty stalls and sideshows in the face of such competition.

Longstaff accused Max of the theft of the cat, and in return was accused of attempted murder (to which Longstaff merely shrugged). Max, bolstered by a battery of eyewitness accounts, accused Tom of the destruction of the cage. The young girl's father, who by this time had been sent for, accused Tom of abandoning a defenceless young lady, and sacked him on the spot, handing him a pound note for that month's wages; after that he accused almost everyone else there of something or other, until in the end he even threatened to sue the cat. Several bystanders claimed that Petronella had made off with the cat before the constable arrived. This much was true; she had spirited it back to her caravan where it had been locked up safe, and it was only the will of the mob which forced her to fetch the animal back to the scene of so many crimes. Meanwhile, it was claimed that the tent had been packed too full with people, and that these fairmen had no respect for the public safety; moreover, their tents were too small, and dangerous, difficult to get in and out of, and in short were a disgrace. It was even pointed out that the travellers' own living quarters were no better, as if this had some obvious bearing, and had Petronella not at that moment arrived back with the cat, a fist fight would have broken out between fairmen and patrons. The arrival of the Cat-Icarus, now a legal as well as a zoological exhibit, quietened things down for a while.

Tom for his part made a series of long and meandering accusations against the cat itself. But these were hardly taken seriously at all, since the poor boy seemed to be blaming the entire course of his unfortunate life on the animal, and in mentioning the workhouse he only added to the general forlornness of his complaint. It was Tom's insistent claims which finally wore the constable's patience away to nothing. Flipping his notebook closed, he took the cat in his arms and announced that anyone who was unhappy with this was welcome to spend a night in the cells as well.

With that he marched off, not quite sure whether a crime had been committed, the cat under his arm.

IV

Broadbent paced up and down outside the drawing room. Inside lay his daughter, still weak and confused after her ordeal at the feast, attended now by the family doctor, who ministered her with salts and quantities of a dark tonic which smelled suspiciously like liquorice and brandy.

It was not that Broadbent had been ordered from the room in the name of modesty. Rather, he had sent himself out to try and cool down, since his temper was still boiling hot, and in such a state he could tolerate no one in his sight. Tom had been his groom since the boy had turned fifteen – a good five years ago – but Broadbent had dismissed him on the spot, there at the fair, without even a ride home. For all anyone knew, the ex-groom was still in Dewsbury, chuntering to himself about the cat.

Broadbent was angry. He had been so enraged, after learning what Tom had allowed to happen to his daughter, that he felt sure he would horsewhip the boy to death. He was also angry with himself, for having permitted his daughter to visit the fair with only a half-witted groom for protection. It was common knowledge that at fairgrounds virtue is rarely found but frequently lost, and Broadbent's decision

132

to let her go had been surprising and wholly unexpected. He, like most people who find themselves suddenly rich, had developed an excessive concern for the virtue of his children, a preoccupation with high probity which seems to have something to do with a vague notion of nobility. A similar obsession with virtue could have been seen in those nouveau-riche homes of mill owners and merchants across the land; when their sons and daughters inevitably fell from this unnatural grace, either as an act of rebellion or simply as a consequence of living, then the parents would despair, unable to explain their child's attraction to base and unworthy things.

Broadbent's daughter, though, had not fallen so much as been let fall, and the ignominy cut even deeper. She had been buried beneath a pile of low people, at a fairground sideshow, not two strides away from an incident of common thuggery, in the proximity of gypsies, and dangerously close to a mutant animal. She had been crushed half to death there on the wet ground, and now he felt that the family name itself had been trodden into the mud.

Tom was to blame for all this. However, Broadbent was a compassionate man, and was one of those people who knows compassion to be amongst their principal virtues. Though his mill served to shorten the lives of all who worked there, and though the wages he paid meant that his employees were forced into cramped and insanitary slum dwellings, so that their beds crawled with bugs the year round, and their children, those that didn't die young, grew up with constant coughs and running noses, and though even in the worst stages of an illness the mean conditions of their lives denied them decent medical attention, so that they frequently died from ailments which started out as no more than head colds or tickly chests, despite this, Broadbent was a compassionate man. So as soon as it was clear that his daughter had come to no lasting physical harm, and that she would be compelled to live with only the psychological scars inflicted upon her by such a trauma, he turned his attention to the problem of Tom. He got thinking about the groom's engagement, not more than a few months before, to a scullery maid at the workhouse. It had ended when she went suddenly mad and had to be sent to an asylum. Broadbent knew this because it was he, keen to ensure that Tom did not go the same way, who had paid for the girl's swift removal.

Tom had not properly recovered from the loss of his fiancée, becoming nervous and withdrawn and almost a mute. Once or twice Markham had sent word that he had been hanging around the workhouse, asking people where Alice had gone, which provoked great sadness there, since they had all been terribly moved by her inexplicable descent into madness. Moreover, none of them knew where she had been taken, only that it was an asylum some distance away. So, Tom's very presence at the workhouse had become an unwelcome reminder of the whole sorry affair, and Markham put a stop to it.

Now, as his temper cooled, Broadbent saw that Tom's life had taken an unfortunate twist, and that a young man could be seriously harmed by such a thing. He reasoned, perhaps correctly, that if a temperamentally insecure young man were thrown out on to the street with no trade but that of groom to his name, then the likely outcome was tragedy. The problem, of course, was that the idea of Tom returning to work at the Broadbent home was out of the question. For one thing, his negligence had brought humiliation on the family; and for another, Broadbent himself could not be seen to back down from a decision already made, because there was only so much honour to play with, and the Broadbents were using theirs up rapidly. He sent for Markham.

Naturally, Markham did not welcome the suggestion that the workhouse should now offer Tom employment, however proficient his grooming skills. Broadbent, though, was an important and influential benefactor, and though the men discussed the ins and outs of the matter at hand for more than an hour, they both knew that it had already been decided: Tom would become assistant overseer at the workhouse, at the institution's expense. And here lies a small detail worthy of attention. The workhouse functioned like any other establishment, paying a regular wage to its employees. However, its superintendent was a kind of general manager who saw to it that the place cost no more than it should, and was himself paid according to his own efficiency. In other words, a good part of Markham's salary came in the form of a sort of inverse commission, so that if budgets were exceeded, his own earnings fell. By this mechanism the benefactors had always managed to keep the workhouse expenses under the tightest rein. Or, more accurately, Markham had always been so afraid of the monthly outgoings that he spent every last drop of his energy in making sure that not a lump of coal nor a single candle was used unnecessarily. That is, he made everyone's life unimaginably tiresome and frugal for the sake of his own pocket. Like it or not, then, Markham would have to find the means to employ Tom. Immediately, he began to think of ways in which an assistant overseer's wages could be shaved from the workhouse budget, which was already pulled as tight as normal logic and invention could pull it.

The men's conversation at this point took an unusual turn. Tom's destiny having been settled, they moved on to a more general discussion of the boy. Gradually, events at the fairground were described by Broadbent in more and more detail until the cat, despite being in Broadbent's eyes a far less significant element in the whole fracas than the brawling gypsies and other low types, made its inevitable entry into the narrative. Markham felt the hairs on the back of his neck prickle at the first mention of the animal, and the thought that it might still be alive sent a cold shiver around his body. Then, with Broadbent's eloquent description of Dewsbury Feast fresh in his thoughts, Markham suffered what could only be described as a flash of genius; an idea that came from nowhere, fully formed and perfectly balanced, an idea so brilliant that he excused himself as soon as politeness allowed and rushed back home to begin making plans.

Meanwhile, the trap was sent all the way back to Dewsbury in search of Tom, together with a brief note from Broadbent explaining the new arrangement with the workhouse. For his part, Tom had not left the fairground. He had fallen in with some of the fairmen who had helped to clear up the remains of the Cat-Icarus tent. Now, three or four hours later, they sat around inside another, larger tent and drank bottled beer which Tom sent out for by the crateload until, after several crates had been brought in and consumed, he had no money left for more. The men caroused in an idle way, without much animation or joy; or perhaps the events of the afternoon had provoked in them a kind of thoughtfulness, for it was certainly true that *that* kind of thing did not happen often, even at a fairground.

The tent where they now drank was a large one, with a sawdust floor and a raised boxing ring in the middle. From time to time Tom would climb up on to the dais, muddling his way through the thick ropes which hung around its four sides, and challenge Pedro Rocca to a fight. Pedro 'the Rock' Rocca was a professional boxer, though he fought only amateurs; all day long he would prowl around outside his tent, grizzling more or less menacingly, hoping in that way to lure someone into the ring, any spirited man who fancied his chances against the bald and somewhat ridiculous-looking Pedro, who was not only dressed in a yellow silken robe, but was bald and easily fifty-five years old. He was, in fact, exactly the right age for the job, because many a young man, with a girl on his arm and bunch of rowdy friends behind him, would reckon such an old-timer to be easy pickings. And sometimes Rocca did get hit. Now and then an enthusiastic youngster would land a punch. Just one, usually a glancing blow which obliged him to take his opponent more seriously and mount a proper defence. Excitement would rise around the tent, and more paying customers would pour in through the doors, the word having spread instantly that another victim was ready for the slaughter, the new crowd keen for blood and glory or, if not both, then at least the blood. Rocca would play with the newly emboldened victim, drawing him in, ducking his ridiculously predictable punches, and pulling all his own so that it appeared that a real fight was taking place. After a few minutes, when no one else came through the tent doors, he would wallop the lad square on the temple just hard enough that his legs gave way beneath him and he found himself instantly on the canvas. No one ever chose to try and beat the count after that, so Rocca was saved the need to apply any further persuasion.

Now, as Rocca relaxed for the evening, he was being taunted by Tom, who had of course bought the beer, so a little tolerance was called for. However, the alcohol seemed to render Tom dangerously short of judgement, since the more he drank the more earnest were his invitations for Rocca to fight. The others did their best to ignore him, thinking that he must be suffering some form of nervous reaction to the Cat-Icarus incident. Perhaps it had been the fearful sight of the cat itself, they thought, not without a certain jealousy, since if the cat really was such hot stuff then Petronella and her two partners had been in possession of a living, flying fortune.

From the ring Tom now went too far. He called Rocca a coward and a crybaby, and possibly also made reference to the boxer's mother, though no one heard this clearly enough to confirm what had been said. The bald man staggered up off the floor, stood his bottle carefully on the ground, and walked over to the ring, where Tom was jigging about with both fists held up at face height as if in readiness. When Rocca got to the stage, instead of springing up onto the dais he simply reached under the bottom rope and, with one arm, swiped the boy's legs from under him. Tom fell without a sound but with an expression of great surprise on his face. Rocca then pulled him off the canvas by his feet, heaved him on to his shoulder, and carried him out of the tent, dumping him on the wet grass outside. Then he returned to his bottle of beer. No one said

anything, and in a minute or two they had forgotten who
Tom was.

*

Catty must have got a very good opinion of policemen. Not
every cat can say that, perhaps. But for three weeks at
Dewsbury Central Police Station, food and affection were
in limitless supply.

Each morning a mountain of breakfast scraps was put
down for the new visitor, and throughout the day there was
a never-ending series of meals and snacks and elevenses
and tea breaks. The Dewsbury Constabulary, it seemed,
marched on its stomach, and there were some substantial
ones. Hardly an hour passed without the laying down of
newspapers and pencils for a fresh round of gorging, always
washed down with sweet tea, and always a saucer of it put
down for the cat. The poor thing had no choice but to leave
whole plates of titbits untouched, and this eventually served
as a gentle hint that a cat's needs are really quite modest in
comparison to a policeman's.

As far as affection was concerned, the cat was overbur-
dened with it. The constables there must have been recruited
according to their sentimental tendencies, for though hardly
a crime was detected or solved in those three weeks, even
the toughest amongst them would turn to gibbering fools
when petting the winged cat. Perhaps policemen have some
special, urgent need to express their feelings, because they
cooed and babbled, down on their hands and knees, as if it
were their own first-born child.

After three weeks, though, the cat was taken away.

V

Sergeant Harold Devitt of the Dewsbury Constabulary looks so anxious that anyone might think him a novice. Fifteen years' service as a police officer to his name, fifteen years of ham sandwiches and sweet tea that have lent him an almost buxom rotundity. But now he doesn't know where to put his pudgy hands, and his stomach has curled itself up so tight that he can hardly stand up straight. His jowls quiver, and points of sweat glisten on his forehead and on the ridge of his nose; he is, suddenly, all humidity and leakage, and under his uniform he bristles and chafes with a sour, nervy dampness as he tries to explain about the cat. In front of him sits a police officer of a higher rank than any he has previously encountered.

There have been two complaints, both lodged according to the correct procedures. Joseph Markham, who moved more urgently on the matter, turning up at his solicitor's the very day after the incident at the fairground to prepare his legal challenge, has accused Longstaff of the theft of a winged cat from the workhouse. No concrete explanation of how the cat had then found its way to the fairground is given, but there is a whole section in his

140

submission which describes Mr John Longstaff as a noto-
riously unconventional businessman, and which includes
a signed statement from an ex-stable hand claiming that
Longstaff beat a horse to death with a wooden club; other
statements allege that he kept only improvised financial accounts, and that he regularly overcharged clients
and became abusive when they refused to pay. There is
even a description, lengthy and showing the hallmarks
of Markham's own prolixical style (though it is unsigned
and therefore inadmissible), of the ramshackle hen house
that Longstaff built and maintained, and insinuates that
more than one of his customers found him to be of dubious
and unsteady character, indeed just the kind of man to
whom it would occur to steal a winged cat for the purposes
of making money. John Longstaff, it is suggested, made
a deal with Petronella to share the proceeds from the
fairground attraction.

This theory is contradicted by Longstaff's own documents,
which arrive several days later. In them he claims that it
was not Petronella but two young gypsy men who stole the
cat from New Court, where the animal had been living of its
own free will, having arrived there unexpectedly the very
day that Longstaff and his family moved in. One of these
two gypsies is described in great detail. However, no names
are given, since by the time Longstaff set out to find them
again, the fair was gone, and all that was left where the tent
had stood (and fallen) on the great open field in Dewsbury
was a pile of boxwood splinters and a black-and-gold sign
announcing the Cat-Icarus. Longstaff, being not wise in such
matters, punched and ripped and kicked the sign to bits until
it was worthless as evidence.

'Well, Sergeant,' the senior officer says, 'what's it all about?'

The presence of so high-ranking an official (from head office indeed) is a consequence of the widespread publicity which the case has received. In the weeks since Devitt attended the scene of the collapsed fairground tent and its many attendant altercations, local newspapers have been full of speculation as to how the case might be resolved and, crucially, who will get the cat. From the start Petronella is favourite to carry off the prize. For one thing, descriptions of her appearance and general demeanour make her a sure winner in the eyes of the reading public, and a seemingly endless succession of accounts of her immense size and physical strength keep the newspaper editors happy right up until the trial itself. And with every new mention of this woman-mountain, she gains a little bulk, slowly expanding until she exceeds the boundaries of what is credible. Finally, there seems little doubt that she, like the cat, is a mutant, possibly (as one excitable young feature writer proposes) a strange case of Siamese twins with a single head. The suggestion takes hold, and soon it becomes commonly agreed that her girth is so great that no other explanation can be taken seriously but that she is some sort of multiple being. This line of reasoning develops into a general discussion of whether such a mutation has ever existed before, and within a fortnight the matter is clear: Petronella is the only living example. Since not a single photograph of her can be found, old images of Chang and Eng Bunker, the original Siamese Twins, come to adorn every article on Petronella. Long accounts of P. T. Barnum's 1862 European tour (in which the twins were exhibited to great acclaim) appear in even the most humble news-sheets, and it is noted that the famous conjoined brothers from Siam had, in 1862, attracted the interest of royalty, a point which allows the citizens of Dewsbury a kind of vicarious pride. The more salacious journals also mention the double marriage of the Bunker brothers, and that between them and their two wives they produced no fewer than twenty-one children, as if this statistic in some way legitimises the gypsy woman's claim on the cat. Alongside pictures of Chang and Eng are placed diagrams of the possible configurations of Petronella's own double-bodied form, showing how with just a little more bodily cohesion, plus the loss (or concealment) of one head, her great mass can be explained. But it is pure speculation, and the mystery of what exactly lies under those voluminous gowns – now referred to as 'mystery-robes', 'ghoulish garments', 'horrendous habiliments' – sets Dewsbury (and, it must be said, most of Yorkshire) afire with shivery speculation. On top of this, journalists agree that her mystical and shadowy line of work is most likely to bring her into contact with *a world of freaks, monsters and magic*. This much can hardly be denied, and there appears, in addition to the interest in Petronella, a new fascination with the fairmen and their exotic lives. Pictures of travellers' carvans are published, together with plans of their interiors. *Could* you *live in a place like this?* asks one headline, and beneath it are printed some recipes which, it is suggested, might be cooked in such cramped conditions. A week later the correspondence columns fill up with letters of praise for the fairmen's wives, since the horror of cooking dinner in so confined a space seems to many readers something worse than slavery on the high seas.

Despite all this free publicity, though, Petronella has got

no benefit from it. Neither has she so much as made a claim on the cat. She disappeared along with the rest of the fair's itinerant community the next evening. Devitt, aware of this likelihood, made sure that he interviewed her soon after the events of that memorable day. In fact, he made his way back to the fairground the very next morning.

He was invited into the caravan, and Petronella took up position in the armchair, spreading herself about in the usual way until she became part woman, part furniture, part caravan. Max was sent for and after what seemed like an extraordinary amount of time, he skulked in like a scolded dog and leaned against the door, as if he might bolt the minute Devitt looked the other way.

'Okey-dokey,' the sergeant began, hoping that this, his first interview on the case, would be the simplest. 'The Cat-*Icarus* . . . How did it come to be here?'

In returning the very morning following the disturbance, Devitt had caught Petronella and Max unprepared. After things had quietened down the previous evening Max, now fearing that his new attraction was ruined and that he was most likely to be tried for larceny, even if Longstaff didn't get to him first, had spent the rest of the night steadying his nerves on port wine and India ale and, not being a regular drinker, anything else with a likeable name. So when Petronella embarked on her story, telling Devitt exactly how the cat had been offered to her for twenty pounds by an unknown gentleman somewhere on the road from London several weeks ago, and how she had no idea who this gentleman was, though she gave a very full description of him, and even quoted parts of the conversation which had passed between them, when she began all this, then, there had still not been time to settle on a common alibi with Max, who she had not seen since the previous day and who, even now, showed signs that his drinking had gone on not only into the early hours, but on and on, into the later ones. Petronella, though, got quickly into her stride and, unencumbered by the need to keep to an agreed story, let her narrative flow free.

'And the gentleman *assured* me,' she said, 'that the cat was originally from France—'

At this point Max, already confused, intervened.

'France?' he said through a hiccup, and then belched, filling the caravan with sweet, alcoholic fumes, which in their sickliness added a strange hint of dubitability to the whole story.

'France? No, no, further than that,' he continued. 'From Araby she flew—'

'She?' Devitt said.

'She,' added Petronella quickly, seizing on this one opportunity to concur with Max, although the truth was that neither she nor her adoptive nephew had any idea as to whether the cat was male or female. And they were not the only ones.

'So,' Devitt said, having already used up several pages of his notebook to no obvious effect, 'it is a *lady* cat then?' And only as he noted this down did it occur to him that neither had he asked himself, the previous evening, what sex it was.

'She flew to us from the East! And,' said Max, before stopping to swallow, as if preparing to say something of great import, 'she is a magical, a magical animal and appears and disappears and you can't know anything about that cat!'

Thus Max's story began, without much sense of where it might go next. Discovering that he had an enwrapped audience, he became loquacious, and wouldn't stop. Petronella's eyes implored him to shut up, since with every word he undid another piece of her alibi, oblivious to the contradictions he was weaving. He described the cat's magical appearance six months ago at a fair in Hull, where it was said it had landed on a ship from the Indies (by this time he was even contradicting himself), and how the animal was the friend of bats and vampires throughout the continent. Devitt, by this stage more interested in conserving the blank pages of his notebook than in the any notion of the truth, sighed with impatience.

Then, without warning, Max shut up mid-sentence, on his young face the surprised look of a drunk who suddenly realises that he has been talking. Devitt's sigh, together with the bored, sorry look in his eyes, told Petronella that not a word of her story had been believed either. They had come to an impasse, and the police officer mumbled something about continuing his inquiries and returning to talk to them again within the week. However, both he and the gypsy knew (for she was a fortune teller) that within forty-eight hours her caravan would be many miles away, and that she would have ceded any claim on the cat.

Devitt could also see this far into the future. When it came to looking into the past, on the other hand, his sister had done all the work. For she had recently been a visitor to New Court, where along with a group of friends she had paid tuppence to see John Longstaff's flying cat, though apparently on that day it wouldn't fly due to an unfortunate airborne collision with a Canada goose that very morning, which had unnerved the animal and, in addition, may have sprained one of its wings (the cat's). Petronella, then, was lying. She and Max were very probably guilty of the theft of the cat, but on what grounds could Devitt detain them? And since they were travellers, how could they ever be found again once they rode out of Dewsbury? All in all, the sergeant told himself, the theory that the cat had wandered of its own accord from New Court to the fairground was a far more satisfying one. And if the distance seemed too much for a cat to have managed, then perhaps the thing had flown after all.

Devitt next went the ten miles from Dewsbury to New Court, where he happened to catch the Longstaff family all together, having what looked like a funeral lunch. Longstaff himself came to the door, eyes sunk deep into his shallow, colourless cheeks, and his body only just holding itself together, as if it might fall apart and collapse into a pile of withered pieces if you so much as loosened his necktie. Inside, the other three Longstaffs were in a similar state, mourning the loss of their cat as if it were dead. Flora had developed a nervous twitch, and as she tended to her daughters, stroking their hair and running a calming hand across their small shoulders, she blinked involuntarily, perhaps from tiredness or anxiety, looking as if she had not slept for a week. The girls were mute, and hardly raised their heads when the policeman came into the parlour. They bore the numb faces of those who have endured a pain so great that the soul itself has been sullied by it and will always retain some shadow of that suffering.

Devitt was offered tea, and when he took his cup he found that the tea itself was stone-cold. At last the painful subject of Catty was raised. Heads dropped lower still, and tears welled and trickled. Longstaff, with his voice for the main part holding steady, managed to recount the story of how the cat had arrived on the very first morning that they were at New Court, and how the poor under-nourished thing had been taken in as a pet. Meanwhile, his daughters sniffed quietly, and Flora fussed about with plates and cutlery, her twitch getting worse as the story unfolded.

'Now,' Devitt said, 'tell me about the workhouse.'

For a moment Longstaff gathered his thoughts.

'Haven't been there in three months!' he said at last, as if this might be the end of the matter.

'Three months?'

'Aye, three months. And I've never heard of Markham before yesterday, when that halfwit kept on about him. I sold eggs to the cook up there, and I stopped going when I got rid of the hens.'

'Three months ago?'

'Three months ago.'

'From the Towers!' said one of the girls suddenly, as if by speaking, her pain was momentarily lifted.

The three adults looked at the girl, whose eyes were big and swollen and pleaded to be believed.

'Catty flew around at the big building, and then came home for tea!'

'The Towers?' Devitt asked, who knew nothing of the area.

'A *big* building!' one of the girls replied, pleased that the policeman was listening to her and sounding proud of herself.

'With towers!' added her sister. And then they smiled, forgetting their woes.

'With towers?' said Devitt. 'A big, *big* building?'

'Oh yes!' the two of them cried in jubilation. But then, turning to each other, they burst into such loud and harrowing tears that their mother in the end had to take them out of the room.

'So, the cat flew here from a big building with towers?'

'Yes, it flew all the way!' Longstaff said sarcastically.

'It did!' came a high-pitched reply from the door, and then more howls of distress, the sounds disappearing as the distraught girls were taken down the corridor and into another room, and the door shut behind them.

'It flew here,' Devitt repeated, and noted the fact down.

Longstaff stood up, unable to contain his rage any longer, pacing up and down on the parlour carpet, his feet never once touching the wooden floorboards beyond its limits, which were painted a sooty black; backwards and forwards he went, as if the limits of the carpet were the only means he had of keeping his temper under control.

'The bloody thing came here when we did and it stayed. That's it. Nothing more to it than that.'

'The same day you arrived?'

'Yes! And what of it?'

'And, the cat became a pet, you say?'

Longstaff stopped his pacing and turned to Devitt. 'Did you see the girls, eh? Their faces? All bloody night like that, they've been. All night and us up with 'em as well. All night and all morning. And every bloody night since they stole the cat!'

Devitt kept taking notes steadily, nodding a little, his

pencil scratching out its wickerwork of single words and odd phrases, all tied together with arrows and question marks and thick underlinings.

'And,' said the policeman, sensing that Longstaff, like his daughters, was reaching some kind of emotional hiatus, 'it was not an exhibit when it was here, then? Like at the fairground, a *business*?'

'It was a pet,' Longstaff said, bringing both hands up to cradle his face, as if to pull away the mask of anguish and fatigue that he could feel lying there like coal dust and clammy sweat.

A clatter of footsteps approached, and in a matter of seconds the two girls were back, breathless and giddy, bouncing on their feet and knocking into each other. Their mother arrived a moment later, just in time to see them get to the table. One of them held the hems of her dress close to her, as if she were concealing something against her stomach. And her sister, wincing with infantile delight at every breath, began to take handfuls of coins from the dress and deposit them on the table: farthings, old and new, and halfpennies and pennies, some as dull as mud, the occasional glint of a silver sixpence amid the expanding pile of brown metal. So many coins came from the dress that the pile soon spilled halfway across the table, each new fistful dropping with something between a tinkle and a thud onto the rest, and the odd coin rolling to the floor, one of which came to a stop at Devitt's feet.

When the dress was emptied the two girls stood to attention in front of the money, slightly in awe, but their faces also straining with a silent joyous laughter which seemed almost to be painful around the eyes and mouth.

Longstaff brought his hands away from his face, the fingers dragging with them any last remaining equanimity. His expression froze, lower jaw protruding a fraction, eyes glazed and inattentive.

Devitt shifted in his chair. Then he smiled at the girls: 'Catty?'

'Yes,' they whispered. 'Catty!'

Devitt next visited the workhouse, where Superintendent Markham not only supplied him with enough material to fill the remaining pages of his notebook, but stopped periodically during the telling, repeating those words which merited special attention, and making sure that the policeman was getting them all down.

'Ah, that cat!' he said, shaking his head, rising from the chair in his office and stalking about the room. The memory so pained him that he could not sit still as he talked but had to shake the sadness continually from his bones. 'Four years I kept that little creature, four years. You know, the day it was born, right here in the kitchens, there were those who wanted it drowned. But I wouldn't have it. You can ask any of 'em. They'll tell you. Four years it stayed, and the day its mother died I . . . well . . .' and at this point he found it impossible to continue.

'And, after the four years?' said Devitt, as quietly as he could.

'Eh?' said Markham, as if awoken from a reverie. 'What happened next? Why, that scoundrel Longstaff stole it. The very day he stopped bringing the eggs, if I remember correctly. The same day.'

Devitt made a note of this, and Markham was able to give

him the exact date. And when asked why the theft had not been reported earlier, Markham was majestic.

'There is, sir, a difference between true feeling, and responsibility to the law. *And I for one know it*. Just a cat, that's all it is, a deformed one at that. But to us it is family. It is . . . *loved!*'

Devitt scribbled furiously, trying to get the whole sentence about *responsibility to the law* down verbatim, since it appealed to him, and he thought it might be of use later on.

'That was a sad day for us. First, the old ratter died, which broke our hearts. And then,' and here Markham may even have cleared his throat in order to disguise unmanly sentiments, 'its poor, deformed kitten . . .'

'Which was four by this time . . . ?' said Devitt.

'Four, but still a kitten to us! Defenceless, of course. It depended on us, the little mite. Stolen and taken to a circus. You know, our young scullery maid Alice was so upset that she had an attack and went mad.'

Markham now explained how Alice and Tom were both present, four years earlier, at the discovery of the winged kitten; how their romance had been nurtured through those four years, growing and strengthening along with the cat, which had been born at the same moment as their deep, ill-fated love. The theft of the cat had not only pushed the poor scullery girl into a state of madness, but had clearly sent Tom the same way.

'But I have hope!' Markham said, hoisting a pointed finger into the air as if to puncture the atmosphere of gloom which his own pathetic narrative had created. 'Tom tried to liberate the cat from that monstrous fair. But it was an act of affection, of true feeling, not madness. And when the cat is returned to its home here with us, I feel sure that the poor boy's recovery will begin. You know,' and here he made a proud little cough, 'I have decided to take the boy in. He'll come and work with us here. No, Longstaff has forced one innocent young person into madness, but perhaps, Sergeant, I might be able to save a second from the same fate.'

Markham made the slightest bow. His story was told.

Since the investigation began, Devitt had come to regret his part in the whole affair. Petronella had disappeared, but against this there was a growing clamour in the newspapers (and, indeed, amongst his colleagues) in favour of her keeping the cat. And as the days passed, public support grew for the gypsy woman, whose photograph had still not been procured (she was by now in Clapham, taking a sabbatical from the fairgrounds) and who, as a result, had grown in physical as well as psychical stature, finally becoming 'Petronella, last of the Romanies and Queen of the Spiritual Kingdom' but also, sometimes in the very same publications, 'Petronella, mutant Siamese mystery' and 'Petronella, hideous double-bodied mammal-woman!'

Devitt began to find himself suddenly awake in the cold, silent hours of night, wheezing, his arms aching. There was only one dream, but it came to him now with a worrying regularity. In it he is walking down a dusty street, perhaps in Mexico; the sun burns him like scalding porcelain against the skin, and around him is a wall of noise – distant piano music, shrieking women, the odd pistol shot, a cockerel at full cry. In the midst of it all, as he continues down the street, he feels the dry dust under his feet, the gritty crunch of uneven sand, and in his mouth the taste of it, fine and bitter. People move past him going the other way, men and women in twos and threes, laughing, grimacing, as if drunk and on the edge of some act of unnecessary violence.

Devitt looks up towards the sun. Its heat cuts him, like razors in each fold of his screwed-up face; and against the sun's white glare are tangled stains of black, flashing one after the other across his vision, their shapes fractured and irregular, each one like a sudden ragged tear in the screen of light. He realises that his arms are moving, his hands turning hot then cold, and looks down to find that he is juggling. He can see, below his fast-moving hands, that his feet are still taking him forward; his back is upright and stiff, and he is juggling cats as he goes. He is shocked that he can walk and juggle at the same time, and for a moment suffers a flush of anxiety lest he drop one of the animals, which he notices are alive, their limbs in motion as they attempt to stabilise themselves each time he tosses one up in a high arc through the burning air. But then, just a second or two later, he is once again calm. There are three cats, all black, or at least that's how it seems, and he senses that not only is his juggling regular and assured, but that the cats feel this too; they land in his outstretched palm without discomfort, letting themselves fall onto their backs or their bellies, quite without their normal instinct to land paws first. As they hit his hand, he whisks each one sideways, his arm down low, and then launches it again quickly with a flick of the wrist. On he goes, past saloons and sideshows and tethered horses that shake their heads to get free of the flies around their ears. Then he sees Petronella, bigger than ever, as big as a horse at least, sitting under a parasol which itself seems to stretch right across the space where a building should go. She wears the same enormous drape of a dress, and he peers at it, forgetting the cats. Under the dress there are shapes that he cannot account for, big, rounded forms, and between them angles and bulges and valleys, and – does he see? – the flutter of two hearts. Her eyes beckon him over, their stare luscious, more inviting than any woman's he has ever seen, and her breasts are huge and swollen, two, four, twelve of them perhaps, for they bobble and multiply, a moving pontoon of flesh for her tricky, tempting head and its many chins to rest on. He is about to say thank you, feeling his burning face turn into the beginnings of a smile, when around him someone screams. Then another, men and women together, their cries full of drunken terror. He is no longer walking forwards, and now, panicked by the noise, he looks up and sees one of the cats rise from his hand in a steady ascent. On reaching its apex it takes flight, dashing free into the air and circling above the heads of the crowd on the street before making its way up higher. Devitt then sees that another of the cats has already escaped, soaring high in the sky, until it finally disappears towards the sun. Before he can stop it, the third and last cat takes flight and is gone.

'Well,' says Devitt, and can think of nothing to say, no obvious way of beginning. Because although the senior officer in front of him wants the full story, there must be a proper place to start, and Devitt has no clear idea where it is. He has carefully weighed the evidence after interviews with Petronella and Max, Longstaff and family (twice), Markham (three times in all), as well as a futile meeting with Tom (who Devitt thought quite beyond recovery, which made Markham's commitment to take the poor, mad boy in look like an act of even greater kindness). After all this, there seems to be no obvious point of departure, and in the end Devitt relies entirely on Markham's words: Longstaff is a scoundrel. Such a conclusion is hardly the way to open a report, so Devitt does his best to reconstruct events leading to the fairground debacle, relying (perhaps too enthusiastically) on several dozen of Markham's other choice phrases, and for the main part keeping New Court as the centre of the action. The senior officer is very grateful for this, since he has previously made it clear that his good friend Mr Broadbent is to be kept out of the case altogether; and now, having made the effort of coming personally to see the investigating officer, he is especially pleased to note that Devitt does not find it necessary to mention either Broadbent or his daughter once in the long, rambling account of events. Devitt, over the previous three weeks, has been left in no doubt as to what should and should not be uncovered in the case, so he is doubly nervous about the results of his investigation.

All in all the interview goes well, and it is duly decided that John Longstaff will be charged with larceny, to be tried at the Quarter Sessions. Whereas the more modest Petty Sessions would have been the natural place to hear a charge of stealing a cat, by now it is clear that the case has come to represent something beyond simple theft. There is intrigue and an attractive grimness in every last detail, and the Petty Sessions could never confer a sufficient gravitas, nor indeed would the courtroom be large enough for the crowds expected at the hearing. Broadbent could easily have used his influence to limit press interest in the case. However, the best way of keeping his daughter's name out of the whole affair was to let unbridled speculation over Petronella reach its dizzy heights; in this way, when the public realised that the case was not about a mutant gypsy fortune teller, but the far less compelling claim that a removal man had stolen a cat from a workhouse superintendent, then the business would be quickly forgotten.

VI

Inside the courtroom of the Leeds Quarter Sessions, Markham had already given his evidence, a performance which in its combination of raw emotion and dignified resolution had moved several people to tears, and he was now squeezed into one of the cramped stalls to watch the rest of the trial, along with what seemed to be half the population of the city. Every inch of occupiable space had been filled at least twofold; men in pinching suits were squashed so close together on the benches at the back that they rocked endlessly from buttock to buttock, since there was only room for them to set one down at a time, and it was only through a tense, muscular kind of shuffle against neighbouring buttocks and thighs that even this much contact with the bench could be achieved. Standing room was under the control of one stern, worried-looking court sergeant, who marshalled the door at the back of the room and would allow no one in until another person went out, such was the intensity of the crush of bodies standing everywhere; people threw themselves shamelessly towards any spot of floor which suddenly opened up and showed itself to be big enough for two feet. In the press stall journalists sat brazenly on top of each other, their legs criss-crossed in a tangle beneath them, and one eager pressman after another would claw and hoist himself to the top of the pile, balancing precariously there for a minute or two before he was dragged down into the mêlée of limbs below as someone else clambered over him on his way to the summit.

Towards the front of the courtroom, where a little more decorum was in evidence, bodies were squeezed so tight up against one other on the benches that people could feel their neighbours' hearts beating – one on each side – and could hear the endless clicking and cracking of elbow and knee joints right up and down the row, as people squirmed and wriggled in search of an illusory moment's comfort. When occasionally someone stood and left their place, the entire row would shake itself loose, relieved arms and legs easing into an inch of freedom, before everyone settled back in their places and found themselves no better off than before. Once when this happened a man who was standing in the crowd by the door came forward to take the vacated space; only, when he tried to slip himself in, the row would not or could not yield, and after a full minute of trying to lower himself down on to a sliver of wooden bench no wider than his forearm, he gave up and tiptoed back to the crowd by the door, where his standing position had already been taken, and he found himself politely but firmly jostled to the back, next to the sergeant.

The first of Longstaff's daughters was called. Flora and the two girls had been waiting outside the courtroom, the mother so afraid that she could hardly move, but her daughters oblivious to what was happening within. Both had been told that they must tell the truth, and this had been repeated so often since the date for the trial was known that they had begun to recite the phrase to themselves, until finally it seemed meaningless and something of a game.

Inside the court, the girl was led by an old, whiskery official to the witness stand, where she was allowed to kneel on a chair, and it was some time before the sighs and mumblings of sympathy died down enough that the magistrate could make himself heard. When he did begin to address the witness, it was not at all certain whether she understood or not, since she bowed her head so low that her chin pushed into her chest and her eyes looked straight down to the floor. And then, as she scanned her immediate surroundings, slowly bringing her eyes up to find lines of polished shoes and the carved, dark-wood feet of court tables and desks, she saw it: a cat cage, made of wickerwork with a wire grill at the front. Catty lay inside, slumped down on its paws, not so much an exhibit as a bored onlooker, struggling to keep its eyes open and showing no signs of discomfort at all. The girl's heart leapt and, seized by a sudden excitement, she looked right around the courtroom, as if this simple act would be enough to get Catty back, just as soon as all the adults knew whose pet it really was, and all about New Court and the wings and the charabancs and the Towers.

The magistrate gave her a series of easy questions: her name, her age, where she lived, did she know what it meant to tell the truth. In response to this last question the girl, despite her seven years, gave the magistrate a short speech, impressing upon him the need always to tell the truth. Longstaff watched his daughter as she grew in confidence, and could not help but smile, knowing that even the most mean-spirited person would be persuaded by her delightful (and delighted) innocence. With each further answer she cast a glance at the wicker cage, and the whole court could see the glow of love in her eyes. There was such fondness in her every word that the court could easily imagine the warmth of the coals in the hearth, the winged cat on the rug and beside it a seven-year-old child, the two of them together in a breathless, feline contentment which seemed to represent something sacrosanct, a scene never to be spoiled by interruption. Oh, the cat was hers! The cat was loved! And Longstaff was an innocent man!

'So, tell me,' the magistrate said, now regretting the need to extend the interrogation, 'is Catty a boy cat or a girl cat?'

She looked confused, and sought the eyes of her father, who could do nothing for her. He pushed himself down hard on to his seat, as if chained there and unable to move, knowing that he could not leap up and rescue his brave daughter.

'It's . . . Catty!' she said at last, but the murmurs around the courtroom grew, and were by now not altogether fond ones.

'And Catty,' the magistrate said, in a tone which could not have been gentler had he whispered it through cotton wool, 'that's a funny name for a cat, isn't it? Does it have a real name, like, let's see, like Thomas, Richard or Harold?'

Sniggers could be heard from the crowd, and Longstaff tried desperately to find the chuckling culprits, knowing that in other circumstances their heads would already be split open. He gripped the edge of his seat with both hands to confine the rage within him.

'What is it called, then?' the magistrate repeated, but by

this time his gentleness seemed like irony, though not to the girl. Her lower jaw began to shake, and her eyes fluttered, trance-like, until she appeared to be on the verge of an infantile madness. Everyone in the place would have called the proceedings to a halt, had it not been for the curious feeling that she was about to answer, and that her answer was the key to everything.

'Thomas!' she cried, and immediately laughed out loud at the magistrate. And then all the court laughed along with her. One or two at the back broke out into applause, but were quickly told to stop.

The girl was led away to great acclaim, and Longstaff, who had passed in those few minutes through so great a torrent of different emotions that he could hardly remember a word of what his daughter had said, laughed as well.

Next came the second of the Longstaff girls, perhaps a little disappointing in contrast to her sister, since she turned white and shook visibly at the very sight of the courtroom. As the magistrate spoke to her it was obvious that she barely understood; her head moved jerkily about and she found it impossible to fix her gaze anywhere, being so frightened by each new thing she saw that she shifted her eyes straight away on to something else.

After several minutes it became clear that a sort of torture was being enacted there, and her mother was called for, who was allowed into court even though her own evidence had not yet been heard. Leaving her other daughter on the knee of a court clerk, Flora took up position next to her child in the witness stand and did all that could be done with a small white handkerchief to comfort her in front of the now silent audience. After the mother had been warned that she must not prompt the child, the questioning continued. The very same questions were asked, and though the answering was slow and hardly audible, and also thoroughly unconvincing in its delivery, the same answers were given. But already, the court was getting restless, for now only one question mattered. When it came, the magistrate did his best to repeat it word for word, and even to imitate the tone of voice he had employed with the previous witness.

'What is the cat called?' he asked, having made the very same comments about the name Catty, and once again mentioning Thomas, Richard and Harold (though no one thought it very witty a second time).

The child looked puzzled and turned to her mother for support, almost disappearing into Flora's embrace, until the magistrate had to ask the question again just to make sure that the girl was still awake. She shook her head as if deluded, her breathing so fast and shallow that had she fainted there in her mother's arms no one would have been surprised. But now not a single person, apart from her parents, wished the questioning to end.

'Bessie,' she said in a low, low voice.

The magistrate craned his neck to hear, and had to hold a hand up to stop mutterings from the room developing into something more excited.

'Bessie!' she said again, as her mother looked on with undisguised horror. 'We call her Bessie!'

Longstaff jumped from his seat and began shouting.

'We call it Thomas-Bessie!' he bellowed right at the magistrate, who was banging his gavel harder and harder, because by now the court had erupted. The Longstaff girl was terrified, and the mother, herself in a state of terror, made her way out of the room, daughter under her arm, as the uproar intensified.

'We call it Thomas-Bessie,' Longstaff shouted again, louder still, turning to the court, 'cos we didn't know if it were a boy or a girl!'

By now even the gavel was useless against the swell of noise, and eventually, through means of an improvised sign language, the magistrate indicated that Longstaff should be restrained; it took two officers to pull him back down to his seat. More officers were called, since several members of the public had to be thrown out of court, which was in danger of becoming a riot. Through all the commotion Joseph Markham, in his seat to one side of the courtroom, sat as still and quiet as did Thomas-Bessie, who lay patiently in the wicker cage, hardly lifting an ear at the tumult.

So much noise. The whole place filled with cries and screams and shouting. The poor girl was taken away, weeping and clinging to her mother. That was the last I ever saw of her and her sister. I tried to watch them go through the side of my cage. But it was useless. I could only make out a mass of bodies, a crowd of big, dark shadows through the gaps. The sound of heavy footsteps shook my cage and echoed in my head until I could do nothing more than close my eyes and wait for the chaos to go away.

VII

There's a nagging chill around Tom's neck and in the soles of his feet. He keeps close to the towering walls of the main building, partly to shelter from the wind, which blows down from the great sycamores beyond the old outbuildings, down into the massive body of the workhouse, and also so that when his feet begin to take him towards those outbuildings he'll know it and will try to resist. For three weeks he has tried, without any success at all, to stay away from that disused stable with the wooden platform in it. He goes there every day, sometimes two or three times in a single morning, slipping in through the half-opened doors, buckled on their hinges and lodged fast in the ground, where dandelions and thick, bushy grass seems to have glued them for ever to the earth. Each time he creeps back into the place his chest deflates with a fizz of released nerves, and in those first few moments he wears a big, stupid smile, his breath heavy and irregular with the panting of silent laughter. When he moves further inside, towards the wooden stairs, he begins to blubber, suddenly and with no chance of stopping himself, until even if he makes it over to the stairs all he can do is collapse down on to them and weep.

He has been at the workhouse three weeks. After the day at the fairground he had found himself penniless, homeless and jobless. It was Markham who had taken charge of him, offering him a job, explaining that he would come to the workhouse and earn his keep there. Only, Markham had put it in a peculiarly compelling way. 'Whatever happens,' he had told Tom, who was by this time frightened half to death at the thought of his sudden destitution, 'you're coming to the workhouse. One way or another,' Markham announced, seeming to relish the nice inference which one could but draw from what he said, 'one way or another you're coming to us!'

Tom for his part did not need reminding of this. Though, for him, the shadow of that place cast an extra and more pene-trating darkness across his soul, and in his desperation he almost fancied that being an inmate there might be prefer-able; only in this way, he thought, by being locked up, would he ever manage to tear himself away from his most power-ful memories; and even as he nodded in agreement with Markham's take-it-or-take-it offer of work, Tom felt himself being drawn back to that vermin-pit of a stable, and to the wide-eyed, screaming face of Alice, her limbs in spasm, as she lay trapped, delirious with fear, beneath his panting body.

In the three weeks since his arrival Tom had struggled to discover exactly what his new job was. There had been no mention of wages, but neither had there been much in the way of work, and he began to skulk about the place on his own and do his best to keep out of the way. Markham had all but disappeared, spending whole afternoons in his office drafting legal submissions, or in conference with his solicitor. The rest of the workhouse staff distrusted the boy, and he felt the cold absence of Alice in the kitchens and in the expressions of all those who had known her.

He was sent on one or two errands, but quickly got the impression that these jobs had been devised for him, and would otherwise not have existed: since when did the workhouse send a boy all the way to town to buy furniture polish? Or to a bakery three miles off just to return a couple of old pie dishes (which puzzled rather than pleased the baker on receiving them so unexpectedly)?

For the last three weeks Tom has not slept more than an hour without the return of those two scenes which have come to replace all other images in his young, shattered mind. One of these is of himself, nearly naked, on top of Alice, high up in the old stable. In the other he is in the tent at the fairground, and watches the canvas collapse onto his own exhausted body. Sometimes the two images come together and vie for prominence in his weak, jittery reality. The cat wanders nonchalantly centre stage, cool and proud, looking calmly on at the chaos around it; the winged cat that has now become a factotum of evil, fulfilling every office of malice in his imagination, coming to represent the totality of horror and madness and cruelty in the poor boy's head until in the end the thought of it never leaves him, and he carries its fearsome presence with him constantly, both when he sleeps and when he wakes, and all those times in between; finally he yearns to see it, to replenish and strengthen its memory, until slowly it begins to supplant Alice in his thoughts.

Now, after three weeks, he creeps around the outer walls of the workhouse, and there's nothing for him to do but steer himself away from his hopeless addiction. He feels himself turning towards the old stables again, and he falls forward like a drunkard, stumbling ahead of himself, trying to decide where he's going, confused at the ground in front of him as if it's foreign, or has just then appeared.

The wind picks up, and now the smallest finger of it, if it gets down into your clothes, is painful. He is buffeted by a sudden gust, stinging his eyes and sending him sideways. To steady himself he puts a hand against the wall. The bricks, red but baked darker with soot, are warm, the temperature of a comfortable body, and they are as smooth as unblemished skin as he runs his palm across them and feels with the tips of his fingers that the thin lines of gritty mortar between the bricks are warmer still. He walks on, following his hand until it reaches a set of doors wide enough for a carriage, but which he knows lead to the furnace room. He has passed them every day since he came, and has sometimes heard the faint clanking of water pipes, or the just audible hum of the furnace. Today, though, the wall itself is warm, as if the fire has been stoked up twice, like a heart which one day begins to pump faster and more intently. He pulls open one of the doors and steps inside.

By this time John Longstaff is on his way to jail, where he will do six months' hard labour for larceny. Even before he leaves the court buildings, having kissed his wife and daughters goodbye, Joseph Markham is on his way home, the wicker cage by his side, Thomas-Bessie the famous flying cat now his legal possession.

When he arrives at the workhouse, an ebullient Markham springs down, abandoning his horse there in the yard for someone else to deal with, and skips like a child all the way round to the back of the building, the cage bouncing against his leg in the wind. Even before he takes his coat off, he has decided, he will take a look at the brand new trap.

Tom is already inside the furnace room. The temperature there is almost unbearable and the hot air rubs against his wind-pricked cheeks like sandpaper. His throat and lungs feel as if they are crammed full of old, dry carpet, and he has to strain to draw breath. The furnace door is fractionally ajar, and through the inch-wide gap tiny licks of flame curl out against the dull iron door, providing what little light there is in the place. He moves around, pushing his feet forward slowly in the semi-darkness across the stone floor, sensing the crunch of coal fragments underfoot, imagining how the dark expanse in front of him looks, as he waits for his eyes to become accustomed to the dark. He moves off, away from the source of the heat, the insistent glow of the furnace following him, pushing through his clothes on to the backs of his legs and arms, and sees in a corner a fleck of something vaguely familiar. The dim, yellow light from the flames is intermittent, yet it catches something golden in the corner of the room. It flickers in and out of vision, winking at him, insinuating its presence, a distant curve of gold, half a ring, a neat semicircle twinkling in the dark. He edges forwards and makes out a little more, more gold, a bit at a time, first an outline, then more curves, and a series of neat, regular uprights. He cannot quite believe what he sees, so familiar and so mesmerising that he goes on, forwards, even when his eyes first make out the words, painted in large gold script: *The Cat-Icarus.*

Behind him the doors are dragged wide open, and the room is suddenly filled with light. A shriek of wind rushes in, exciting the furnace, and flames belch from it in a sustained burst. There at the door, against the cold light, is Markham and the cat.

For a long second Tom looks at the cat, whose white-and-ginger face and ears can be seen through the wire mesh at the front of the wicker cage. And in that second his body turns to liquid from the inside: acid wells up in his stomach, burning through the walls and dripping down onto his kidneys and his bowels; adrenalin comes from nowhere, a fast-travelling goo that saturates his flesh, pumping it full and juicy, until it comes away from bone and he collapses, first to his knees, then toppling over onto his face. From his lips a thick, bubbling saliva flows, soaking into the coal dust on the stone floor.

Markham watches the boy for a while, but then seems to make a snap decision, for he tosses the cage to the ground and walks from the room in disgust, closing the great doors behind him. Deaf to the harrowing, pre-pubertal screams which can be heard from within, he takes his keys from a coat pocket and locks the doors, then marches off with a very heavy and disconsolate step to his office.

Tom's filthy, devilish cries of anguish are muffled by the wind, which by now has risen to a gale and pummels the brick walls of the workhouse with such force that no one dares venture outside; even if they did they would hear nothing of Tom.

Markham, when he reaches his office, has already begun to regret the effort of winning back the cat from Longstaff. He regrets it because though his victory in court has been resounding, it has come almost to nothing. He had no desire for the animal, just as he had no desire to take Tom in and give him work. The cat is merely a way to offset the cost of giving the boy a job, although it promises much more than this. For Markham, after long consultation with the workhouse solicitor, who claimed again and again that the law in this area was on many points unclear – prevaricating, or so Markham thought, until it seemed that even the word *cat* had no secure basis in law – had decided that if the workhouse (that is to say, he) must provide for Tom, then Tom must turn a good profit. So, a travelling sideshow had been constructed for the cat, designed to fit on the back of a pony and trap, to be taken to fairs and feasts and any other place where paying customers might be found, there to exhibit the famous Cat-Icarus. By now every person who read a newspaper or indeed had spoken to a person who could read a newspaper, from Nottingham to Newcastle, knew of the winged cat, though few had seen so much as a photograph, although it seemed that almost everyone *knew* someone who had actually seen the thing fly, or at least who knew someone *else* who had seen it. The cat, in fact, had been seen by practically no one since the now infamous day at Dewsbury Feast, when its presence had caused so much trouble. Since then it had become a living gold mine, although at the moment the gold itself lay unmined. It was, of course, Tom who would extract the lucre on Markham's behalf.

However, he now realised that Tom was mad. And if the boy was going to flop to the ground in a gurgling heap *every* time he laid eyes on the animal, then someone else would have to take charge of the Cat-Icarus sideshow, with its new, shining cage and bold gilt sign (which included a few grand references to antiquity, but nothing like the original). Markham contented himself somewhat with the thought that he still had his potential gold mine, and only the thought of how best to dispose of mad Tom remained.

But at this point something occurred to him: mad Tom and the cat were now locked in the furnace room together, and the furnace mouth was just the right size for the wicker cat cage.

Meanwhile, Tom had at last regained enough consciousness to crawl across the black, stone floor to the doors, still gurgling from fear, moving ponderously like an injured animal. He hauled himself to his feet, his body slumped against the heavy wooden doors, which shook so violently on their hinges in the wind that he believed they were trembling out of fear for him. Before his eyes a series of jumbled images danced in a wild kaleidoscope: the cat, Alice, the furnace, the gold lettering, filling his soul with a hatred so intense that even John Longstaff would have withered under its power. For a moment Tom flayed out his arms, as if the raw loathing inside his body could no longer be contained, his head rolling loose on his shoulders as he entered a new and deeper delirium. Then, as he turned and stumbled forwards, he caught sight of the wicker cage again, and even before his lips had hardened into a cruel grin he grabbed the cage and ran with it the three or four strides over to the furnace. In one great twist of the body he yanked open the heavy iron door, and with the other arm swung the cage back ready to hurl it into the flames, which now spat into his face with such fury that he felt his eyelids begin to peel away and the hairs in his nostrils sizzle and disappear. Then, as he prepared to throw the thing into the fire, he realised that the cage was empty, its wire door hanging open: the cat was loose in the room with him.

The cage fell from his hand and hit the floor. At that exact moment he felt the brush of a furry wing against his neck and, spinning around so quickly that he lost balance and crashed down on top of the cage, he saw the cat hovering above him in the fiery red light, its wings as huge and meaty as an eagle's, and claws that could take a baby's head clean off. He may have fainted, or simply curled up there, but sooner or later he was staggering to his feet again, running and clattering from one side of the place to the other in bursts of lunatic energy, his arms spinning like rotors, trying to beat off the cat, which he could sense right above him, hot and rampant, its feet tangled in his hair, its crackling breath cold and steely in his ears. He ran into walls and scrambled halfway up them, his hands beating into the crumbling brick, his fingernails ripped clean off, his voice shrill and hoarse, pleading to be saved.

Markham was sprinting down from his office to save the cat, two of his men behind him. When they arrived and unlocked the doors, Tom already had his arm inside the furnace, right up to the shoulder, and was quite clearly trying to climb in. The flames nibbled at his skin and turned it a blotchy maroon, and the hair on one side of his head had disappeared, leaving the scalp grey-black, welted and wrinkly.

They dragged him out on to the floor. His arm was so charred that it was impossible to tell whether there had been a sleeve on it. His hand was like charcoal, puffed up and scored with lines of blood, the flesh laid open, glistening. He trembled, and from his eyes ran a thick glaze, oozing from him and turning his face crusty. Next to him on the ground, not more than three or four feet away, was the wicker cage, and on top of it sat Thomas-Bessie, looking on, its head cocked slightly to one side. Watching.

VIII

Out from the fire, and he was mad already. There, back where
we started. I stood and watched as he burned. I smelled it. But
they dragged him out. Then it was just me. I pulled myself up
into a ball and waited. Wait, and you'll see things . . . Soon
it was regular meals, and back to normal. Find yourself a
quiet spot. And watch. That's where it'll happen. In front of
your nose.

John Longstaff did his six months in jail. When he was
released he found that his men, who at first had tried to
keep things running for him, had all left. Flora had sold
most of the furniture to makes ends meet, and New Court
was once again grown over with thick grass, so tall and lush
now that it covered the old sink, and only when the wind
moved the grass did the white of its ceramic surface blink
through. For several weeks he sat at home, not allowing
himself even a short trip away from New Court. Those six
months had given him time to contemplate injustice, and
to indulge himself in fantasies of revenge. But the thirst
for violence was so strong in him that, once reunited with
his daughters and his wife, he feared even laying eyes on

Markham, or indeed on anyone who might remind him of the whole affair. So, he wisely contained his anger inside the stone walls of his own house and waited for it to subside. Only slowly, over the months that followed, did he begin to venture out into the world, where he eventually threw himself again into commercial life, though with a degree less vigour than before, now always expecting some small disappointment in the course of things and not baulking in the least when success was hard to come by and even harder to build on.

At the workhouse, by contrast, Markham's accounts had turned rosy. Though Tom had not burned himself actually to death, he had demonstrated his own irredeemable madness, and as such could clearly not work in any capacity. Markham explained this to Broadbent, who was still anxious about publicity surrounding the cat, and it was decided that Tom should be put quickly and discreetly in an asylum, as if the boy were no more to them now than an old carcass, to be got rid of before it started to fester. Broadbent seemed to have no option but to finance this himself, and the matter was left at that, dealt with in a handful of clipped sentences between the two men.

As for Thomas-Bessie, the new Cat-Icarus trap was soon brought into service. Markham quickly saw what an excellent investment he had made, and after each outing to a fair he returned to the workhouse with his pockets stuffed full of money. However, as the riches mounted, the more distrustful he got of anyone who came into contact with the animal. Fearing an attempt to steal it, he had no choice but to let it sleep in his own private lodgings, although the sight of those wings set his nerves jangling, and brought back such feelings of guilt that he often stayed awake half the night, fully expecting to feel at any moment four claws sinking deep into his eyeballs, tearing his throat open, dragging out his heart. In the end the cat exerted so potent an influence on his mind that the little nest he had created for it there in his parlour came to resemble a shrine, complete with velvet cushions and several dishes of his best china, which he replenished three times a day with the most exquisite offerings of fresh rabbit, cream and as much sweet biscuit as he could fit in a dish.

*

The weather is mild, with just the hint of a breeze, and the distant promise of sun. The patient is wheeled out to take his first breath of fresh air for a month. Half his face is covered in bandage. When he attempts a smile the skin above and below his lips feels as if it is shot through with deep needle wounds, and even around his good eye the flesh won't move as it should. One arm is in a sling, and the hand is wrapped up so well in bandage that it appears twice the normal size, his forearm like a white barbell. The nurse keeps a hand on his shoulder and chit-chats to him about this and that, but neither of them listens to the words, which drop around them unnoticed on the wind.

She parks the wheelchair next to a bench and sits down, her hand still on Tom's shoulder. Together they look out over the gardens of the asylum, which extend as far as he can see, ending at the edge of a wood which marks the limit of his damaged vision. From time to time someone in the familiar grey patient's uniform wanders past them on the grass, one or two of them accompanied by nurses, but others on their own, moving slowly, without much impetus, as if they have forgotten what it means to move directly towards something.

Tom's head shakes from side to side, which gives him the appearance of being constantly in disagreement with the world. But his eyes are hollow, and have no shade of opinion to them, no trace of right or wrong, which is at first unnerving, even for the nurses, who are used to ignoring the whiff of madness on a person. Then his eyelids begin suddenly to quiver, as if he's straining to focus on a far-off image. He holds his head stiller, not quite still, but as still as his muscles will allow. The nurse notices this, and when she looks to see what he is peering at, there is a young woman in front of them, not in the distance, as his eyes suggest, but close up, a few strides away.

It is Alice, although she is known to the staff here as Bunny. The name began as a private joke between nurses; Alice would shuffle about inquisitively, her nose twitching, and she seemed hardly to comprehend anything at all, constantly rediscovering everything as if for the first time – cups, tables, doors, people – and showing a reserved kind of delight in each discovery. After a while it was clear that she responded equally to being called Bunny as Alice, pulling a face of mild surprise whenever someone addressed her, as if the sound of her own name was utterly novel.

The nurse thinks that she might introduce Bunny to the new patient, who is out of the hospital ward for the first time since his arrival. However, there is no need, because Bunny moves across the grass towards them, her little nose busy, her eyes alert and quizzical. She comes right up to the wheelchair and stands in front of Tom, swaying slightly as she examines him from both sides, looking carefully at the dull white bandages on his face, and paying particular attention to his arm in the sling. His head begins to shake again, and from his mouth there is a wheeze of breath and following it the slightest fragment of a voice; after that there is nothing, and he stares ahead, past Alice, into the mid-distance. She seems to laugh. Reaching out with her hand she touches his face, laying her fingers so delicately on his bandaged cheek that he hardly feels them there. She shuffles closer, takes her hand away, and sits down on the grass beside him.

THE DONKEY WEDDING
AT GOMERSAL,

recounted by an inhabitant of that place

I

Gomersal is a village in the West Riding of Yorkshire, in the north of England. For centuries it has been a cloth-making place, and though it has never exactly tasted greatness, several times in its history it has known the sound of greatness being tasted nearby. One brush with eminence came in the year 1724 when the famous novelist Daniel Defoe is said to have travelled here on his journey through England and Wales. He had been previously in Halifax, a wool town of importance some six or seven miles distant, and was on his way to Leeds, the principal market for finished raw cloth in the region. After reading the account of his travels, though, I cannot ascertain certainly whether the great writer actually trod the ground of Gomersal; he might never have left his carriage (or horse), and all we have to go on is a tempting passage with which he fills that small space on the page between Halifax and Leeds:

> And this brought me from the villages (Birstall, etc.) where this manufacture is wrought, to the market where it is sold which is at Leeds.

181

Gomersal, of course, is one of 'the villages', and as the reader can see, Birstall is another, though at that time Birstall was within our township, and might then count as Gomersal by another name. What Defoe's words accurately achieve is to locate us on a significant road, squarely between places of import. So, though it might appear that we are betwixt and between, as the phrase goes, in truth we are at the centre of things. And that's the way we like it.

Several more times in history have we nearly grasped celebrity and magnitude. In 1860 a committee of notable Gomersalians proposed an extension of the railway from Batley through Birstall and Gomersal and thence to Bradford. The London and North Western Railway Company considered the project favourably, no doubt impressed by the sum of £15,000 which had been got up by subscription. I hardly need say that such a line would have opened us up to all the major points in the country, to Liverpool, Manchester and London. But Parliament would not pass the bill, and we were left without rails. Batley, which is only three miles away, had already got its station, and was beginning to see the advantages, growing in size and wealth quite disproportionate to its importance, which has always been scant. Meanwhile, we in Gomersal and Birstall were left as we always were, though we got our railway in the end.

Another dalliance with high renown came in 1872, when a travelling circus chose a site just past the limits of our village, on the low ground outside Cleckheaton, which is our nearest town. I well remember watching the great tent being erected there, though I was still a boy at the time, and how we strained to hear the animals growl and roar in their heavy cages, which were covered in tarpaulins, as the caravans arrived. Over the following week we all paid at least one visit to the circus, and many of us young lads begged to be given money for a second and third ticket.

People came from all around, from right along the Spen Valley and from as far off as Morley on the other side. Alas, they came and witnessed what was, even to an impressionable village lad, a sorry sight. For the circus had but a handful of rarities, amongst them a single lion, which was dull and grubby and would roar at nothing unless its keeper beat it over the head with a wooden staff that he had for the purpose. I will not here go into the rest of the sorry menagerie, for it really was a most dispiriting show, and was only excused by the activities of a troupe of clowns, which kept us amused pretty well. However, it was out of fascination with this lion, and despite the rest of the show, that many of us returned a second time, and also because circuses were in the news at the time, as I will mention presently.

During the Friday evening performance, which was to be the penultimate one in Cleckheaton, the lion escaped. It happened right in the middle of the show, but since the animal was not on display just then, its absence at first went unnoticed. By now we were all keen to see the droopy old thing, and it was with a mixture of mock compassion and bravado that we boys had squeezed on to the thin wooden benches inside the tent to get another look at this tame and unmenacing king of the jungle. One or two, I seem to remember, had resolved to try stroking it, and others (myself included) had composed rhymes of derision to shout at the poor bag of bones. But the lion had disappeared. The circusfolk did their best to conceal the fact, but as the performance went on it became clear that something was amiss, and though we were well entertained by clowns and a pony rider, who would repeat the same few tricks again and again, the ringmaster himself wore a look of intense agitation and perspired so liberally that his scarlet tailcoat showed it.

Eventually word got out. Someone must have overheard the commotion backstage, and in what seemed like only a few seconds, panic swept through the audience. We all scrambled down from the benches, which were banked up high against the walls of the tent. And here the confusion really began. Most of us pushed outwards in a natural desire to escape the confines of the marquee, but once outside, in the dark of the evening, we rushed straight back under canvas, reasoning that if the lion was running free then the only place where it definitely would not be found was the tent itself. There we remained, huddled and chattering, with many of the younger ones in tears, which set the women off crying too, and one or two of the men, if I recall. Some people actually climbed back on to the benches as if to safety, perhaps thinking that the lion would never be capable of scaling so great a height.

Now this is what I mean by a dalliance with high renown, because within ten or fifteen minutes the animal was tracked down and recaptured. It had wandered off and was found on the banks of Spen Beck, drinking quietly, and showed no resistance at all when it was led back into captivity. Had it but taken a bite from someone whilst at liberty, or even mauled them a little, we would surely have found ourselves firmly on the map. As I have said, circuses were prominent in the newspapers at the time, and I well remember how a mishap with one of the animals could get a place thoroughly known: the 'snapper of Manchester' was still fresh in our minds, though really it was no more than a tame crocodile that had eaten the toes of one or two bold circus-goers in that city; then there was the tragedy at Northampton, where a lady was flattened to death by an elephant, which intended no harm but had a sore foot and stumbled onto the poor woman, who it was said had ventured too close. By comparison, our own brush with rampant wild nature was no more than negligible.

I do not want to labour the point, but let us just say that though we have never truly seen greatness, we have been several times touched partly by it. Not only did Defoe pass by, but our village provided inspiration for the lady novelist Charlotte Brontë, whose book *Shirley* is set in Gomersal, though I have never read it myself, so I cannot say. However, since the Brontë sisters became known for their books, it is not Gomersal that has got all the interest but Haworth, a village on the far side of Bradford, where they lived for many years with their father and their drunken brother. I have heard that many's a day when packs of book lovers can be seen treading the cobbles there and generally making a nuisance of themselves. Yes, there is little doubt that Haworth is to be for ever associated with the Brontë girls, but we in Gomersal have our place in literary history too, and though this is not much understood, those who know, know.

Gomersal also has an interesting religious history, and in this respect no year is more significant than that of 1851. It was at this time that the Moravian Brethren were celebrating the centenary of their chapel in Little Gomersal. Strictly speaking, the full constitution and privileges of the Brethren Unity had been granted back in the year 1755, when the Gomersal congregation was declared a full 'settlement' under the direction of the Elders' Conference at Fulneck, a Moravian settlement some three miles away in Tong village. Thus, 1851 was not so very significant for them, although it must have been in their minds because a year earlier, in 1850, they installed a pipe organ in their chapel.

This century, which even as I write is coming to its glorious end, has seen a great swelling of Nonconformist fervour of all kinds, and innumerable chapels have been erected since Wesley stirred the country up with his preaching. However, whilst religious Nonconformity of one sort or another has its place, and no one could deny it, there is nevertheless something about the word 'village' that evokes in the English mind a certain image which can only be complete if it includes that surest of symbols, the village church, by which I mean of course an Anglican church. And there is no room to doubt but that the building of St Mary's Church in 1851 was a thing of great significance for us. It is also of import to our story, so I will go into the matter here in some small detail.

By tradition of history, Gomersal has been on the periphery of the parish of Morley, and, before 1851, those who sought Anglican worship had need to slip down Church Lane (the very name tells us as much), or make their way across Monk Ings fields to St Peter's of Birstall, the church of our neighbouring village. However, we were eventually given our own district within the parish, and thus St Mary's was erected in Gomersal. The site chosen was near Hill Top, whose name is again self-explanatory. It is the high point of the village, and

separates Great Gomersal, the village proper, from Lower or
Little Gomersal, an altogether more modest place, really no
more than a hamlet. Hill Top is traversed by the old road
from Halifax to Leeds, most certainly the route taken by
Defoe on his historic journey. Dropping down from Hill Top
to the west, the road leads to the Spen Valley, where one
finds Cleckheaton, the nucleus of much industry, being a
place where many wool mills have been built; continuing
on through the Spen Valley and beyond, the traveller will
eventually come to Halifax. Descending to the east from Hill
Top one takes Church Lane a steep mile down to Birstall,
aforementioned village, and on to Leeds. It is in Birstall, as
I have said, that St Peter's Church can be found, along with
two public houses which have both at some point been called
'The Black Bull', and both of which will be important as our
story unfolds. For the moment, though, let it suffice to locate
these points on our map of the village, and move on.

The year 1851 is one that will be remembered for all these
things. And at London, we should not forget, there was a
great exhibition held that year, and they built a palace
out of glass. Indeed, 1851 has prospered in the common
memory these forty-odd years, and shows no sign of being
forgotten. But in Gomersal the real reason is not the new
church, nor the Moravians, nor the glass palace at London.
It is because of the Donkey Wedding. Had Defoe by some
miracle chanced upon us that year, and stopped at any
point between Cleckheaton and Birstall on the road which
joins those two places and which runs through Gomersal,
then I think it likely that his diaries would have contained
a good few pages on the events of that day. For nobody I
have spoken to can recall anything similar before or after;

and I might say that I have spoken to the village's oldest inhabitants, whose memories stretch back as far as the great European campaigns against Napoleon and the Luddite rebellions of the same period. Incidentally, the history of these uprisings, they say, are dealt with admirably by Miss Brontë in her book, and I shall not let them detain us here, other than to remark that we played an important part in those momentous events too.

The story of the Donkey Wedding has a good deal of history to it, which I cannot omit. Some time before 1851 it happened that two people, a man and a woman, found themselves both in their middle years but without spouses. There is an old saying in Yorkshire, and it goes: 'Once ye'r wed, a penn'orth o' sausage costs tuppence.' This is indeed true, as many readers will be able to confirm. But we ought not forget another fact about wedlock, though sadly I know of no adage to illustrate it: once you are married, the rent is shared between two. Here the reader might thoughtfully consider his own wife, who, whilst she may spin or sew, as the saying goes, she often brings no money into the house, so that the benefits of marriage are by this tally not exactly what they seem. However, we should also bear in mind that in a place where a great deal of factory work was available, where indeed the whole ancient enterprise of weaving and cloth-making generally had been transformed by the advent of the great mills, many women did work, some would say as hard as the men.

Ruth Kent was born at the beginning of the century. She married a butcher, who was some years older than she, and they lived together in a cottage in Little Gomersal. One day this man got the religious feeling in a bad way. At that time such things were not uncommon, since Methodists and other Nonconformists were doing a fine trade in attracting converts to their chapels. But his wife, a redoubtable woman, and close to six feet tall, would have none of it, and neither did it occur to her to be ruled by her husband and worship out of obedience to him. Thus, he turned to religion alone, and in particular to the Moravian Brethren, who by that time were well established in the village. He would attend their regular 'love feasts' (for that is how they call their prayer meetings), going alone. However, a husband attending these love feasts without his wife was presented with a very real dilemma: the Brethren organised their meetings in a special way, with separate seating for married and single people (this second group further divided on the lines of the sexes), so that our poor butcher was out of place wherever he sat. This, I regret, is all I know on the subject, and I have not been able to find out where he did sit, though I have spoken of the matter to Minister McLearry, recently retired Minister of the Brethren, and also to the present incumbent, Minister Elliot, but to no avail; it was a long time ago.

Ruth held the Moravians in high contempt, considering all things from across the English Channel to be dangerous and harbouring a dark enmity. This is a common feeling hereabouts, since many have not travelled nor are acquainted with foreign tongues. Indeed, I need hardly recount the tale of the Hartlepool monkey, which is most illustrative of the point, for I doubt that anyone can be unaware of this sorry tale. However, for the entertainment of any reader not familiar with the history of the north of England, and further to show what a definite fear and suspicion of all things foreign has infiltrated the public consciousness here, I will give the facts of the case in as few words as I might. What happened was this: during the Napoleonic Wars a merchant ship was wrecked in a storm off the north-eastern coast of England. It was in those days quite normal for seamen to have a little monkey on board as a pet, to provide some manner of affection on the long, loveless voyages. One such monkey was found washed up on Hartlepool beach after the storm, nearly dead from drowning, but its heart still beating despite everything. The townsfolk, though, were so stirred up with fear of the perfidious foreigner, and so ignorant of him to boot, that they built a gallows there on the beach and hung the poor animal, thinking it a Frenchman.

Perhaps, then, Ruth shared this island mentality, this distrust of all that lies beyond our shores. In any case, she would have nothing to do with the Moravians, although by this time it could hardly have been said that the Brethren were foreign, being mainly normal folk from roundabouts. Nevertheless, a steady stream of brothers did come over from the Continent and join the Gomersal community, and also the one at Fulneck (which had been established earlier); they were mainly from Bohemia and, of course, Moravia. It turned out that in 1829 this fine example of international understanding showed its worse side, for the Black Pox was brought over with the Brethren, and several Gomersalians died as a result, among them Ruth's husband, who was well short of forty years, and had been in good health up to that point. So, we might perhaps think of Ruth's refusal to follow her husband to prayer as having some wisdom in it after all.

After 1829 Ruth lived as a widow, but refused to accept

charity of any sort. Provision for the poor in our village has an interesting history, which I can hardly do justice to here. But let me say this: in those days workhouses were becoming more numerous throughout the country. At the turn of the century the idea had arisen amongst those who paid the poor rate within the parish that charity was not a good palliative to poverty. Amongst the poor were many who would let themselves drift into idleness and hardship, for they knew that easy money awaited them. A deterrent, not an amelioration, was needed, and a workhouse was the solution, for it provided the poor with a simple choice: either hard labour on the inside, or a more concerted effort to find the means of subsistence on the outside. Indeed, I well remember how the poor used to call them 'Bastilles', so disagreeable were conditions therein.

With the appearance of a workhouse, then, charity for the idle disappeared. And we know that a workhouse generally eased the sometimes severe financial burden placed on the ratepayers of a parish, who in this way were released from their ancient and most disadvantageous responsibilities to the Poor Law. Needless to say, it was the ratepayers who were in general most keen to see a workhouse built, as a way of persuading needy citizens that there was no easy relief from the struggles of life, to which we are all subject, rich or poor.

Gomersal, then, finally got its workhouse, and I am proud to say that my own grandfather was one of the worthies who saw that it was built, to the benefit of my family ever since, for at last we escaped the harsh burden of Poor Law payments. However, I might also mention that Ruth never went near it. No, with a commendable presence of mind she took up her dead husband's knives and cleavers, still in mourning as she was, and marched first to one butcher's shop and then on to the next. In the end, she got as far as the other side of Cleckheaton, in fact right up the valley side and on to High Town, some two miles away from Gomersal at least, where she entered a pork butcher's and, as she had done with no success at a dozen shops before, strode up to the counter and laid her tools out in front of her.

'Learn mi to cut up a pig,' she said, 'an' ah'll work fer' nowt an' do yer cleanin' an' all.'

Ruth Kent could not, if my conjecture is accurate, have been a handsome woman. She was shockingly tall and, at that moment, was dressed all in black; a sharpened cleaver lay not two inches from her hand, and the impression must have been an arresting one. But it was just her manner; there was no threat in it. The butcher at first stood there, the soles of his boots pressed hard into the sawdust, his hands buried in the front pocket of his apron, stained with old blood and the brown slime of offal.

'Ah best get mi wife,' he said, and disappeared through a back door.

Ruth had previously been a spinner, a craft which she had learned from her mother. In those days many women spun wool in their own homes, one of a series of old offices undertaken by villagers on a freelance basis, although most often these workers – card-setters, combers, spinners, – supplied a particular weaver. In the ancient way of doing things, the weaver might expect his wife to spin, as well as his daughters, and indeed this was the case with Ruth, whose father had been a weaver of modest but respectable means.

By 1829, though, the great wool mills were already established right along the Spen Valley, and the old, venerable crafts were in decline. Ruth's mother, who was by this time old and widowed, had been spinning wool since the Americas were still ours; she had spun on and on whilst first Robespierre then Bonaparte tore France in twain; she had produced her fine yarn morning and evening through the Luddite rebellions of 1812, never stopping to consider how she herself was the very embodiment of all that the Luddites were fighting for; and she had hardly paused between bobbins as news of the victory at Waterloo arrived. Years after that, when her daughter married the butcher, she was still spinning, at the age of 72. But by then both mother and daughter knew that things were changing, and spinning no longer provided a stable living. Soon after her daughter's wedding, old Mrs Kent died, at a grand age. Not long after that, Ruth's husband also perished, as I have described.

There is a streak of intense self-reliance in the Yorkshire psyche, and though not everyone has it to the same degree, those most possessed are unstoppable. One sees it sometimes, or hears such stories as make one believe that it is perhaps a kind of madness, for there is surely a point at which blind tenacity goes beyond what is really a virtue. Ruth had such a spirit, and as far as I can deduce, would have seen no wisdom at all in the phrase 'the golden mean', for being at the middle of something meant to her only that there was still half of it left to do. Being widowed, she decided that since her husband had left her nothing more than a case of butcher's knives and a few cuts of fresh meat, she would put the tools to good use. Perhaps she sold the meat for a small profit, or gave it away. I don't know this.

Of course, butchery is a man's employment, and she was prudent enough to know that this, and also her age, were against her ever getting a proper apprenticeship. However, by the time she had marched into her twelfth butcher's shop, in High Town, and pleaded to be taught how to cut up a pig, she at last found a pair of sympathetic ears; not those of the pork butcher himself, but those of his wife. She took pity on Ruth. In fact, it is more than likely that she recognised Ruth, for there would have been few young women six feet tall and in mourning going about the Spen Valley with a set of butcher's knives, and by that time everyone knew the sad case of the Gomersal Black Pox.

For the next three months she was taught how to turn a dead pig into gammon, chops, belly pork, bacon, ham joints, shanks, loins; how to scrape out the liver, heart, lungs and everything else that lurks beneath the hoary surface; to remove the trotters, cut away the pizzle and all other extremities, hack off the ears and snout, pick away the cheek-meat; that is, she learned how a pig, which previously she had understood to be an animate thing poking around a farmyard in one piece, was in fact no more than an assortment of savoury cuts awaiting the frying pan.

The butcher, being a businessman, made sure she paid for her lessons; she scrubbed and cleaned and generally did what was asked of her, and sometimes she went a fortnight without getting her knives into a fresh carcass. And one more thing: no pork butcher will ever divulge his darkest, most arcane secrets, least of all to a young woman who has plans to set up on her own. No, he never taught her how to make sausages, for that is a sacrosanct affair, and a butcher can be ruined if his recipes get out but once. I suspect that even a butcher's wife is not privy to this knowledge, and I have some evidence which seems to confirm this, which I will mention in the following pages, since it is very pertinent to the story.

Over the weeks of her ad hoc tutelage, Ruth had become good friends with the butcher's wife, who was by all accounts a kind woman and also one of those persons with a good deal of that Yorkshire tenacity which I have described. It happened that this woman was thinking of going into business herself, and although her husband's shop was in High Town, she had noticed that in the Spen Valley there was a rapidly growing mill population, and equally there was a growing need for general provisions. Her idea was to set up in a small way, selling what few basic things she could get locally, but mainly a selection of the cheaper pork products: bacon, offal, trotters, cheek, brawn, black pudding, dripping. She was keen to share the work, and Ruth was of course only too happy to find a partner in whatever kind of undertaking. So the two of them rented a little shop down in Cleckheaton, near the Punch Bowl Hotel, and they soon prospered.

However, though they progressed quickly to pie-making and curing their own hams, which naturally they got from the butcher's shop in High Town, the butcher himself – who was delighted with his wife's new business – would not allow them to sell sausages, since he saw sausage sales as the cornerstone of his livelihood, and genuinely feared a drop in sales, although the two shops were a good mile apart. Finally, about a year later, he relented, but would only supply them with an inferior product, and this led to some marital strife for him.

Here our narrative gets thin, and I will be brief. Ruth did well in the shop, and it became a permanent fixture in the lives of many of those who worked eleven or twelve hours each day in the wool and shoddy mills nearby. Somewhat strident in comportment, she matured into a woman who, whilst stern, had a welcoming sort of seriousness to her, one of those people in whose company one always feels more contented than can really be accounted for. The shop did good business, though it remained a modest enterprise. Fifteen years later the two women were well known throughout the valley, and their premises had become one of the constant points of reference for those living and working in Cleckheaton.

Ruth's partner was older than she, and by this time was getting too weary to have any true ambition. After fifteen years Ruth, who was herself in her middle years by now, was taking the lead in running the shop. One day she decided to treat herself, and took the train to Leeds. Her plan was to buy some fine clothes, because she now had enough money for a few luxuries, though in fact little opportunity to show them off, since she was no churchgoer.

She arrived in the great city and marvelled at the vast shopping arcades and markets, at the bustle of people there in respectable coats and hats, and generally got a good opinion of Leeds, which she had never been to before. However, she was not exactly enchanted; she felt no sense of awe, and did not experience that immediate yearning to return which one sometimes feels even before leaving a new and exciting place. Before long the task of buying clothes became perfunctory, and seemed to her simply a matter of trailing from one shop to another and wondering whether there was any difference between the products on offer in each.

Then, as she turned a corner, she smelled something familiar: pie crust. For years she had been getting up at dawn and preparing meat pies for the shop, which over the years had become one of its great attractions; that smell was ingrained in her imagination, and as she turned the corner she momentarily lost her footing and had to rest against the wall, for a sudden disorientation led her to believe that she had travelled through time and space or, perhaps more cruelly, that her shop had dragged itself behind her all the way to Leeds, like the ball and chain on the leg of an escaped convict. However, when she had recovered her balance of mind, she followed the smell, which was slightly different from what she knew: sweeter, saltier, fattier, meatier, as if all the aromas of her shop, from the bacon and brawn to the singed crust on a mutton pie, were churned together and rose, hot and greasy, on the air.

The smell was coming from Enoch Evans' Pie Shop, a smallish shopfront which boasted a narrow window with nothing but individual pies in it, lined up like regiments of foot soldiers, ten or eleven rows deep, each pie a golden yellow, and behind, on a banner which stretched across the back wall of the interior:

Pork Pies: the finest tasting pie in the country!
Fresh every day. There's 'snout' better!

Pork pies? Ruth had never heard of them. The staples for centuries had been meat pies, generally filled with offcuts of beef (but often containing a more varied marriage of fleshes), and mutton pies, which were the firm favourite of most people, not least because they kept for days on end. Pork had never been a common pie filling, and the reason was obvious: there was no part of the animal left over for a pie. Which bit, from the snout to the rump, was not in some way already a part of the daily sustenance of people? Was it bacon perhaps, or liver and cheek? The ears and the entrails, or the chops and the trotters? What part of the pig was in the pie?

There was only one way to find out. In she went and got herself one. It was still warm from the oven, and it cost her nearly twice what she charged for a small meat pie, though she put this down to city prices. The shopkeeper, who may have been Mr Evans himself, looked so much like the animal he traded in, with a big, squat nose and fat red jowls hanging low, bristly and well fed, and the faint trace of a grunt each time he inhaled between words, that there seemed little doubt but that he lived very well on a diet of these *pork* pies. He said something jolly as he took the order, and handed her a paper bag as if inside it was a true delight, something to keep and cherish for ever. She was overwhelmed by the smell of the shop, where the sickly odours hung thick and meaty, and she escaped to the street as soon as she could, wondering what to do with her pie. However, she soon noticed that, despite the smell, there was in fact a steady stream of customers going in and out, and many of those on the way out already had their teeth into the crust of a pie as they stepped back on to the street, heads buried in the paper bag, as if they were hogs snuffling for truffles there.

Ruth found herself a seat some way off, and sat down. Opening the paper bag with care, she uncovered the pie and noted the shiny glaze of its crimped pastry top, how the glaze itself took one's attention and seemed to tickle the imagination into greedy fantasies. She had never seen a more beautiful, a more alluring pie in all her life. She held it up close to her face and breathed in the rich aroma of warm, fatty pork; with her fingers she felt how the pastry casing, though firm and hard after baking, yielded slightly when squeezed, promising a crunch and a soft inner life all at once. She took a bite, small and judicious, like a professional, and chewed slowly. There was a crumble to the crust, and then the taste of good peppery pork fat oozed out and into her cheeks. She chewed faster and faster, the remaining pie held up to her mouth, ready. Another bite, not so slow and not so small, crumbs of moist pastry dropping down, coming to rest on her best coat. And another, until there was one quarter of the pie left between her greasy fingers, which were covered in warm meat jelly that glistened in the sun. She deliberately kept that last quarter of the pie back, telling herself that from this she would be able to copy the recipe, having decided right there on the bench that pork pies were the future. But she could not resist this last piece; it sat forlornly in the grease-stained bag, a teasing remnant of decadence, a fragment which, by its unexpected survival, seemed to accuse and tantalise. She nibbled at it, telling herself that an eighth would do, that she didn't really need so much pie in order to make her own, that she would reconstruct the pie, however small the bit she had left. Each time she removed another crumb of the pastry, each time she pared down that nodule of pork filling with her teeth, her faith in the memory of the pie became stronger. Soon there was nothing more than a thumbful of pastry left, which she popped back into the bag before that too disappeared.

For a moment she sat quite still, trying to discern the heart of the taste more precisely. The basis of the pie's astounding deliciousness: was it bacon? Was there pork dripping in the pastry? (There evidently was, judging by the stains on the paper bag.) Was it the spices, or herbs, or something completely unknown to her? And in that moment, after a life of diligent struggle and hard work, she came to know true satisfaction, for it seemed miraculous that such a pie could have been created at all. But since it had been, that it existed at all, there in Leeds, it seemed impossible that it had not been created entirely for her. She opened the bag once again, and emptied the last crumbs into her mouth.

She then went back to the shop, bought herself a half-dozen more, and took the train straight home to begin her examination. And it was only by the strictest and most severe act of self-control that she arrived in Cleckheaton with as many as two pies still uneaten.

*

Two years later William Walker moved to our very own Spen Valley, though of course no one could have guessed the importance of his arrival at the time. Nevertheless, here he came. And who's to say it was not, one way or another, the most signal thing ever to happen in these parts? I for one should not care to judge, since there is a great deal of history to compete for that accolade.

Whatever the significance of his arriving, though, we can say with some certainty that amongst his first discoveries here was a small pie shop across the road from the Punch Bowl Hotel that was a Mecca for the new 'pork' pies. Colleagues at his new place of work would fall into delirious reveries each time they mentioned them, reminding him that he should pay the shop a visit, as if in giving this advice they were simultaneously reliving the exquisite taste of their last pie.

Ruth had arrived home from Leeds with her two remaining pork pies that Monday afternoon, and sliced each one into a hundred pieces, laying out little piles of the four main constituents of a pie: the crumbly outer crust, the soft inner pastry, the meat jelly which lined the pie's casing, and the minced pork meat itself, which nestled within the layer of jelly inside the pastry casing. She even picked at the glaze in an attempt to divine exactly its composition. And after innumerable trials and tests and false dawns, after excitement at the wonderful aroma which spilled from her oven was once again dashed as another disappointing batch finally emerged, after all this she eventually discovered everything there was to know, and inevitably the moment came when her pork pies were ready to put to market. There was only one difference between hers and the originals, which a traditionalist might have called sacrilege. It was that Ruth's pies were made in pie tins, which was all she knew, whereas the ancient manner of doing a pie is to 'raise' the pastry by hand around a wooden mould. This matter of the raising of a pie is full of controversy, and the less said about it, the better.

West Riding is a place where people are set in their ways, and though the new style of 'pork-filled' pie in Ruth's shop window might have been the best in the north of England, it took several days before the first one was sold, to a young man on his way back to work in the afternoon, who in truth only bought it because he was not paying attention. But after the first it was only two minutes until the second was sold, because the same boy, having eaten the first pork pie ever to be sold in Cleckheaton, sprinted straight back and got himself the second; he would have bought more, but didn't have the money. His testimony was enough to persuade three or four workmates to try one of Ruth Kent's newfangled pies for supper, and after that sales rose so fast that soon the shop began to remove other items from its stock list, such was the demand on Ruth's time to keep up production.

When William Walker arrived in the town, a couple of years after this, it might well have been said that he found himself in the true centre for pork pies outside the big cities, with the exception of Melton Mowbray itself, where I am told the whole thing began. Certainly, few places at that time were hooked on the pies, because it wasn't until some years after this that the pork pie really took hold of the nation and became a solid favourite.

William had never tasted a pork pie when he arrived in Cleckheaton. He was not from these parts at all but hailed from Bingley, a place which has an old connection with us, for the weft and warp from the Gomersal Cloth Hall mill was in olden times taken by donkey all the way there to be woven, a journey of some ten miles, and then brought another ten miles back. Old Joe Rush of Bingley did the driving of the laden donkeys, and he was a simple man, famous for letting his animals dawdle, so much so that a common expression in our village was, 'Thou't as slow as Joe Rush fro' Bingley', which means that you go one foot today and the other tomorrow.

So William Walker arrived in our part of the world and took up the position of engineer at Heaton's shoddy and mungo works in Cleckheaton. He got himself some pretty mean lodgings, although it was generally thought that he deserved better, both the shoddy works and the lodgings, because it is said that he was a man of great talent for technical things.

Cleckheaton is not such a large place, though of course it is important in its way, and it should hardly surprise us that William soon found his way into Ruth's shop, where it is said that he took such an immediate liking to the pork pies that afterwards there seldom passed a day without him calling in twice. He was a short man, rather stout of body, with a face like a full moon, always smiling, his forehead and cheeks shiny-pink and tight, and he seemed constantly to be taking delight in some small thing or other. Ruth looked at his round face, eyed the bulge of his belly, and thought that if she pushed his head down hard enough he might spin around until he whistled. But at the same time she was wooed by him, by the smack of his eager lips as she handed him his lunchtime pie, his speech already crackling with saliva, his stubby fingers caressing the pastry crust through the paper bag in joyous anticipation, bouncing slightly on his toes as if he had just been given a bag of glittering jewels. And how he loved to talk about the pies! What a crust yesterday! Such a tasty filling today! It made her heart jump, each morning and again in the evening, that he could say such things, could be made so easily and completely happy, this round man who never frowned.

And the pies got better. She knew that they had improved, because in the end it became impossible to make enough of

them. Three years after her fateful trip to Leeds, and to
Enoch Evans' Pie Shop, she found that there was no longer
space in the shop window for all the pies. Gradually, she
was obliged to jettison the shop's offal and bacon, until in
the end the display was a carpet of crust, and the pies had
to be stacked on trays, one tray right on top of the next,
piled seven and eight high on any bit of spare surface that
could be found. People would buy them hot, straight from
the oven; baking times got to be widely known, and some
of the smaller workshops nearby actually scheduled their
dinner breaks in such a way that the workers could make it
early into line for a pie. The shop rarely had a single pie left
when the door was eventually closed late into the evening,
because after the wool mills shut up for the night, generally
at seven or eight o'clock, great swathes of people descended
on the place, pushing hard to get inside, with those outside
bobbing up on tiptoe to see how many were left, and often
shouting in through the door if they spotted someone they
knew nearer the counter who might secure one. It was known
that several of the local mill owners sent out for pies on a
regular basis, often getting upwards of a dozen at a time;
and, though Ruth was discreet, if a groom or some other
servant came in at a busy time for a large order, she could
not refuse, and sometimes she had to send her last pies to
the mill owner, in full view of his hungry employees, who
that night would go without.

William lived near the shop and always managed to slip
in when it was empty. He was freer in his movements than
other workers, being an engineer. It is said that a mill
owner is never happier than when he sees his engineer
idle and with his feet up on the table, for this means that

all is well and the mill is running smoothly. At Heaton's, where William worked, old rags and bits of scrap cloth were churned up and formed into a kind of cloth again. The production of shoddy and mungo is not at all glamorous, and there were rumours that William had been a brilliant inventor who had been taken on at Heaton's after falling on hard times. The truth was more prosaic, though. He had been widowed, his wife dying whilst carrying their first child, which also died. Having no family left in Bingley, he had removed to the Spen Valley in search of a new life, having been given a personal recommendation from his previous employer, which got him easily into his job at Cleckheaton, and indeed it might have got him a job anywhere at all. When he tasted his first pie, in 1848, William had been alone for nearly a year.

By this time some serious problems between the butcher and his wife had arisen. First, it was the sausages, as I have already mentioned; over the years this difficult issue was never resolved between them, and brought them a great deal of argument and unhappiness. Ruth could do nothing about it, and simply got on with running the shop, where it was now clear that the future was in pork pies. Whilst her partner bickered about sausages, she persevered with the business, until there was no one in the Spen Valley who would have denied that her pies were the finest around, and that her crust was the best to be had. Indeed, that crust lives on in the memory of all those who have tasted it. A savoury crust it was, but not too fatty; its lightly crumbling edge fell in delicious flakes on the tongue, salty-sweet and its inner side soft and white, lined with a meaty jelly in which the pork itself nestled. Of course, people everywhere talk in this way about their own local pies, because a decent pie stays in the memory: that is the nature of a pie. But Ruth Kent's were exceptional. Moreover, they only ever got better, never a bad one, never a poor batch, with popular estimation growing and growing. Both women profited from all this, but the butcher's wife had become old and weary from the constant battle with her butcher husband, and finally both she and he argued their way into exhaustion and retirement, and would spend the remainder of their lives passing sarcastic comments to each other about pork products. By the time William Walker had become a regular customer in the shop, then, Ruth was most often there on her own, and found that she rarely had time to think about anything other than pies.

One afternoon, just after lunch, when people had made their way back to work, William Walker called in at the Punch Bowl Hotel and drank a pint of beer. He stood alone at the bar, and in his mind he went over a single sentence that he had spent most of the morning bringing to a state of perfection. He went over it so much that, when he drained the last of the beer from the tankard and the barman asked him if he wanted another, William replied: 'If there wer' iver a time yer might fancy tekin' a walk, 'appen on a Sunday . . .'

At this point he stopped. There was a pause, before each man looked up slowly at the other.

'Ah mean . . .' William said, but really he didn't know what he meant.

'Another?' the barman asked, and began to fill William's tankard without waiting for an answer. They watched as the beer rose, a thin ring of bubbles running up against the dark pewter, ahead of the brown ale. And William was lucky, because his ideal sentence had taken the barman so much by surprise that after the silent pint had been poured, the exact wording had been lost from memory, and both men were searching their heads to find a convincing misconstrual.

'Ah mean,' said William, having a second go at it, 'shooting.'

'Aye, aye!' the other replied eagerly. 'Shooting!'

'Yer go after rabbits round 'ere?'

'Oh aye! Sundays, nah an' then,' he said, not stopping to think that he had never owned a gun in his life, nor had he set a rabbit trap since he was fifteen, and that in any case few people went hunting any more for fear of the consequences.

'Well,' William said, 'one o' these days!'

'Aye!'

'Cheers!'

'Cheers!'

The barman shuffled away as quickly as politeness would allow. William brought the tankard right up to his mouth. A drop of sweat rolled across his bald pate, gathering speed as it ran down his blushing forehead and onto the ridge of his nose, and fell with a plop into his beer. He looked around the bar, sure that everyone must have heard it. But there was no one there. He turned back to his ale and started drinking.

Another pint after that and he was at the pie shop. He had a cigar in his mouth, thinking that it might impress Ruth, though he couldn't stand the taste of tobacco so left it unlit. He paused just outside the shop door and set about making sure that the sleeves of his jacket were straight, and that his braces were not tangled; he adjusted his tie, and finally made a pretty wholehearted job of tucking his shirt into his trousers. But the beer took away any precision in his actions, and as he stumbled through the shop doorway he was still trying to tuck a shirt-tail away, his whole torso skewed awkwardly, arms twisted behind him.

'My God!' Ruth said, having watched his ridiculous preparations through the window. 'What's all this in aid of?'

'If yer wer' ever . . . ah mean, if ever *you* wer' . . . a Sunday . . . time on a Sunday if there wer' . . . *if* a walk, ah mean . . . ah *might* . . . *you* might, ah mean . . .'

He continued like this, stuttering on through half a phrase before losing himself and having to begin afresh. Time, like precision, had become blurred in the Punch Bowl, and his monologue went on for quite a while. As she listened, her elbows on the counter, and her chin resting on her hands, the first curls of a smile appeared at the edges of her mouth. In the end his babbling petered out, but before he got too choked up with shame she leaned right across the counter and kissed him on the cheek.

'Sunday,' she said.

A customer entered the shop, and William, who was dumb with surprise, edged backwards until he was outside, his eyes never leaving Ruth's. She for her part had discovered a new way of smiling, her face falling into an unfamiliar configuration, a smile which began with a warm tension across the cheeks, and spread up past the eyes and down along the neck and arms, spilling into the chest until her lungs were full and airy. The newly arrived customer pulled at his collar and coughed, since he was in a rush, and thought that unless he broke the spell now, he might stand there all afternoon, ignored.

The first invitation had taken William over twelve months to work up to, and in fact his timidity was only finally overcome because of the beer, which he hardly ever drank, and which gave him an unusual courage. But he could not always be drunk when he saw her, and in the following days he was so abashed and unsure of where things really stood between them that he conspired to visit the shop only when it was certain to be busy. Out of the corner of her eye Ruth would watch him sneak in, pushing close up to the backs of other customers as if he were hiding, trying to conceal himself until the last moment. As he got to the front of the queue she turned immediately around to get his pie, in such a way that he needn't say anything at all. When she handed over the heavy paper bag, she found herself grow even taller, and her arms tingled with energy; like a child who has been told not to smile she stifled her grin, and said the price of the pie as he handed her the money, although of course everyone knew the price, and her voice was low and secretive.

Over the next few days, and without either of them realising it, the whole thing turned into a little ritual. His manner, whilst still diffident, became a touch eccentric, quizzical almost. Then one day he winked as he got up to the counter, a kind of mock gravity about him, and she gave a little curtsy in return. This lasted a full week, so when Sunday arrived they were both unsure as to how they might put aside their game and become normal people again.

It was a hot day, and he called on her at two in the afternoon. By this time she was living in the rooms right above the shop, since it had become necessary to be there almost every hour of the day to keep production up, and

209

besides, it was more economical that way. She opened the door and stuck her head out. She wore a plain green dress and a small straw hat. On her nose there was a smudge of flour, which gave William a dilemma, because although the sight of it appealed to him, it was cruel to let her go out with it still there. So he tapped his own nose, which she at first thought a comical gesture, but then, seeing that he was staring directly at hers, she sensed that something was wrong. She wiped the smudge away with a laugh, though she had turned pretty red in the face.

Now she began to worry about her appearance, but in a strange, erratic way; with her hands she beat at her skirts, and threw her head around in all directions, trying to spot any blemish or other imperfection, as if suddenly nothing about her was likely to be all right. Eventually, after getting them both uncomfortable with this display, she said: 'Yer'd best come in any'ow. Ah'm not ready.'

William paused, but she had already disappeared into the back of the shop, so he followed.

Inside there was a heavy smell of animal fat, something stronger than cooked bacon, not quite rancid but nearly enough to make an unsuspecting person wretch.

'Ah'll 'ave to be back soon,' she called out from the back room. 'It niver stops 'ere, yer know.'

Her speech was punctuated by metallic rattles and the odd dull thump, which could hardly be the sounds of someone getting ready to go out. Not knowing what else to do, he went over to the counter and, stepping behind it, looked into the back room. There she was, the sleeves of her green dress rolled up to the elbow, her hat still on. She was mixing pastry.

'Won't be a minute,' she said over her shoulder, and returned to the bowl.

William stood in the doorway, looking at the room, which was in fact a kitchen. It was small, no more than ten or eleven feet square. Yet in it there was every possible tool of the pie-maker's art: big earthenware jars of flour stood on the floor, which was inch-thick with flour round about; a table with a small hand mincer bolted to its edge took up one side of the room, and below the mincer on the floor a bucket half full with brown and grey mince; on the table lay hefty lumps of fat-streaked meat, some of it run through with gristle which glinted in the afternoon light, and knobs of white fat hanging from thin sinews of a filmy material which at places adhered to the meat; there was plate after plate of raw lungs and hearts and every other part of an animal's insides, each exotic variety sitting in its own liquid, and this having dribbled over the lips of the plates, running onto the table top and forming streams which met and mingled with the juice from other dark parts of the animal in a complex system of bloodways covering much of the table's wooden surface, and those few islands that were left dry showing the murky brown stains of earlier blood. To his left was an oven, which reached almost to the ceiling. The oven was cold, but crammed full of pie tins; small individual ones mostly, but one or two larger than the rest, all empty, and pushed inside so haphazardly that they looked as if they were jammed fast. He saw more tins on the top of the oven, again in a confused arrangement, and they actually touched the ceiling, which was so high that not even Ruth could have reached without a chair. Then, as his eyes became accustomed to the clutter and mess, he saw yet more pie tins, littering the floor in one corner, stacked after a fashion, but the stacks irregular and unstable, and in a sink opposite, a mound of tins rose a full three feet above the top of the sink itself, blocking out most of the window behind.

William shook his head in disbelief. To the steady rhythm of Ruth's pastry mixing, his eyes skipped from one site of devastation to another, from blood-oozing offal to piles of unwashed tins, their insides scaled with grease and bits of brown crust; big pans lay here and there, brim-full of a thick, viscous slop that must surely have been the same stuff which, in a solid, pastry-wrapped form, he devoured with such relish twice a day.

But it wasn't the bare realities of pie-making that threw him into shock, since he worked for a shoddy manufacturer, and the foul and the festering were as food and drink to him. No, it was the chaos, the sheer disorganisation that offended against the cool logic of his engineer's mind, the absence of design, the anarchy, the helpless confusion all about. He felt also a sense of shame, at having stolen past the counter, to the inner sanctum of the shop, only to be disgusted by its imperfect realness, so utterly different from what would finally appear in the shop window. And on top of all this, he was in no doubt that until things improved he would not enjoy another pie, that the sight of this awful mess would come back each time he took a bite, clouding his senses and numbing his taste buds.

In an attempt to understand how such a situation could possibly continue day after day, he asked Ruth some simple questions, about baking times and batch sizes, how meat was ordered and prepared; the kind of things that seemed natural to him, those numbers and facts which were, in a way, the basis of the enterprise itself, a job being really no more than quantities and processes, to be laid down and followed. Yet when he asked all this, Ruth found it difficult to answer. Either she didn't remember how often the oven was fired in a week, or she simply didn't know. Batches? How many what? When? How? She simply had no idea, and as his questioning went on it became clear to him that she was exhausted, weighed down in a haze of chaotic drudgery. By chance he looked at her feet and noticed that her shoes were lopsided and ingrained with flour and covered in fat stains; he saw how her hands were raw and callused and that her forearms were just skin and thick, ropy muscle underneath. As they talked she continued mixing, and her head rocked gently on her shoulders.

William ascertained that she was preparing pastry for a large batch of pies, which were normally ready late in the evening, but went into the oven at dawn the following morning; whilst these were baking she would make another batch to go into the oven directly after the first lot came out. Only in this way could she hope to satisfy demand much past lunchtime, and she would then make more pies in the afternoon, during the slack period, and this final batch would go in at five o'clock, to be ready for the evening rush. After closing the shop for the night, the whole cycle would start again.

He was horrified, and instantly regretted that he had tried to entice her away from this unremitting toil for even an hour's leisurely stroll, because it was time which she patently could not afford to lose.

'Well,' he said, taking off his jacket and rolling up his sleeves, 'it sounds like yer could do wi' a bit of 'elp.'

With that he stepped over to the sink and set to washing the dirty pie tins before she had a chance to stop him. As soon as she saw him there, the pile of tins towering above his head, and he staring up as if he were about to mount an attempt on the summit, she laughed out loud.

They turned to their work in earnest. And as they worked they talked, chatty and fast, as if in the shared rhythms and clatter of the kitchen there was more space for conversation. He for his part was intrigued by the job in front of him, looking on the dirty tins as a new and testing problem awaiting his solution, and because of this he chatted casually, without much thought, on and on, until the washing up was done. Only then, as they stood back, drying their hands on old scraps of rag and admiring their work, did they realise that each of them had for the first time talked about the death of their spouse; and, when they saw each other's eyes, with surprise they found a trace of redness there.

From that day on, the evening work was shared. William would call around after finishing at the shoddy works, and together they would eat a light supper of pies and pickles followed by fruit. Then they would make a start on the big overnight batch. With each visit he would have new questions, some of which confused her, whilst others annoyed her with their pedantic insistence on some small point of detail. How long can a raw pie be left? How many trotters to a quart of jelly? Is dripping bought by the pound or the stone? Are all the crimps on the pastry top of a pie really necessary? How far can one reduce the egg content of the egg-milk glaze before the final colour of the pastry changes? Is there a special implement for putting the two little air holes in the top of each pie? Does pepper go stale?

No! In the end she would tell him to be quiet, and, because of his natural timidity, he would immediately shut up, though it was not long before he piped up again, and in the end she would answer whatever he asked. For several weeks this went on, and in that time he only washed tins and mixed pastry and asked questions. But he was remembering everything, and there grew in his head a plan, a compilation of all the facts about the shop, and a host of calculations and estimates that, at least to him, were as obvious and straightforward as tying one's shoelace, the kind of simple arithmetic that almost worked itself out, hardly logic at all, just common sense. One evening, after the pies were done, he took a piece of paper from his pocket and told Ruth to sit down.

The gist of it was time. He had worked out that from every drop of energy which she put into the making of pies, half a drop was wasted through bad planning and bad organisation. The mincer! She shrugged, as if to say it was a common enough item. But he knew better, and had sent off for a catalogue from the manufacturers which included illustrations of a dozen larger mincers, all of which would save time and effort. The tins should be kept tidily on shelves, and he pointed out where these shelves would go, and read out the precise dimensions which they would have, and thus exactly how many tins would be housed on each shelf. It was nothing more than a hour's work to put them up, he told her, and rubbed his chin. And the flour! The flour? How on earth can there be anything wrong with the . . . The storage pots are too deep, and too low on the ground. Keep 'em higher up, and save your-self bending down for every spoonful. No doubt about it, 'cause it's two hundred times a day that you bend right down there!

At this point she threw up her arms, exhaling air loudly through her teeth, though really she was keen to hear the rest. And the rest, it turned out, was more important. The oven needed to be bigger, and a proper firing timetable established. Batches should be all the same size, so that oven space was fully used at all times, and thus the minimum of coal burned. And pastry should be made by someone else.

Ruth now looked down at her lap, and brushed a flour mark from her apron. He claimed, all with carefully worked-out figures, that the simple expedient of taking on an assistant, along with the other changes he suggested, would liberate more than half of her working day, leaving her free to expand the business, or indeed to do whatever she pleased. Of course, he also had a pageful of ideas for expanding the business.

It was all too much for her. She thanked him for his kindness, ushered him to the door, kissed him on the cheek, and shut the door behind him. That night she went straight upstairs and flopped down on to the bed. It was already late, and an hour after that she was still lying there, fully clothed, her fat-stained shoes on her feet. She looked at the clock. It had stopped, but she knew that there were just a handful of hours before she had to be up again and firing the oven. She closed her eyes, drifting in and out of a dizzy sleep.

'E comes 'ere and teks a look at all this an' knows nowt abaht it cos 'e's niver bin up afore dawn bakin' pies in 'is life an' pokes 'is nose in my business tellin' mi stuff ah can't 'elp as if ah can bring 'is wife back an' that's all it teks an' why ah dun't know cos 'e thinks shoddy an' pies go on in't same way

216

does 'e but thi dun't an' it teks time to learn yersen all this though 'e dun't think so but wi've all on us got us own ways o' goin' on an' this is mi own an' no one else thinks bad on it but 'e reckons 'e can do better 'e does from nowt just a few old knives is all ah 'ad *nowt* mind yer an' no one in't world t' 'elp me just like 'im an' 'e comes 'ere an' sez ah got it all wrong oh aye terrible ah'm doin' it t' oven's too small an' t' glaze an' t' flour pots an' t' 'oiyles in't pies an' what else ah dun't know . . .

It was already light when Ruth woke and found herself still in her green dress on top of the bed, shaking with cold, and under her stiff body the eiderdown and bedspread churned up and hanging down to the floor. Cursing William Walker she leapt up and ran downstairs, still three-quarters asleep, and began firing the oven. She moved in a dazed frenzy, working by touch because her eyes were so tired that it made her sick to use them, and a headache ran from one ear to the other like a rib of cold metal pushed through her head.

She hurled a bucket of coal onto the burning wood and slammed the door shut. She staggered across to the sink, shaking in the chill of the kitchen, gripping the icy ceramic as she swayed in and out of consciousness.

Some time later, finding herself still at the sink, a small sound poked her back into consciousness. There was something wrong. The oven was packed full with pie tins, which were now heating up and, being empty, beginning to warp. Grabbing a cloth she opened the door and started pulling them out. They fell about her, one or two catching her dress and leaving brown marks, and others sizzling as they hit a patch of dampness on the floor. When they were all out she got yesterday's uncooked pies and put them in, knowing that she was at least an hour behind schedule, possibly more. Then she began picking up the hot tins from the floor, stooping down and recovering those that had fallen by the flour pots, leaving little trails where they had rolled in the thick layer of flour. But there was nowhere to put them, and in desperation she flung them anywhere, not looking where they went; they landed on the meat table, in the sink, and others simply fell back to the floor. In the end she gave up and escaped from the kitchen, as if she were unable to do anything else to remedy the situation.

That morning she leaned hard against the counter of the shop, straining to keep herself awake, her face so drawn and colourless that many customers asked her if she was all right. She said that she was, though in fact there were by eleven o'clock no more than one or two dozen pies left, and she would have to shut up shop as soon as they were gone, because she had no strength to make more. Through those first few hours of business she cursed William Walker so severely and in so many ways that she made herself ill with bile, which rose in her spiteful throat and threatened to drip from her mouth and on to the serving counter. This was his fault coming here and making everything his business which isn't at all with his little bald head thinking himself such a know-all and that pot belly of his like a piglet's and if he thinks he's setting foot in here again . . .

Just then a young man came up to the counter. Without thinking she reached for a pie. But he said: 'The kitchen through here, is it?'

She was beyond exhaustion by this time, and simply

nodded and looked past him, though there was no one else waiting to be served. He went through to the kitchen before she could stop him, and when she followed, she found that he was marking distances out on the walls, using a long, wooden ruler, and putting neat pencil lines here and there, then, after taking more measurements, adding other pencil marks to form small crosses on the whitewash. It was all over in a minute, before she had time to understand who he was. Then he left, winking at her as he went, his body full of a jaunty, youthful bounce.

She hobbled back to the counter, finding that her legs were about to give way, and began cursing William Walker again, the words filtering through her cruel, pursed lips, which fizzed with spittle and hissed with such venom that had anyone been there to see it, they would have immediately called for a doctor, and perhaps would have waited outside whilst he came. Some time later the boy returned, carrying under his arm a number of wooden planks, something short of a yard in length, and in his other hand a tool bag.

It occurred to her to block his entrance to the kitchen, but before she could summon up the strength to move, in walked William, a bunch of flowers in his hand, and an imperative, workmanlike expression on his face. She slumped down on the counter and burst into tears.

Within six months the shop had increased production by 40 per cent. Ruth had taken on a young assistant who did the late shift, and the kitchen had benefited from new shelves, a bigger oven and various other improvements. The preparation work had been moved to an adjoining room, which boasted a larger mincer, as well as an area for storing ingredients. Pies were now being sent out to other shops, and indeed many shop owners had to be turned down, since both Ruth and William favoured a policy of prudence and steady growth over unbridled expansion.

Despite all this, Ruth found herself with a working day that was almost cut in half. At first she could not tolerate leaving the premises with only her new assistant there, and was constantly in fear of returning to find two hundred blackened pies, or no pies at all, or, worst of all, bad pies. But there were no bad pies, and gradually she was able to tear herself away. She now discovered that the world around her was there to be enjoyed, and that evenings could bring true pleasure, rather than being just the early commencement of the next day. Walker had advanced her the money for several of the costly improvements, and he had a perfect excuse to call round each day after work to see how his investment was going.

So there we have it. Ruth Kent and William Walker together built up what became over the next few years the most famous pie shop in the area. But let us return to an earlier matter, that of the economies of cohabitation. It was but a long year after this, when the cost of Walker's improvements had all been repaid in pie sales, and the business was flourishing as never before, that the two of them decided that since they were in each other's company so much, and I suppose liked it that way, then William might as well move in and live there above the shop too. Of course, this is quite a normal thing to pass between a man and a woman, and I can think of nothing more natural. Only, in their case it was not so natural as it might have been, because they never got married first, but lived together just as they were, Walker and Kent, quite openly and without apparent shame. And this was the start of the Donkey Wedding.

II

As I have mentioned, Yorkshire folk have a rare tenacity, and this is wont to show itself in times of great crisis or need. Well, in the year 1851 one such crisis arose, because it was just then that the truth about Ruth Kent came to be widely known: she was cohabiting with William Walker. He, it is said, kept up his own lodgings to begin with, and was held in such high opinion right across the town that this scandalous change of domicile was not at first suspected. Also, his natural modesty and discretion led many people not to believe the rumours, and it was a number of weeks before the whole affair was uncovered.

Even for a mill town, the normal waking hour at the pie shop was early, being in general somewhat before dawn. In this way the unmarried couple could arise and set about their business without being noticed. Walker, after firing the oven and warming himself in front of it, would be off to the shoddy works before most people were out of bed. He had always been a diligent type, so no one found it surprising that he now began to arrive at work somewhat earlier than had been his custom.

However, the truth will out. And it was confirmed one

Saturday evening when there arrived at the shop a cart, and on it the contents of Walker's lodgings – trunks, boxes, odd items of furniture – all of which seemed to announce that he and Ruth were no longer of a mind to conceal the nature of their arrangement.

Abraham Thornton, an overseer at a large Cleckheaton mill, witnessed the removal that evening. He was just then out for a stroll, but raced straight home and got ready for his regular visit to the Punch Bowl, already bristling with outrage, now in possession of real concrete evidence.

That night he sat in the pub and denounced this sinful couple first to his companions, and then, as the tone of indignation in his voice attracted the interest of others nearby, to anyone else in the place who would listen.

'It in't reet at all!' he said, shaking his head so violently that the rest of his body followed, and ale slopped over the rim of his tankard down on to his boots. 'It just in't reet!'

'Leave 'em be!' came one rejoinder.

And then another: 'What's it to do wi' thee? Thah's nobut meddlin' in other folks' business.'

What with Abe Thornton's indignation, and the equally vociferous opposition to it, there came a point when the entire front room of the pub was drawn into the argument.

Ruth Kent's previous marriage was taken into consideration and counted in her favour, for it seemed that she had been married a Christian, and her husband had been one of the Moravians, who were a very religious lot, though on the strange side. However, little was known of Walker; that he had fled Bingley some years before was common knowledge, and theories as to why he had taken flight now came one after the other. Each scandalous suggestion, though, was shouted down in a torrent of liberal-minded derision and a general feeling of goodwill towards the man, who everyone liked. The only thing that could really be said against him was that he didn't let his business be known to everyone else, which in such cases of popular justice always counts against a person.

The discussion intensified, and before long the inhabitants of the pieshop had become a side issue, and the question was one of laissez-faire generally. Was it a good thing? Should man be allowed to act as it pleases him? Or is he by nature an obedient creature? One sage even brought Jeremy Bentham into the discussion, but was shouted down by a majority of pie-lovers, who knew nothing of philosophy but felt that in some way this might be an attack on Ruth Kent, which would naturally put their favourite supper at risk.

Thus the question was debated, until somehow the moralists put forward a very persuasive point: that only through marriage could the pie shop avoid public censure and thus definitely survive. Their reasoning was perhaps not as sound as it first appeared, because the magistrates had no powers to take action, and really there was no legal issue at all. However, there was a religious aspect, because many of the mill owners in the area were strict Methodists and their approval was always better to have than to want. (By the by, I might here add that John Wesley preached in Gomersal several times towards the end of the last century; really, I should have mentioned it sooner, for undoubtedly it was something of great import in our history.)

The next morning Abe Thornton arose with a thick head. He staggered to the kitchen, still in his nightshirt, and could do little more than sip at a cup of sweet tea and

wait for things to settle down inside his skull. Despite all
his protestations the previous evening, which towards the
end of the night had included several inaccurate quotations
from the Scriptures as well as a partial rendition of the
wedding service itself, despite all this, Abe himself was not
a regular churchgoer, a point which had in fact been raised
in the Punch Bowl. To this Abe had made a fine defence of
himself, drawing a distinction between true religious spirit
and mere servitude to the calendar, until in the end it seemed
that he was in fact speaking on the side of the laissez-faire
tendency. However, he quickly righted his arguments by
claiming that marriage is a civil responsibility and part of
a social contract, and that man by entering into wedlock of
his own accord shows himself to have exercised free will by
choosing to follow the path of moral rectitude.

Now, as he sipped his tea, he contemplated the difficult
interview he had to make. The outcome of the debate in the
Punch Bowl had been that he, Abe Thornton, would pay a
visit to the proprietors of the pie shop and enquire into their
intentions as far as matrimony was concerned. How could
anyone judge the matter at all, until it was known exactly
what was going on above the shop?

Just then, with the cup of tea right up to his lips, he felt
something strike the back of his head, and in that second the
world disappeared from view. Against his face was a dark,
itchy cloth; it wrapped itself around his head and neck, and
fell into the tea, so that the hot liquid rose up into its fibres
and wet his chin and mouth; with the tea dampening the
cloth he began to discern the familiar whiff of tobacco and
ale and old perspiration. Someone, it seemed, had thrown a
pair of trousers at him.

Let me say here a few words about women. For sure it is that there are some rare and noble ones, and who knows really how they compare to us men as a general thing, being so different from us in their countless ways. But let it be said of the women in the world that some are fine and some not so fine, and thus far in this story we have met one or two of the better examples.

However, Abe Thornton had the misfortune to be married to an altogether wretched one, a woman of a character so mean and niggardly and so wanting in the normal feminine arts, in common civility, in all that is amiable and delightful, that it would hardly be going beyond what is truthful to call her a hag, and a baggage, and such a trout that it is a wonder any man could have taken her as his wife. Who, at this early hour of the morning, and on a Sunday, would do such a thing as to throw a pair of trousers at the head of a man, in his own home, quietly suffering the effects of a heavy night?

Mrs Thornton, it seemed, was not the only woman who had ever been in the habit of going through her husband's belongings whensoever it pleased her. On this particular morning she had investigated the pockets of her husband's trousers to find that there was hardly a penny in them. The truth was that, as the leader in the debate at the Punch Bowl the previous evening, Abraham had bought more drinks than he intended. In the end things had gone as far as buying 'rounds', which as anyone familiar with the public houses will cede is a dangerous practice, since the buyer gets a drink 'in' for everyone, but seldom does he get the same number back in return. I have heard that there are even those who, whilst they take their free drinks with great good cheer, have no intention at all of getting 'in' a round of their own, and happily pass night after night in the company of more generous souls, hardly ever laying out a penny. That night, finding more money in his pockets than he had remembered putting there, Abe went further down the road of buying 'rounds' than normal, until the recipients of his kindness, who of course numbered many more than he normally drank with, were surprised as each new foaming tankard arrived for them, gratis.

Abe pulled the trousers from his head and neck, getting them tangled up with the cup in his hand until there was tea everywhere apart from in the cup. He threw down the steaming garment and was on the verge of rising from his seat and taking an angry stride over to the door, where his wife stood, her arms folded in front of her. But in the end he didn't. Even before the two of them exchanged words he knew what had happened. He had gone out to the Punch Bowl in a rush the previous night, and in his swift preparations had grabbed some money from the tin in the kitchen, money which was for all domestic expenses. That night, of course, had been Saturday – pay day – and the tin was full. In his haste, then, he must have taken too much. Suddenly he remembered the clamour at the bar each time he reached into his pocket and ordered more drinks, how the cheers rang loud and the slaps on his back came two and three at a time; people who he was sure he had never before seen in his life leaned into him, staggering against his body like puppets in the wind, thrusting their wet lips to his ear and babbling their words of gratitude.

He closed his eyes and, though he was never a very religious person, prayed. When he was done and opened them again he saw that his wife had the tin in her hands, and was holding it upside down, its little painted lid swinging loose on its hinge. He felt a sudden pull of nausea from deep within his stomach, and might have succumbed to it right then if the tin had not at that moment flown across the room and hit him square on the bridge of the nose.

There ensued a scene which the reader can only guess at, for Abe had indeed spent all the money in the house on beer, and the two of them had nothing to live on for a week. How the poor man endured such a barrage as he surely got, on top of the ill effects of the drink which he was suffering from, is a mystery. But somehow he did survive, and after the shouting and the hysterics were at an end, the two of them quite calmly took all the food that they had in the house and placed it on the table in the kitchen. There was half a loaf, three or four potatoes and two strips of belly pork, which were destined for the Sunday lunch, along with a few carrots, a half cupful of milk left over from yesterday, something near to an ounce of lard, several pickled onions in a jar, which floated in vinegar so old and murky that to eat them would have been almost courageous, half an ounce of tea, sugar in the bowl and a quantity of flour. Only then did they ask themselves: how do we manage with so little food in the house, for we are not poor, and we live well enough, and we no longer have children to feed? How can it be that there is not more to eat here? And the answer was obvious. Like most people roundabout, from the lowliest mill hand to the skilled engineers, much of what was eaten came from pie shops, the pies being cheap and filling, and, what was more a necessity to some than to others, hot, because many were the families that had no oven. Of course, Ruth Kent's pies, in addition to being all of this, were delicious, so pie consumption in the environs of her shop was naturally somewhat higher than the average. Pies. That is what they ate. Pies.

Later that day Abe Thornton strode out through his own front door, went right past the Punch Bowl without so much as looking at it, and crossed the road to the pie shop. He was invited into the kitchen, where Ruth and William were at work. Their unexpected guest shuffled in as far as the doorway, his hat in both hands, as if by holding it out in front of him he gained some measure of seriousness, almost as if he were at a funeral. Neither Ruth nor William seemed much interested in him, and they turned their backs to continue working. Something wasn't right, and although Abe Thornton had never before gone past the shop's counter and into the kitchen at the back, he felt a tingle of novelty in the air, and were it not for the sight of that tall, familiar woman, bent over a mixing bowl and giggling as the little fat man tossed cherries into the air, he would have guessed that he was in the wrong shop.

After watching them for a while Abe's senses came at once together; the place was filled with the smells of candied orange peel and cinnamon, of moist, peppery nutmeg and the sticky-sweet fug of raisins and sultanas left to soak. It didn't take a genius to fathom the truth of the matter: they were making a cake, and judging by the quantities of almonds and dried fruit that sat about in deep, capacious dishes, and the piles of eggshells that lay discarded on the table, dribbling their last drops of glistening white, and more shells on the floor trodden into the floury mess there, it was going to be a good cake.

'Catch!' said William, turning to Abe and throwing him

a candied cherry, which, since he still had his hat in both hands, bounced off his chest, bobbled on to the crown of the hat, and fell on to the floor. Both men watched it drop. Ruth stopped mixing and turned around to see what was going on. William blushed, and mumbled some sort of explanation, which no one understood. He shrugged and threw another cherry at Abe, who looked on, immobile.

Ruth raised a hand in mock admonishment. It was thick with cake batter, which dripped off her fingers in big slippery lumps and spattered back down into the bowl. The sudden movement of her hand caused a glob of the stuff to fly off from the tip of one finger, spin through the air like a sycamore wing, and land with a tiny pat on William's bald head. He stood dead still for an instant, those quick eyes flicking first to Ruth, then upwards, as if he could see right through his forehead and up onto the shining pate where the offending slime now lay. Like a good engineer, he was trying to work out if it were possible that this had been a deliberate act, whether Ruth could have taken aim with the intention of the mixture landing just there. Ruth saw his careful, calculating eyes at work, and immediately knew what he was thinking. She took her hand, extended it until it hung directly above his head – which, since she was so much taller than he, was merely a matter of holding her arm out in front of her – and finally brought her palm down onto the crown. The sticky contact was made, and William, who even now was gasping for air as laughter took over his entire body, grabbed a handful of cherries and launched them at her. Several hit her gently in the face; others got stuck in her collar, which was unbuttoned because of the weather, and one or two fell inside her dress.

There now began a scene which Abraham could scarcely conceive of as an act of affection, indeed could scarcely believe was happening at all, for it involved a great deal of cake batter on the one hand, and on the other a very disproportionate quantity of dried fruit. Through it all, the two of them seemed to have forgotten the onlooker, who stood in the doorway to the kitchen, his body utterly motionless but for the jaw, which fell open by degrees until it rested on his necktie.

The two combatants reached the entrance to the store-room, and only then did they remember that Abraham Thornton was still there in the other doorway. Somewhat abashed, they looked at him and, noticing his red cheeks and the way that he tried to keep his eyed fixed towards the floor, but that he kept blinking up involuntarily, Ruth said: 'Don't fret. We're mekin' a weddin' cake.'

And with that she took the opportunity to wipe the back of her hand on William's face, smearing him further with batter.

'St Peter's,' William added, digging his fingers into Ruth's waist with such force that she doubled over, howling with pain, and the two of them toppled through the doorway together and disappeared down on to the floor of the store-room.

'Tek yersen a pie!' came a cry, amid the giggling.

'Aye, tek a dozen! Yer't first t'hear it!'

Just in case Abe were in any doubt as to the offer, Ruth then came running through into the kitchen, breathless, with a plate stacked high with pork pies. She pushed it into his arms, explaining that tonight they had a few left over and that he might as well have them, though to Abe it seemed more like a celebration gift, since no one had ever known Ruth to have a single pie left over, Sunday or not.

William reappeared, wiping his head and neck with a towel in an attempt to remove the thickest of the batter, which was now drying, leaving a thin, light brown film on his skin. He told Abe that they had been that morning to St Peter's Church at Birstall to have their first banns read, and that they'd be married two weeks tomorrow, on Monday the 4th of August. They would have got the banns read sooner, and had meant to do it before William moved his things into the shop, only they never seemed to get around to it. There was always so much else to do rather than to go to Birstall to see the vicar. And besides, it was a formality that they reckoned they could live without for a week or two, since they had both done it before.

Abe nodded, mesmerised by the besmirched head of William, which moved as he spoke but which Abe could hardly believe was human, since with its light covering of cake batter all over it looked more like the head of a marionette dangling from the arm of a distracted puppeteer.

Still quite unable to say anything, his face seized up with stupefaction, he bowed solemnly and backed out of the kitchen door. He turned and sprinted from the shop, the plate of pies held out in front of him, in addition to the hat, which he clung to with finger and thumb. Ruth and William, who still knew nothing of his reason for his visit (though later they would guess it) watched him leave, and then they both collapsed laughing on the floor, surrounded by a light scattering of cherries and sultanas.

When Abe Thornton arrived home his wife had moved

from anger to a kind of tight-mouthed impatience. She had resolved not to speak to her husband at all, and as the door opened she flew from the room, as if the sight of him was too much for her to bear. But, seeing what he had in his hands, she stopped short of escaping and looked at the pile of pies suspiciously over her shoulder.

'An' 'ow much yer payin' for that lot?' she asked, in that cynical way that some women have of always looking for the worst side of everything, and no doubt thinking that her husband had got the pies on some form of credit not to his advantage.

'Nowt!' Abe replied, which were the first words that had come out of his mouth since before he entered the pie shop. 'They was free, an' if yer dun't want 'em, ah'll 'ave 'em missen!'

True, he had been somewhat shocked by all that he had witnessed between Ruth and William, but by the time he arrived home his mind had changed and he was now set on the idea of paying homage to that soon-to-be-married couple. And though he did not know exactly what form the homage would take, just thinking of it made him bold and generous; the wrath of his wife was as nothing to him, and he went so far as to flaunt his booty, waving the plate of pies right under her nose as if tempting her to take one.

'Idiot!' she said, swiping a pie from the top of the pile and devouring it there as she stood, holding it in both hands like a squirrel and gobbling it down quick.

When Abe put the remaining pies down in the cool cellar, he noticed that the belly pork had not been touched, nor the half-loaf of bread, so it must have been out of sheer hunger that his wife had taken the pie, which well illustrates the depths of her hypocrisy.

That evening Abe, now stuffed to bursting with savoury crust, strode to the Punch Bowl and convened the debating circle again. There were fewer men there, since it was a Sunday, although once it was known that Abe Thornton had returned to the theme of weddings the place soon filled up, and Abe, who was of course penniless this time, found that some of yesterday's 'rounds' were repaid to him, and that he could drink all he wanted on the goodwill he had lain up the night before.

The news of Ruth Kent's marriage to William Walker was greeted with universal approbation, and Abe took advantage of the moment to make a little speech on the glorious estate of marriage, which I must say I cannot imagine him having the courage nor the imagination nor indeed the bare-faced cheek to do, after what he had put up with at home. But he did his best, and concluded with what was in essence the beginning of the Donkey Wedding.

'So, there's nowt that's more fittin' than we do summat special on't fourth o' August,' he said, 'cos they're a bonny couple an' on top o' that them pies . . . well . . . ah ask yer all, what'd we do wi'out 'em? Fer't pies alone we ought to do summat!'

As to the celebrating of a wedding, most people were in agreement; if Walker himself was disinclined to organise any sort of festivity, then there was no harm at all in someone else getting up a party in honour of two such well-liked people. However, as to the suggestion that the pies themselves were to be honoured, there was less enthusiasm. For though they were without doubt very tasty pies, no one could imagine just what a strong affinity with those pies Abraham Thornton had acquired, and his speech seemed to border on the insane.

Now, in these parts it is not uncommon for there to be pie-eating competitions and other activities based on the humble pie. Most people at the time would have known of the great celebration pies made at Denby Dale. The first was made over a century ago, in honour of the King, and later on there was another one in Denby which I am told contained two sheep and twenty fowl, to commemorate the Battle of Waterloo, and a third in 1846 (which must have been still fresh in the minds of many people in 1851) to celebrate the Repeal of the Corn Laws, this pie said to measure some seven or eight feet across. What the good people of Cleckheaton did not know in 1851, because it had not by then happened, was the disastrous Denby Dale pie of 1887, made to commemorate the golden jubilee of Queen Victoria, which was over eight feet across and filled with game, rabbits, fowl of all kinds, pork, veal, mutton and just about any other carcass which they could lay their hands on. The resulting pie was, and this I have on good account, so rank and foul of smell when it was finally cut into, that not one portion was eaten, but the whole thing, which must have been enormous, was wheeled out of the town to some place nearby and there buried with great ceremony.

Most of those listening to Abe in the Punch Bowl had heard of such festivals and, of course, they had all heard of wedding breakfasts, which happened almost by the week in the Spen Valley and usually ended with a good deal of revelry amongst the working people. But they had never heard of the two things – pie festival and wedding breakfast

– being mixed together, and really no one had the first idea of what Thornton had in mind.

Slowly, as the ale ran free, at least for Abe Thornton, it became generally accepted that a special effort should be made for Ruth Kent and William Walker. At a point in the evening when enthusiasms were at their peak, a committee was formed and charged with the task of organising the wedding. But since by that stage everyone was pretty drunk, they all voted each other on to the committee, so really they were no better off than before the voting, and in the end Abe proposed that a second 'inner' committee of 'wedding sergeants' be formed, which most people agreed to, and immediately he was voted 'captain'. In this way they proceeded; the plans themselves were made, foremost amongst which was the concept of surprise, for it was thought imperative to their success that the whole thing be sprung on the couple on the 4th of August, so that the honour be made most satisfying to all concerned.

For the next two weeks the sergeants met in the Punch Bowl, a little enclave of them huddled around a small table in the corner. These private meetings put the rest of the committee into a state of frustration and jealousy, and some threatened to give up their places. Abe, seeing the danger of this, rushed decisions along as best he could. He allotted responsibilities to both sergeants and ordinary foot soldiers, a total army of fifteen, although many more besides enlisted as assistants. The captain himself was to lead the wedding procession, which naturally was to start outside the pie shop and go through Cleckheaton, up the hill to Gomersal, and down Church Lane to St Peter's at Birstall. Others were in charge of the constituent parts of the procession – human, animal, vehicular – and various other aspects of the great

day. All in all there were fifteen areas of responsibility, so
that one might ask whether in fact the whole thing had
been based upon a true plan at all, or whether things had
been added simply in an attempt to keep everyone on the
committee happy. Of course, this is all in the past, and the
best that one might say is that, great plan or not, there must
be hardly a person alive who would not pay good money to
have been in Cleckheaton on the 4th of August that year to
witness the wedding of Ruth Kent to William Walker, which
was really not their wedding at all but the idea of Abraham
Thornton, which has been known ever since that day as the
Donkey Wedding, and which I will now recount.

*

It was the morning of the wedding, very early. Young John
Thornton, who was no relation to Abe, rushed his donkey
up Church Lane, all the way from Garfit Lane to Hill Top
at Gomersal, and right down the other side into the Spen
Valley, where Cleckheaton lay waiting for him. With a short
stick, the boy, who was only eleven years old, prodded and
poked at the animal's hefty flanks, which were swollen with
good eating, for the donkey was as much a pet as a worker,
though it did its full share of graft in the Thornton household;
but since old David Thornton, the boy's father and the beast's
master, was one of the last hand loom weavers thereabouts,
it is probable that the animal itself never did anything too
energetic down at Garfit Hill from one year to the next.

With the boy was Mark Ball, a little younger still, but old
enough to drive a donkey too; his animal was smaller and
less barrelled about the middle, and the way it jerked and
trotted along of its own accord suggested that just to be afoot

in the morning with nothing tied to its back, and no cart to pull behind, was cause enough for celebration.

The two boys kept up a good pace, and the sun, which at six o'clock on a bright August morning was beginning to cut through the cool, shadowy trees that lined much of the route, its sharp yellow rays low and dazzling, promised a hot, prickly day.

They arrived at Moorbottom in Cleckheaton and made their rendezvous with some half a dozen men who had just finished their patrol. An all-night watch had been necessary because of the scale and complexity of the operation. To make sure that each part of the plan fell into its place, preparations had begun the previous night. In addition to this, another patrol was stationed near to the pie shop, so that if William or Ruth ventured out during the night for any reason, word could be got back to Moorbottom and all traces of what was to come quickly hidden away. However, the real reason for this patrol was to secure the pie shop as discreetly as possible. The question of whether the bride and groom were to be willing participants in the events which were about to unfold was a very urgent one, given all the energy and fuss which had gone into the organising, not to mention the subscriptions which had poured in and which had gone on such things as feed for the animals and other sundries too numerous to name; after all this what was most pressing was that the two lovebirds did not manage to get down to the church on their own, or, what some people feared, did not escape completely, for in that case there was no sure way of knowing if they would choose ever to return to the town at all. Ruth and William had by now come to understand that something was afoot; nudges and winks had come their

238

way on a daily basis over the previous fortnight, and though they would have preferred there to have been nothing for folk to wink and smile at, with a sense of resignation they both realised that they were trapped, and that a wedding breakfast had been got up.

By seven o'clock some ten or fifteen men had gathered outside the Punch Bowl, although Captain Thornton was absent, as indeed were his sergeants. Those who were there laughed and occasionally popped inside for a glass of something; the owner had put out plates of bread and butter and slices of black pudding to be eaten cold, all paid for by the committee. The sun rose higher, and where there was no protection it got to be stinging hot, so that before long the ale began to take effect, and the men's low-voiced chattering turned into the beginnings of choruses, which had to be quashed immediately lest the sound reach the pie shop.

A young lad then came running, his chest heaving as he stopped, knowing the importance of the news he brought, and hardly managing to get it out between gasps. As soon as it was said, all those assembled pulled themselves into action in an efficient manner and disappeared. The boy, whose job was now done, and who had no one there to congratulate him on his part in the proceedings, stole into the pub and filled his pockets with bread and black pudding, which the landlord didn't mind at all because it had all been paid for. He returned to the front court of the pub and waited there alone, knowing that he had found himself the best spot in all Cleckheaton. Within five minutes the black pudding and bread was all gone from the boy's pockets. He licked the butter from his fingers and nibbled at his nails, each one with a thin crescent of dark pudding under it, and waited.

By about half past seven the sun was well into its stride. William Walker put both mugs of tea down on the little table next to the bed and went over to the window to open the curtains. Ruth, he knew, had been awake for hours, so he threw the drapes right back. The room was flooded with a bright, burning yellow, and Ruth had to bring a hand up to shield her eyes from the light. Below, the road was deserted, but there was a static hum in the air, something summery and promising as William looked out towards Cleckheaton, along the road that would take him through the town and on to Birstall, and bring him home with a wife. He stole over to the bed, where Ruth still had a hand across her face. Sitting himself down on the edge of the bed, he lifted her hand and kissed her, first on one eyelid, then on the other.

'Mr Walker, ah can do wi'out that sort o' thing at this hour o' t' mornin',' she said, keeping her eyes closed, her mouth curling into a smile, her large teeth showing through.

He grabbed her around the waist through the sheets.

'At this time tomorra mornin' yer'll be Mrs Walker, an' mine a' do as ah please wi', mornin', noon—'

A brass band struck up. The sound came from some way off, but almost immediately it got louder, as if the players were running forwards as they played. It was a two-step, and a lively one; the bounce of its rhythm rose up into the morning sky in waves, and it seemed as if some new, foreign air was being poured into the warm valley, filling it with a strange excitement, mingling with the sun's yellow rays and turning Cleckheaton blithe and mischievous.

The band approached, and from his vantage point outside

the pub the boy sat enthralled. Each beat of the bass drum sent a new and stronger shiver of anticipation down his spine. And then they came into view, resplendent in their uniforms, marching in formation round the bend in the road briskly towards the Punch Bowl. In front of them was a white horse, a huge animal which appeared to be adorned with flags. As the music got louder and louder the boy made out Abe Thornton on the horse's back, which was indeed bedecked in ribbons and colourful hanging cloths depicting heraldic motifs in red and gold and black. Thornton himself sat erect, his chin high in the air; he had on a crimson military jacket with brass buttons and a white sash, a maroon cummerbund with ornamental tassels, grey trousers, and boots so shiny that they threw off flecks of sun as his horse moved in short, well-controlled paces. On his head he wore a magnificent black shako helmet with green plumage, and from his hip dangled a sabre in its gilt-and-black sheath which just three and a half decades earlier might have been slicing through a Frenchman on the plains of Waterloo. The band was twenty or thirty strong, and included several euphoniums and a bass drum at the back, plus an assortment of flugel horns and baritones and a good number of cornets, which of course led the way. On each side of the band rode two of Abe's sergeants, and another took up the rear; they also sported old military uniforms, though not all had genuine plumes, and they must have represented three or four different regiments, such was the contrast between each of them. For the main part, though, their helmets were of a kind.

Ruth and William were now at their bedroom window, though they had drawn the curtains again and could only peep through the narrow gap that remained; he crouched a little and she leaned over him, so they both got a tolerable view. The band passed directly beneath the pie shop, marching at a good pace on its way to the pub, and many of the musicians seemed to look in the direction of the shop as they passed by with their mounted guard.

'What the—' William said.

'Must be a—' Ruth mumbled back. But William had already noticed something else.

The music was now so loud that the boy outside the Punch Bowl, who had never heard such a thing and at such close quarters, put his hands to his ears, though he was laughing as he did it. Then something took his attention, and he turned to his right as six donkeys emerged from the side of the pub, dressed in pink and yellow finery, and pulling a large cart, which was ablaze with colour and had been stacked with boxes three or four feet high. So much bunting hung from it that there was hardly any of the cart left to see, and on the top, which formed a kind of dais, two large chairs had been lashed. Even the harnesses which attached the six donkeys to the cart (in two lines of three) were festooned with bunting and little flags, which flapped as the cart inched forwards into position, aided by five or six men with sticks, who all wore their hats, one or two with ribbons in, and big gaudy sashes across their chests.

Turning again, the boy saw that coming up the road behind the band were more donkeys, many more, and all of them transformed into things of beauty by ingenious arrangements of flowers and cloth and ribbons. They were herded along by yet more men, again with ribbons in their hats and sashes across their bodies, all of them jogging along

242

merrily in the morning sun, and at such a good pace that there came a point when it seemed that there must be a collision right outside the Punch Bowl.

Just as the band got to the end of its two-step it arrived at the pub and came to a stop, and immediately after it the herd of donkeys also arrived. Abraham Thornton now took charge, unsheathing his sabre and directing people here and there, sneaking up behind any loose donkey and nudging it back into the group with a gentle tap to its rear end, and generally knocking things into shape. From the sidelines the whole scene looked like chaos, with band members holding their silver instruments up high above their heads as if to protect them from the animal throng, and the mounted escorts circling about nervously this way and that, one eye on the mêlée and the other on their leader. To cap it all, there emerged a second donkey cart from somewhere or other, pulled by a pair of colourfully dressed animals. This cart had two poles tied to it, one on each side, across which was hung a banner. On it, in red letters edged in blue:

Who could have thought it – the Jovial Crew!

Beneath the words was a painting showing a great crowd of people, some waving their hats in the air, others dancing.

The procession fell suddenly into place. Or at least it seemed to happen suddenly, because Abe Thornton raised his gleaming sabre high above his head and there fell a hush. The band began playing again. Abe took up his position at the front, and off they all went after him, the band going first, then the smaller of the carts, with its colourful banner, the loose donkeys following that, and finally the wedding chariot itself, which brought up the rear.

Ruth was enjoying the spectacle so thoroughly that, despite being still in her nightclothes, she had drawn the curtains full back, better to admire the festive scene; besides, the action was now up by the Punch Bowl, and the window was no longer directly in view.

'Come on!' she said. 'We'll just 'ave time to see 'em set off afore we 'ave to go!'

With this she flew about the room, eager to get dressed quickly, so that she would catch at least a moment's fun down at street level.

Meanwhile, William remained at the window, weighing up the odds, divining the meaning of the mounted guard and the band, the banner's cryptic slogan, and the two chairs placed high on their cart.

'Ruth, love,' he said, and had to repeat himself before she took any notice.

'What?' she said, returning to the window.

'They're comin' for us.'

The Jovial Crew was no doubt a thing to behold, but one aspect was more eye-catching than the rest: the free-walking donkeys, which numbered some twenty beasts, carried fully grown men on their backs. The bright sashes, it appeared, signified that a person was allowed his own mount, and twenty men now did their best to remain on theirs, though they had no saddles, and in addition many of the riders had taken some ale already, and this, plus of course their general mirth, led many to pay insufficient attention to their animals, with the result that half of them had taken at least one tumble before the procession had made its way the short distance from the Punch Bowl to the pie shop.

Ruth and William watched all this from their upstairs window, and were now gripped by fear, because although they were resigned to being at the centre of Abe Thornton's festivities after their wedding, they had not expected anything before the ceremony. All they could say to each other as they saw the Jovial Crew approaching the shop was that there must be something else afoot, some other celebration that they didn't know about, perhaps the arrival of a circus, or a special holiday at a mill, though of course these and any number of conjectures were very improbable. William began looking more closely at the people below, because men like Abe Thornton, and indeed most of those in the procession, should have been on their way to work by now. It was a Monday morning, and how such a gathering could have happened on a working day was baffling. William spotted two or three faces he knew from the shoddy works amongst a crowd of onlookers that moved down the road behind the procession, and who were clearly not thinking with too much urgency about getting to work.

Here let me say a few words about capitalism, as it is generally called, being the means by which the rude and unwieldy stuff of nature is turned into useful and valuable merchandise. For centuries there have been men who take raw wool straight from a sheep and turn it into cloth, and indeed our towns and villages were built on the activity of such men. But as is well known, the last century has seen great changes: where once there was a scattering of individuals – spinners, combers, weavers – who might all have taken their small part in the trade, there is now a mill, and inside it is so much production, which never stops from seven in the morning till seven or eight at night, that some men have become exceedingly rich by it. These men, who are no doubt capitalists, have sometimes been accused of striking a hard bargain with their workers, making them toil hour upon hour in the mills for very small wages, and taking the better part of the profits for themselves. I can hardly go into all this here. But let it be said that the mill owners are seldom as cruel and hard-hearted as they are painted, and on the other hand the common workers often lack even the most basic virtues; one has but to bring to mind the history of the Luddites, who wantonly smashed and burned down mills all over the West Riding, to know the truth about the working man.

Had the Donkey Wedding happened but a few years later, then my own father would have been by this definition a capitalist himself, since he took a small share in a Cleckheaton mill in 1855, the same year I was born (though I myself was always destined for the law, not trade). The capitalists who form part of our story are those mill owners in whose employ were Abraham Thornton and his sergeants. The committee managed to persuade these capitalists that by honouring the wedding of William Walker and Ruth Kent they would be mounting a great demonstration of Christian devotion, and celebrating the end of immorality at the pie shop. Hence, Abe and his men had been given the morning off, and in addition several large donations had come the way of the committee from the bosses, though I am told that none of them came to see the procession itself. Thus, the Donkey Wedding had the support of all classes, and the capitalists in this way showed themselves truly generous; although they also learned a lesson later on that morning which perhaps would lead them in future to look on such generosity with more careful consideration. Certainly, my father would never have granted time off for such frivolities.

Abe Thornton knocked hard on the front door of the pie shop with the butt of his sabre. Three fateful knocks, which from inside the pie shop sounded like a summons to the gallows. The bride and bridegroom finally appeared, having dressed in a rush. A great cheer went up as they opened the door, and the crowds, which lined both sides of the street, applauded with such fervour that several donkeys bolted, along with their mounts, and had to be pursued by the sergeants on horseback.

Ruth and William were duly placed in their respective chairs, which were like two thrones, and really it would have been better had Ruth worn a dress with a train, because she looked quite out of place in such a plain frock. The two of them said little to each other, now accepting the inevitable, and their discomfort soon wore through the expressions of complacency which they tried hard to keep up as the chariot jerked to a start and the whole procession took off again.

After a minute or two's parading it became clear that it was not only Abe and his committee that had absented themselves from their places of work; for as they got closer to the centre of Cleckheaton the crowds got thicker and the cheering, which had begun as a sporadic thing, now rang constantly in everyone's ears, and the band's stirring music had to compete to be heard above the throng. By the time they reached the George Inn, which is right in the middle of town, the bustle to get a good view had become so intense on both sides of the road that the captain and his sergeants were all occupied in keeping the onlookers back, riding up and down the flanks of the parade just to make possible some kind of forward movement. People were streaming out of mills, most of them running; they sprinted across grassland, scaled any wall in their path, and battered their way through lines of bushes as if on a hunt, eager not to miss anything; young lads clambered on to each other's shoulders and up lamp-posts and indeed on to anything that might afford them a better sight, everyone falling about with laughter at the same time. They came from mills right up the valley, from out past the Punch Bowl, and the road into Cleckheaton, which the parade had just followed, was filled with fast-moving bodies flocking in from the peripheries; when William looked behind him, the road was like a river of bobbing heads, and it shocked him so greatly, being at the centre of all this, and hardly knowing what to expect next, that he mumbled something to Ruth to try and take her attention, and thus prevent her from looking back.

By the time the parade had made its slow progress through the town and began its ascent up the hill from Cleckheaton to Gomersal, it was already getting well into the morning. The crowds ahead were worse than those behind, and Abe's white charger had to cut a swathe through the sea of humanity at every turn. The mills, it seemed, were empty; at first, those who were able had crept out to get a peep, but word got around and there was suddenly a most unusual laying down of tools and abandoning of machines, so that production in the Spen Valley came to a halt, and for once the vast machines were silent.

It didn't stop there. Gomersal was ready when the parade, after a long and tiring climb up the hill, arrived there.

Thomas Burnley's mill up at Hill Top emptied of all life as soon as the first notes of the brass band were heard approaching. The workers spilled into the grounds of St Mary's Church opposite, which was just then being built. On and on like this it went, over the hill at Gomersal and down Church Lane, which was where things became very excessive indeed.

Between Hill Top at Gomersal and St Peter's Church at Birstall there is a steep descent of about a mile down Church Lane into the valley which includes Batley to the south-east, where there are a good many mills. Word had somehow got as far as there, and now, as the Jovial Crew came over the hill at Gomersal and began the drop down to Birstall, the entire side of the valley rose up and came to see the Donkey Wedding. They poured out of mills and workshops and houses, swarming over hedge and dyke to be in at the fun. There was such a crowd there by the time the parade had made its way down the hill that the procession could not get through to the church, and was held up until the crowds, which at first took no notice of Abe's sabre, could be persuaded to cede passage.

When the wedding chariot itself got to the church gates, not much before dinner time, Ruth and William were helped down to great roars of jubilation, and the wedding party made its way into St Peter's, where Canon Heald conducted a service behind locked doors, since he was fearful that the church might be overrun. There was, of course, a clamour to get in before the great doors were shut, and the yard of the church was full with the chattering masses. Many of those who found themselves excluded stood on walls and one or two even hoisted themselves up on gravestones to get a glimpse inside through the stained glass, though I doubt they saw much.

However, the Donkey Wedding was taking place not just inside the grounds of the church, but away from it as well. There were now, by common agreement, something over ten thousand people in that corner of Birstall, and may I say that it was later estimated that upwards of twenty thousand souls came to witness the procession all told. With the majority left to amuse themselves down near the church, the Black Bull pub became the centre of all attention, although we might remember that in 1851 it was still called the Chained Bull, owing to another inn across the way at Garfit Hill being called the Black Bull. Both inns were now crowded with drinkers, and it was at the Chained Bull, not five strides from the churchyard gates, that the thirty-two donkeys were housed.

The ale was plentiful, and drinkers spilled out on to the road with their pints, such was the crush inside both pubs. At the Chained Bull, the assembly room upstairs (the pub was used for all sorts of public purposes, including voting) was so crammed with folk that it had to be propped up from underneath, since its floor began to creak, and the ceiling below bowed visibly. One wag noted that never had the place been so full as that on a voting day, although of course few people were voters at that time, which reminds us of the progress we have made in this regard.

By the time the wedding service was coming to an end, few people had much interest in the nuptials, since Bacchus now ruled the day completely. A wire-scale seller called Kershaw was pushed down some steps outside the pub and thought he had broken his neck. But the neck was put right with a few hefty thumps and he carried on drinking. After this there were more skirmishes at both alehouses.

One of these little bouts has gone down in local history. At about three in the afternoon, when a good deal of drinking had been got through, Joe Medley from Littletown stooped down to pick up what appeared to him to be a coin in the grass. He was just outside the Black Bull, I mean the old Black Bull at Garfit Hill, where there was plenty of grassland for drinkers to occupy. This land is used for religious meetings of the revivalist type, and has sometimes had as many as two or three thousand souls there for hymning and prayers. But on the day of the Donkey Wedding there were more than that, for here was the best place to enjoy this extraordinary day, with open ground to sit on, and a little farther off some trees for those in search of a private stroll. Anyway, Joe bent down to recover the coin, and being a young man somewhere in his twenties and sturdy of body, his rump presented a nice target for anyone's boot. This idea occurred to another lad, a few years older, I'm told, and from Cleckheaton, and a boot was duly sent in the direction of Joe's arse.

This was the start of it all, and those of us who have grown up in these parts will be familiar with what happened next, because in the West Riding there is a general rule that when two young men are at odds on some matter, they will immediately fight about it and in this way resolve the disagreement. Of course, they are always encouraged in this course of action by an army of onlookers eager for diversion, and preferring it to be at someone else's expense.

Joe Medley got back to his feet and began the normal shoving and accusing and finger-wagging that such a fracas naturally begins with. But his opponent was for none of this, and brushed him off, saying that if he fancied 'some', then they should do it proper. To this Joe hardly knew what to say, because to him a scrap was a scrap, and could be had as easily outside a pub as anywhere else. However, the Littletown contingent had other plans, and both men, after some heated exchanges, nominated seconds, and the four of them, plus many more besides, marched off to Kenyon's Field, stripped to the waist, and set to with bare fists.

The field in question is right next to Garfit Hill, and is also used for religious meetings, but now it overflowed with a different kind of passion. People flocked in from all around, and the commotion even drew customers away from the pubs, until it was said that there were four or five thousand there to watch, though whether everyone got a clear view I cannot say.

The fight was, by all accounts, a good one of its sort: a burst of flying fists to begin with, and then, when both pugilists had taken one or two hard blows to the head and the first few trickles of blood had appeared, there was much careful stalking about the ring, a greater degree of precision in defence, and more circumspection in attack than either men had before put into a fight. The crowd, as is common at such events, were divided between the desire to see blood run free, and the wish that the entertainment continue longer, for it is certainly true that when two grown men set to with bare fists, if they land heavy punches, the thing will generally not go on long.

Joe Medley emerged victorious, after his opponent had taken 'as much as he could well carry', which is an expression sometimes used hereabouts. In fact, it is said that he had to be dragged away, since his legs had given up on him, though he was still intent on punching the air in front of him. Soon after the fight had finished, attention turned back to the wedding party, which was just then leaving the church, and the whole parade was getting ready for its triumphant return to Cleckheaton, where it was said that more diversion awaited.

Several thousand revellers, who had now given up all thought of returning to their places of work, followed the parade up the hill to Gomersal, and thence down the other side to Cleckheaton. It is said that so many of them tried to get a drink at the Saw Inn, which lies halfway down the hill, that its doors had to be shut.

Eventually, the procession got back into the Spen Valley, where a breakfast had been prepared at the George Inn. As the parade reached Cleckheaton the noise of the band and of the rowdy crew which accompanied it was enough to bring out a good few hundred onlookers again, and so now it was the turn of the George to be overcrowded, and many revellers had to take their pints outside. Indeed, such was the excitement there in the street that a speech was called for. William was dragged to an open window on the second storey, and was greeted by an enormous roar as he stared down at the mob. He did open his mouth, and several times nodded his thanks. But as to actually speaking, he was not up to it, being extremely shy and nervous in front of people. The speech was a failure, although by the time he had been facing the crowd a full minute without a word, most of them had got bored and returned to their beer.

Throughout all this, Ruth Walker remained tight-lipped,

and only once or twice was she cajoled into what might have been called a smile. Her husband was more accommodating, and as the wedding breakfast went on he tried to lay out enough gratitude for both of them, which was made more difficult by Abe Thornton, who was so animated with pride that he kept on asking the two of them whether they were enjoying themselves, though it would have been clear to any sober observer had there been one at hand, that they were not.

The breakfast went on in the usual way. But presently the dreaded rattle of spoon on table announced that speeches were to be given. However, when the captain arose it was not to invite the groom to speak, but to launch into a speech of his own, the text of which he extracted from a trouser pocket, rather ominously, because there was two or three sheets to it at least. He began by running through the usual formalities, and rather wisely complimented the bride beyond what was really truthful, before turning his florid peroration to the organisation of the wedding itself. At this point his theme became so obscure that several members of his own committee began to wonder what he was talking about, though the inner circle of sergeants smirked knowingly as their captain, with a heightened sense of theatre, began hinting at some new surprise.

'It is, honoured guests, ladies and gentleman,' he said, 'a singular pleasure, indeed it is, for there can be no doubt about it, I reckon, a very singular and, if I might be permitted to say, a right memorable one to boot, and what's more, one that's not likely to be repeated 'ereabouts, nor perhaps *could* be repeated 'ereabouts or, nay, anywhereabouts whatever, never, perhaps, what with, ehm . . .' At which point he took a gulp of port, and then another. Some people looked down at their plates, and even his sergeants stared at him in confusion. '. . . what with, if I may say, not a little ironical intent we 'ave prepared, and when I say we, I mean me and these 'ere trusty sergeants—'

The sergeants now crept from the room as stealthily as they might, though one or two of them had taken so much burgundy, which the committee had laid on in large quantity, that their egress was more by stagger than stealth.

'—we 'ave, as I say, yes, we 'ave, in greatest respect, I mean *with* greatest respect, *the* greatest respect, we have made you, Mrs Ruth Walker, fair denizen of the pie shop, muse and goddess of the savoury crust, may I say, nay *must* I say, poetess of the pork-meat, who conjures up our tastiest culinary dreams . . .' At which point Ruth rolled her eyes in undisguised mockery of this hyperbole. '. . . we've done yer a pie!'

There fell a silence about the place that shocked even Abe, who was expecting at least a few gasps of delight to pepper the hush, if not actual applause. But there was not a sound. People at the tables sat dumbfounded, and no one could stifle their true feelings. A host of amazed and horrified faces looked right at Abe Thornton. Moreover, it was not that kind of amazement which might turn at any moment to rapture; it was an anguished, almost wretched amazement at the terrible audacity, the impertinent, not to say inelegant and insulting, suggestion that Ruth Kent (for in their stupefaction no one now recalled that she had been married) be presented with a *pie* to celebrate her union with William Walker, those two who between them, but principally she, had introduced the pork pie into the

255

Spen Valley and had brought it to a state of perfection there, and which now had innumerable imitators in Batley, Hightown, Littletown, Brighouse, Morley, and indeed everywhere except in Cleckheaton itself, where nobody dared. This was nothing but an insult, and a very harsh one.

Then the doors opened, and each pair of eyes in the George looked on in horror as the pie was brought in by the sergeants, who carried it between them on a tray. It was four feet across at least, and sat in a metal dish, itself a good two feet deep. In appearance, then, it looked not unlike a giant pork pie, though a bit flatter. The tray which it stood on was so wide and sturdy that it seemed that the pie must be made of lead, and indeed they struggled to keep it level, though they were five grown men. The crust on top was a light brown colour, and sat on the tin like a flat cap, and one of the men kept a hand on it, as if it might fall off at any minute.

A trestle table had to be brought in, and the enormous pie was placed in front of the married couple, who were frozen in their seats. On the side of the pie dish had been painted: *Thank the Lord for the pies! Thank the Lord for the pie-makers!* As wedding guests saw the words painted there, a general muttering went about the place, and eventually some sniggering.

Just then, as everyone seemed to have got over their shock, the pie looked as if it might fall, and several of the sergeants leapt at it as if to steady the tin, all the time making sure that the crust stayed on. Abe Thornton was almost hysterical with mirth, though his sergeants looked at him as if more haste were needed. He stepped up to the pie, turned to Ruth, bowed low and solemn, and drew his sabre. He offered her the shining weapon.

'Madam, indeed, Mrs Walker, Madam,' to which cheers broke out. 'Madam, for the genius of your pies, and the gift of the newfangled pork pie, which you gave to us all, and which continues day after day to be the delight of all who taste it, and though they toil all day, and life is 'ard, the thought of one of yer pies will keep 'em at it till teatime, and—'

Here there were some shouts of 'get on with it'. Abe cut short his little dedication and handed over the sabre.

Ruth looked with imploring eyes at her husband. But he could do nothing to help. She rose from her seat, the sabre in both hands, wanting nothing more than to take Abe Thornton's head clean off with it, and one or two others in the room as well. However, she resigned herself to cutting the pie. Leaning over the table, she poked the tip of the sword into the pastry. But the pastry did not yield, and she thought that it must be a very strong pie. She pushed a little harder, but again the crust withstood it. Abe was again in fits of laughter, and got so bad that he doubled over, holding his aching stomach, and disappeared from view. At that moment Ruth, who had become sick of the whole performance, put all her weight down on the sabre. This time it did go into the pie, and as the fiery blade disappeared beneath the surface, almost as far as the hilt, the crowd erupted in cheers of delight.

There came a piercing shriek, which cut through the sound of cheering, and brought everything to a sudden halt. The sergeants pulled the sabre out of the pie in a state of some agitation, and Abe, whose giddiness had vanished in an instant, now lifted the crust up, which came away easily because it was not fixed down at all, and was in fact made

257

from a thin layer of plaster and horsehair painted brown. The pastry was thrown aside, and in the tin were half a dozen piglets. They looked up, dazed by the sudden light, and immediately began jumping and clambering up the sides of the pie dish, and up on to each other's backs. All, that is, except one, which was squealing madly, jumping and turning like a pig gone insane, if such a thing exists, and sounded near to death, though it was only his tail that had been partially severed by the sabre, and really it could have been a lot worse.

Within a moment or two all those in the room understood what it was they were looking at, and the conceit was deemed a great success. Abe and his sergeants fell about with laughter, tears in their eyes, and held up piglets in their hands like trophies to the victorious. Ruth could not help a smile, for it was impossible not to look fondly on the little creatures, and even the one with its tail half off was a blessing, for the sword might easily have hit further up and taken its hindquarters clean away, which would have spoiled the fun altogether.

The wedding party finally left the George and made its way back to the Punch Bowl, although the parade was in disarray by now, and most of the band members were too drunk to play a tune together, and each one blew what he felt like all the way along the road. Most of the donkeys had been reclaimed by their owners, and both carts taken away. All that was left of the Jovial Crew was a merry assortment of individuals, some in military uniform, and several of them with a piglet or two in their arms.

At the Punch Bowl more fun was to be had. With the few remaining donkeys, there was racing to the railway bridge and back for the prize of a new bridle; women and children ran foot races, and there were skipping contests, which were very popular and went on for hours.

*

From the window of the pie shop, the music came drifting in, and occasionally the sound of cheering could be heard on the warm evening air.

'Well,' said Ruth, as they sat quietly together, not a sound in the shop but the gentle conversation between them, 'who could a' thought it?'

'Aye,' he said. 'The Jovial Crew!'

They sat back in their chairs and laughed.

'Six piglets!' she said, shaking her head. 'A weddin' present! Six piglets!'

'It 'd a' bin more, Abe told me. 'E wanted *four-an'-twenty*, that's what 'e said, but they 'ad to be small, and that were't biggest dish in Cleckheaton.'

He paused.

'Ah'll tell thee summat, though. Them piglets'll fatten up grand, and think o' all t' pies we'll get from 'em.'

'Pig farmers, are we now?' she said, and was about to smile at the idea of it. But she looked across at him, and there was something in his eye. He was already deep in thought.

ENDPIECE

The first of these novellas, *Eating Mammals*, is really a celebration of the great *Monsieur Mangetout*. I first heard of him when I read that a Frenchman, real name Michael Lotito, had eaten an Apple Mac at a computer fair. This reminded me of old stories about men who, when times were hard, would earn 'free drinks all night' in back-street pubs by eating strange things. I remember one story of a man in Leeds who would bite the head off a live rat, and another (perhaps less plausible) of a man who once ate a sofa, which feat he performed by first setting fire to it, then eating the cinders (sofas in those days were stuffed with horsehair, and would burn down to almost nothing).

However, Michael Lotito (b. 1950) eats for money, not beer. It is said that he can consume up to two pounds of metal filings per day. Over an illustrious career he has consumed fifteen shopping trolleys, seven television sets, eighteen bicycles, a couple of beds and a Cessna light aircraft. He has also ingested a coffin, and is probably the only person who has had a coffin inside him, rather than the other way around.

With all this in my head, I wrote *Eating Mammals*. Some time afterwards, an Indian Brahman told me, without a hint of doubt in his voice, that the *Paris Review* was the right place to send it; he also has a PhD in international relations, and had previously been a graduate student with me. Perhaps it was the international rather than the spiritual element, then, which persuaded me that sending the story all the way to New York was a good idea. Whatever it was, they accepted it.

With *Eating Mammals* about to be published, I began to think about the possibility of writing more 'mammal' novellas. The obvious person to ask was my uncle, Frank Barlow. I was aware that at some time in the past there had been a cat with wings in our family, but I had never heard the full story. However, Frank knew, and over a lunch of roast lamb at the Gables, his house, he told me everything.

The Possession of Thomas-Bessie is the result of that lunch. John Longstaff is in fact my great-great-grandfather. Frank himself heard the story of Thomas-Bessie as a boy from his own grandmother, one of Longstaff's daughters, those same daughters who inadvertently named their cat twice, in court. As an old woman, in the 1930s, she told her grandson about the cat and, crucially, about the court case.

In 1946, by which time Frank was a young man, he managed to see the cat in the flesh, though by that time it was stuffed and in a shop in Scarborough. A couple of decades later he came temptingly close to tracking it down yet again. Since then it may have crossed the Atlantic, although we are not sure about this. It is an intriguing story, and I have used only the very beginning of the life of the cat here. I think that's enough to be going on with.

I now had two mammal stories, and needed a third story to make a book-length collection. It duly arrived.

On New Year's Eve 2001, I was at my parents' house. It was after midnight. I was drinking gin and talking to Susana. She picked up a book which happened to be lying on the sofa (she is bookish by nature). It was *Gomersal Past and Present*, a history of our village published by a local solicitor in 1930 which my father had been showing me earlier in the day. Something took her attention, and quite simply she began reading aloud from the book. The passage was a short account of a wedding at St Peter's Church in Birstall involving thirty-two donkeys. We both knew immediately that this was the third and final story for the collection.

The details in the book were scant, so I contacted our local newspaper, the *Spenborough Guardian*, to see if anyone interested in local history could help me out. A few weeks later a full-page article on the 'Donkey Wedding' appeared in the newspaper. It reported on my interest in the story, and included a photo of me standing next to George Plimpton, editor of the *Paris Review*. After the article was published I was contacted by Frank Kent, who is a descendant of Ruth Kent. I am grateful for his permission to (ab)use the history of his forebears.

Acknowledgements

Thanks to Charles Buice for his editing of 'Eating Mammals' when it appeared in the *Paris Review*; to Professor John Widdowson for his much-valued help with the West Yorkshire dialect; to Frank Barlow, who has kept the story of Thomas-Bessie fresh in his memory since he heard it in the 1930s; to my father Stephen Barlow, for all sorts of advice, particularly on hen-keeping and pie-making, as well as the suggestion of a scheme for the theft of steam-power (complete with diagrams) which was just too crazy to include in any of the present stories. Great thanks to Peter Steinberg, for his perspicacity and encouragement, and for reading earlier drafts of these stories without wincing (audibly); to Nick Davies at Fourth Estate, for bringing everything together with such care and elegance. Finally, to Catherine Blyth, for her constant enthusiasm and a wonderful, unfailing commitment to the text.